Leader of Titans

A Medieval Romance
Book Two in the Pirates of Britannia Series with Eliza Knight
Book One in the Poseidon's Legion Series by Kathryn Le Veque

BY KATHRYN LE VEQUE

Kathryn Le Veque Novels

Medieval Romance:

The de Russe Legacy:
The White Lord of Wellesbourne
The Dark One: Dark Knight
Beast
Lord of War: Black Angel
The Iron Knight

The de Lohr Dynasty:
While Angels Slept (Lords of East Anglia)
Rise of the Defender
Steelheart
Spectre of the Sword
Archangel
Unending Love
Shadowmoor
Silversword

Great Lords of le Bec:
Great Protector
To the Lady Born (House of de Royans)
Lord of Winter (Lords of de Royans)

Lords of Eire:
The Darkland (Master Knights of Connaught)
Black Sword
Echoes of Ancient Dreams (time travel)

De Wolfe Pack Series:
The Wolfe
Serpent
Scorpion (Saxon Lords of Hage – Also related to The Questing)
The Lion of the North
Walls of Babylon
Dark Destroyer

Nighthawk
Warwolfe
ShadowWolfe
DarkWolfe

Ancient Kings of Anglecynn:
The Whispering Night
Netherworld

Battle Lords of de Velt:
The Dark Lord
Devil's Dominion

Reign of the House of de Winter:
Lespada
Swords and Shields (also related to The Questing, While Angels Slept)

De Reyne Domination:
Guardian of Darkness
The Fallen One (part of Dragonblade Series)
With Dreams Only of You

Unrelated characters or family groups:
The Gorgon (Also related to Lords of Thunder)
The Warrior Poet (St. John and de Gare)
Tender is the Knight (House of d'Vant)
Lord of Light
The Questing (related to The Dark Lord, Scorpion)
The Legend (House of Summerlin)

The Dragonblade Series: (Great Marcher Lords of de Lara)
Dragonblade
Island of Glass (House of St. Hever)
The Savage Curtain (Lords of Pembury)
The Fallen One (De Reyne Domination)

Fragments of Grace (House of St. Hever)
Lord of the Shadows
Queen of Lost Stars (House of St. Hever)

Lords of Thunder: The de Shera Brotherhood Trilogy
The Thunder Lord
The Thunder Warrior
The Thunder Knight

The Great Knights of de Moray:
Shield of Kronos

Highland Warriors of Munro:
The Red Lion
Deep Into Darkness

The House of Ashbourne:
Upon a Midnight Dream

The House of D'Aurilliac:
Valiant Chaos

The House of De Nerra:
The Falls of Erith
Vestiges of Valor

The House of De Dere:
Of Love and Legend

Time Travel Romance: (Saxon Lords of Hage)
The Crusader
Kingdom Come

<u>**Contemporary Romance:**</u>

Kathlyn Trent/Marcus Burton Series:
Valley of the Shadow
The Eden Factor
Canyon of the Sphinx

The American Heroes Series:
The Lucius Robe
Fires of Autumn
Evenshade
Sea of Dreams
Purgatory

Other Contemporary Romance:
Lady of Heaven
Darkling, I Listen
In the Dreaming Hour

Sons of Poseidon:
The Immortal Sea

Pirates of Britannia Series (with Eliza Knight):
Lady of the Moon
Savage of the Sea
Leader of Titans

<u>**Multi-author Collections/Anthologies:**</u>
Sirens of the Northern Seas (Viking romance)

<u>Note:</u> All Kathryn's novels are designed to be read as stand-alones, although many have cross-over characters or cross-over family groups. Novels that are grouped together have related characters or family groups.

Series are clearly marked. All series contain the same characters or family groups except the American Heroes Series, which is an anthology with unrelated characters.

There is NO particular chronological order for any of the novels because they can all be read as stand-alones, even the series.

For more information, find it in **A Reader's Guide to the Medieval World of Le Veque.**

Table of Contents

Author's Note vi

The Legend of the Pirates of Britannia.. x

Map of England, Scotland, and Ireland 1445 A.D. xii

Prologue 1

Chapter One 11

Chapter Two.. 22

Chapter Three 30

Chapter Four 39

Chapter Five 52

Chapter Six 59

Chapter Seven... 77

Chapter Eight 85

Chapter Nine 94

Chapter Ten... 113

Chapter Eleven 121

Chapter Twelve 137

Chapter Thirteen.. 155

Epilogue.. 170

Excerpt from Savage of the Sea 177

Excerpt from Lady of the Moon.. 212

About Kathryn Le Veque... 224

Author's Note

Welcome to the second book in the Pirates of Britannia series, but the first book for the pirate group known as Poseidon's Legion. This is the English side of the Pirates of Britannia (Eliza Knight is writing about the Scottish side, known as the Devils of the Deep), and there is a whole lot going on in this story, so buckle up and hold on. It's going to get bumpy from here on out, but in a good way!

This story takes place during the reign of Henry VI, a rather pious man who had mental issues and spent some of his reign trading the throne with the Earl of March, who became Edward IV (Remember Philippa Gregory's "The White Queen"?). This story takes place during that very turbulent time when two men vied for the throne of England.

Now, I've thrown a monkey wrench into the entire situation. Our hero, Constantine le Brecque, is the illegitimate son of Henry V, born before Henry VI. So, technically, he's Henry V's eldest son, and the Earl of March (who becomes Edward IV) – and the factions who want Henry VI's throne – know it. Even though Constantine is a bastard, he could still have a claim to the throne if he pressed the issue. His presence was "tolerated" until he started becoming a powerful pirate, ruling the Cornwall coast and beyond. Now, those siding with Edward are fearful that Constantine might actually press his claim and, of course, no one wants a pirate sitting on the throne of England. They want to get rid of him.

Now, I've brought you up to speed on where we are as our story begins. Constantine is a man with a lot of people hating on him. And, so you are up-to-date on the main bad guys in this pirate world we've created, Constantine and his compatriot, Shaw MacDougall (the Scottish pirate leader) battle Spanish pirates known as *Los Demonios de Mar* (Demons of the Sea) and also a band of French pirates who call themselves The Water Bearers (*Les Porteurs d'eau*).

The French ships are rowed by captives who have had their feet cut off so they can't run away. Really nasty stuff. The Spanish don't do anything quite so bad, as they are more interested in money, but the French just want devastation. They're brutal. Still, both the French and the Spanish are very dangerous enemies of the English and Scottish pirates, as you will discover in this series. They are also dangerous enemies of each other; whereas the English and Scottish pirates have an alliance, the French and Spanish are just out for themselves. Makes for some interesting moments!

Sure, I could make the English pirates brutal and nasty, like the French and Spanish, but that wouldn't make for a very sympathetic or likable hero. Although Constantine and his men don't do anything really nasty in this story, they're not beyond some necessary brutality and even sacrilegious moments. They're pirates, after all. But there is "some" sense of decorum because Constantine was trained as a knight before he became a pirate, so he clings to some of the ideology that he's been taught. Most of all, he believes in honor. At least as much as he can. And he is loyal to the bone to his fellow pirate brethren. There's something to be said about that.

Are there old friends in this book even though it mostly takes place at sea? Absolutely – I couldn't give you a book without someone you knew in it. The familiar face you'll see in this book is Kerk le Sander, who appeared in NIGHTHAWK with Patrick de Wolfe and then appeared as the hero of his own story, THE IMMORTAL SEA. You'll recall that Kerk is, literally, a son of the god Poseidon, an immortal, and he has lived for thousands of years. In this book, he's part of Constantine's pirate squad, a squad that calls themselves Poseidon's Legion – so it's fitting that Kerk is part of it. If there was one man who belonged on the sea, it's Kerk le Sander. Of course, Constantine has no idea who Kerk really is. That's part of Kerk's mystique!

Lastly, there is a holy relic in our story. It sets the entire adventure in motion, there really is a basis for it. It is called the Nanteos Cup and the story behind it is rather interesting. Research indicates that the Nanteos Cup seems to be a true Medieval cup that someone – somewhere along the line – attributed a legend to it. As fascinating as it all is, who's to say that the legend didn't come from some grain of truth? You can check out the story of the Nanteos Cup here: en.wikipedia.org/wiki/ Nanteos_Cup. It makes for fun reading.

As always, I hope you enjoy this tale, so have fun reading about Constantine and Gregoria, and all of the other men who comprise the Pirates of Britannia!

Hugs,
Kathryn

The Pirate factions:

The English faction: Poseidon's Legion

The Scottish faction: Devils of the Deep

The Spanish faction: Los Demonios de Mar (Demons of the Sea)

The French faction: Les Porteurs d'eau (The Water Bearers)

Pirate towns/home bases:

Puerto de los Dioses off the Azores Islands (Spanish)

Trésor Cove (North of Calais, a series of connected caves where pirates can dock their boats hidden inside) – (French)

Clew Bay (Ireland – used by the English and Scottish)

Carantec, Brittany (French)

Scarba Island (Scottish Stronghold)

Perran Castle/Holywell Castle/Mithian Castle in Cornwall (English Strongholds)

Port Eynon Bay, Wales (English/Scottish controlled, also a smuggler's cove)

The Legend of the Pirates of Britannia

In the year of our Lord 854, a wee lad by the name of Arthur MacAlpin set out on an adventure that would turn the tides of his fortune, for what could be more exciting than being feared and showered with gold?

Arthur wanted to be king. A sovereign as great as King Arthur, who came hundreds of years before him. The legendary knight who was able to pull a magical sword from stone, met ladies in lakes and vanquished evil with a vast following who worshipped him. But while *that* King Arthur brought to mind dreamlike images of a roundtable surrounded by chivalrous knights and the ladies they romanced, MacAlpin wanted to summon night terrors from every babe, woman and man.

Aye, MacAlpin, king of the pirates of Britannia would be a name most feared. A name that crossed children's lips when the candles were blown out at night. When a shadow passed over a wall, was it the pirate king? When a ship sailed into port in the dark hours of night, was it him?

As the fourth son of the conquering Pictish King Cináed, Arthur wanted to prove himself to his father. He wanted to make his father proud, and show him that he, too, could be a conqueror. King Cináed was praised widely for having run off the Vikings, for saving his people, for amassing a vast and strong army. No one would dare encroach on his conquered lands when they would have to face the end of his blade.

Arthur wanted that, too. He wanted to be feared. Awed. To hold his sword up and have devils come flying from the tip.

So, it was on a fateful summer night in 854 that, at the age of ten and nine, Arthur amassed a crew of young and roguish Picts and stealthily commandeered one of his father's ships. They blackened the sails to hide them from those on watch and began an adventure that would last a lifetime and beyond.

The lads trolled the seas, boarding ships and sacking small coastal villages. In fact, they even sailed so far north as to raid a Viking village in the name of his father. By the time they returned to Oban, and the seat of King Cináed, all of Scotland was raging about Arthur's atrocities. Confused, he tried to explain, but his father would not listen and would not allow him back into the castle.

King Cináed banished his youngest son from the land, condemned his acts as evil and told him he never wanted to see him again.

Enraged and experiencing an underlying layer of mortification, Arthur took to the seas, gathering men as he went, and building a family he could trust that would not shun him. They ravaged the sea as well as the land—using his clan's name as a lasting insult to his father for turning him out.

The legendary Pirate King was rumored to be merciless, the type of vengeful pirate who would drown a babe in his mother's own milk if she didn't give him the pearls at her neck. But with most rumors, they were mostly steeped in falsehoods meant to intimidate. In fact, there may have been a wee boy or two he saved from an untimely fate. Whenever they came across a lad or lass in need, as Arthur himself had once been, they took them into the fold.

One ship became two. And then three, four, five, until a score of ships with blackened sails roamed the seas.

These were *his* warriors. A legion of men who adored him, respected him, followed him, and, together, they wreaked havoc on the blood ties that had sent him away. And generations upon generations, country upon country, they would spread far and wide until people feared them from horizon to horizon. Every pirate king to follow would be named MacAlpin, so his father's banishment would never be forgotten.

Forever lords of the sea. A daring brotherhood, where honor among thieves reigns supreme, and crushing their enemies is a thrilling pastime.

These are the pirates of Britannia, and here are their stories...

England, Scotland, and Ireland 1445 A.D.

"Up the hill, over the dale,
along the seashore still;
among the waves,
the Sea-God lives,
a thirst for blood and kill."
~ 15th century children's rhyme

Prologue

The village of Carantec
Coast of Brittany
August, 1445 A.D.

SWEET, SILKY, AND *tender to the touch...*

But she tasted like stale ale. And the smell... well, he wasn't a picky man at times when it came to bed partners, so he could stand it. At least long enough for him to get what he'd come for.

"Do not make me wait," the woman begged him, grasping at his breeches in an attempt to pull them down. "I must feel your heated rod between my legs, thrust up into my body. Impale me!"

Had Constantine le Brecque not been so consumed with lust, he might have laughed at that. *Impale me!* He could think of at least three different ways to impale her with his stiff manhood.

Which orifice, exactly, did she mean?

"Patience," he whispered, hand on her breast, pulling at her taut nipple. "All in good time, my lady. In good time."

"*Non!*" she cried, throwing her legs open as wide as they would go and trying to maneuver him between them so she could feel his erection through his breeches. "Now!"

Somewhere, he caught a whiff of rank body odor, more than likely from the bed linens they were frolicking on. It was a seedy room, after all, in a seedy tavern located in an equally seedy town along the coast of Brittany. A fog was rolling in from the sea and the scent of salt and water were heavy in the air, mingling with the dirt of the town and creating a layer of filth that covered everything. Men, women, buildings… even the food. It was all covered with the grimy filth.

But it was the price one paid to visit this pirate's enclave by the sea.

One could find anything here, for a price. Even the wife of a French pirate who, in order to seek revenge against her philandering husband, was willing to deliver most of her husband's wealth to his English enemy on the condition that he would spend the night with her, doing things to her that her husband no longer would.

That was the easy part for Constantine. He'd bedded so many women in his lifetime that one more needy whore wasn't going to make a difference. The act would bring him a great deal of wealth and plant a figurative English dagger in the back of one of his most hated enemies. He'd been negotiating this particular event for almost six months, by way of messages sent through servants, luring the wife of the Dureau Van Rompay right into his own little trap. Only for the money, of course.

Always for the money.

Dureau was the brother of Nicolas Van Rompay, the great French Pirate King, and a particular thorn in the side of Constantine and his Britannic pirate allies. The man had been raiding along the southern and western coast of Cornwall as of late, right into Constantine's territory, and taking what did not belong to him. Constantine had engaged the man when he could catch up to him, using his newly-confiscated 22-gun Flemish warship that still wasn't fully operational, but Dureau had always been a step ahead of him.

Six months ago, Dureau returned to his home port of Carantec, and that was when Constantine began to undermine the pirate where it hurt – in his home, with his wife. If Constantine couldn't get the man on the sea, then he'd most certainly get him on land.

Or, in bed, so to speak.

Dureau played dirty, but Constantine played dirtier.

Now, he had Dureau's wife where he wanted her, writhing and begging for him to impale her in any hole of his choice. But he wasn't going to do it unless she showed him the money she'd brought – *Dureau's* money. That might take some coercing considering how hot the woman was at the moment. She squirmed around like a bitch in heat. To appease her, Constantine dipped his head down and suckled on a nipple, nearly bringing her off the bed.

"Soon, *ma chérie*, soon," he said huskily. "But you do not think this will be so easy without you holding up your end of the bargain, do you? You want something and I want something. Show me your reward and you shall receive mine."

The woman groaned unhappily as she bucked and twisted beneath him. "*Now?*"

"Now."

A heavy sigh. "In my bags."

Constantine continued to tease her even as he looked over his shoulder to a series of trunks and satchels against the wall near the door. The woman didn't travel lightly; she'd come to the tavern with an entourage of six women and several guards. Constantine had seen her arrive but he never showed himself to her attendants, knowing it would get back to her husband. Of course, he wanted Dureau to know, but only when it was safe for Constantine that he should. To have someone run for the husband now would be deadly.

But what he should have known was that he'd already been seen. He was well-known along these shores. Men talked.

And men were coming.

But Constantine wasn't thinking about that now. He was only concerned with the moment at hand, the great deal of wealth he'd been promised, and the fact that the tide would soon be coming in. His ship, *The Breath of Gaia*, wasn't far off shore. The tide would bring it closer in and he could make a swifter escape. He didn't want to linger in this hellhole any longer than he had to.

Kissing the woman's face, her hands, and her shoulder, Constantine pushed himself from the smelly bed and went to the bags against the wall. He began to yank them open as the woman sat up, a frown on her flushed face.

"What are you doing?" she demanded. "Must you look at it now?"

Constantine grinned at her, a devilish gesture that was sure to soothe and tame any female fits. He used the grin like a weapon at times, disarming as it was.

"I must, *ma chérie*," he said. "Business before pleasure, you know."

He yanked open the top of a particularly large and heavy satchel, and was immediately greeted with the great treasure inside. It was a good thing the satchel was leather because of the sheer weight of the contents; gold and silver groats with the face of Henry V pressed upon them glittered weakly in the dim light, some of them hardly used. There were also strands of valuable pearls, bejeweled rings, and a spectacular gold necklace inlaid with precious stones, jade, and chalcedony. Great emerald pendants strung on golden chains or silk ribbons were thrown haphazardly into the pile, joined by exquisite brooches that proudly displayed their ruby gems.

In all, it was a rather astonishing cache and extremely valuable. In fact, Constantine hadn't seen so many rare valuables like this in a very long time and he couldn't help his reaction as he turned to the woman on the bed.

"*This* all belongs to Dureau?" he asked, surprised.

The woman was propped up on her elbows, looking at him with a mixture of lust and impatience. "I took all I could," she said. "There is little left at this point. Not only is that satchel full, but so is the one beneath it. All of it full of my husband's treasures. Take it and welcome, but if you do not come to bed immediately, I may take it all back."

Ignoring her warning, Constantine untied the leather straps on the top of the second satchel and yanked that one open, too. As she'd said, it was full of more of the same and Constantine could hardly believe his eyes. He had no idea the prince of the French pirates, men known as the *Les Porteurs d'eau*, or The Water Bearers, was so wealthy. Their ships weren't particularly fine and they lived in rather unspectacular hovels but, evidently, they hoarded their wealth and didn't spend it on foolish things like fine homes or fine ships.

This put the situation in a whole new light.

Grabbing the satchels, Constantine quickly made his way to the only window in the room, one that faced north over the channel. Lashing out a big foot, he kicked open the wooden shutters, breaking the sash on one of them, and as they slammed back, Constantine thrust his head from the second-floor window.

There were men below, standing in the torch-lit darkness of a damp night. Taking the time to secure the leather ties tightly on both satchels, Constantine tossed out one and then the other to his men waiting below. They scrambled, catching the heavy bags, grunting with the sheer weight of them.

"What do you have in these, Con?" one of the men hissed up to him. "Rocks?"

Constantine waved the man off. "Get to the ship," he said. "But send the skiff back for me as soon as you can. High tide will be here soon and we must push off. Hurry, Kerk!"

Kerk le Sander, an excellent knight and shipmate who had been with Constantine since before he'd taken on a life of piracy, flashed his toothy grin as he grabbed both bags and rushed towards the shoreline where a small ferrying vessel, manned by four of Constantine's men to row it, sat just on the edge of the water at low tide. It was beached, essentially, and as Constantine watched Kerk run for it, he could see the lights of the *Gaia* close by the coast, flickering faintly as the fog rolled in. Soon enough, those lights would disappear, which meant that Constantine needed to leave his situation sooner rather than later if he wanted to make it back to the ship without becoming lost in the fog.

The sense of urgency was building.

"Do you want us to remain here, Con?" Another man below caught his attention. "Shall we wait for you?"

Constantine nodded quickly. "I shan't be long," he assured the man. "Stay out of sight, Gus. Be ready to run."

Augustin de Russe, a very big man with a mean streak in him, nodded seriously. "Hurry, Con," he rumbled, looking about suspiciously. "I do not like the rabble I am seeing. I think I have seen some of those men before, if you get my meaning."

Constantine did. The man meant he'd seen enemy pirates that he recognized, men that possibly belonged to Dureau. "I will," he said, pointing at the man. "But you watch the door. If you see Van Rompay, you will whistle."

"Is he even here in town?"

Constantine's gaze flicked up and down the dirty avenue. "Anything is possible," he said. "Be on your guard."

Augustin's gaze lingered on Constantine before he faded back into the shadows of the small huts and businesses across the dirty avenue. Wrapped in a boat cloak, Augustin blended in nicely with his surroundings. But Constantine knew he had a big broadsword beneath that cloak. Like all of Constantine's senior officers – including a powerful knight named Remy de Moray and a dark ex-priest known simply as Lucifer – Augustin came from a fine family and had been trained as a knight, now finding himself in the odd position of using those skills on the high sea to purse a life of wealth and glory.

But his attitude was the same as the other highly-trained knights on the high seas, Constantine included. Whether they were to have remained on land in the service of a king who demanded they go forth and conquer against other kings and men, or whether they remained on the sea and pursued their own form of conquest and wealth-gathering, it was all the same. They all had to make their own way in life, by hook or by crook. Sometimes, knights did things under the guise of honor that weren't necessarily so honorable.

But no one was losing any sleep over it.

"Come back to bed!" the woman demanded. "You have what you came for and I am growing cold waiting for you!"

Jolted from his thoughts of his men and the glory they sought, Constantine came away from the window.

"I doubt that you could become cold, in any case," he said rather seductively. "But I would like to know where your husband is this night. Surely he is nearby? This is his village, after all."

The woman shook her head. "I left him and his whore at St. Yves," she said bitterly. When Constantine shook his head, not knowing what she meant, she threw her hand around irritably. "The home we share on the outskirts of town. He is home, back in the hills. As long as he has wine and that woman, he will not care where I have gone. But I will not wait much longer for you, *Anglais*, so you will come to me now."

It wasn't a request. Constantine knew he could no longer delay the inevitable, so he leapt into bed beside the woman, rolling on top of her and listening to her seductive giggles. Her hands were in his breeches now, trying to force them down, and he obliged her by unfastening the ties and removing them. When she grabbed his manhood, he flinched because her hands were cold. But her mouth wasn't. When she turned him onto his back, her hot and skilled mouth began to work his manroot in a move that had Constantine rather eager to experience.

Laying on his back and staring up at the ceiling, Constantine allowed himself to give in to the carnal delight of a woman pleasuring him. He had no intention of holding back his release because the sooner he found his climax, the sooner he could leave. Sometimes, he could hold out for a very long time – he had that kind of control. But it depended on how attracted he was to the woman and how much he wanted his pleasure to last. In this case, it would be a fast event and, he was certain, faster than Dureau's wife wanted it to be, but he had a schedule to keep. A ship to board, as it were. And then he had to make it home before Dureau came after him, looking for that massive treasure.

Constantine grinned at the mental image of Dureau realizing the money he'd lost.

But the grin didn't last long. Suddenly, a piercing whistle filled the heavy night hair and Constantine knew exactly what it was. He'd know de Russe's whistle anywhere. Leaping up from the bed, with his erection jutting out from his body like a great flesh sword, he raced to the window only to see de Russe in the middle of the avenue, motioning frantically to him. Constantine knew he had to leave; he didn't question de Moray in any fashion, but he very much wanted his breeches.

Yet, it was not to be. The chamber door suddenly shuddered and, as Constantine leapt onto the windowsill, the door half-exploded in a shower of splinters. The woman upon the bed screamed. It was enough of a jolt for Constantine to leap for his life from the second-floor window, miraculously landing on his feet in the mud outside the tavern. Mud splashed up all over him but he didn't give it a thought as he caught the boat cloak de Russe tossed at him, wrapping it around his body to cover his nakedness as both he and Augustin ran as fast as they could for the cove where the skiff had just pushed off with Kerk at the helm.

Men were shouting from the window of the bedchamber and Constantine could hear Mme. Van Rompay crying and screaming, but he didn't dare turn around to look. Clearly, Dureau's men had somehow discovered their tryst and as he and Augustin neared the shore at low-tide, they knew they'd have to swim for the skiff. Kerk wasn't going to turn it around, and for good reason, but he did order the men to stop rowing as Constantine and Augustin plunged into the icy water and began swimming as fast as they could.

They could hear Kerk urging them on, telling them to hurry, and hurry they did, but Constantine was hampered by the fact that his erection was now being assaulted by icy sea water, so the swim was becoming rather painful for him. Still, he soldiered on, his powerful body plowing through the water until he reached the rear of the skiff. Augustin was a little slower, being that he was weighted down by his clothing, and by the time Constantine was on the boat, Augustin was hauled in a few seconds behind him.

Then, the men began rowing as hard and as fast as they could.

Then, and only then, did Constantine turn to see what he'd been running from and he wasn't surprised to see several men that he recognized rushing into the sea up to their ankles but coming to a halt when they realized they could not catch up to their prey. The light from the village behind them was just enough to illuminate the angry men on the sand, several of them, and he thought he caught a glimpse of Dureau himself. Dureau was a tall man, slender, so his silhouette was a distinctive one. But a shout from the pursuers dissolved any doubt as to who, exactly, had been chasing them.

"Le Brecque!" came a man's angry voice. It sounded very much like Dureau. "You bastard! I will have my vengeance upon you!"

With his men rowing furiously around him, Constantine stood up on the rocking boat to better see the man who was shouting threats at him. "Dureau, my love," he called out in return. "This is all you shall have of me!"

With that, he turned around and bent over at the waist, thrusting his white arse in Dureau's direction. He knew the man could see it, reflected in the weak light of the village, when he heard him laugh. But it was not a happy laugh.

"That is the *best* part of you!" Dureau boomed.

Constantine stood up and turned to face him, blowing the man a kiss. "Your wife thought so, too," he said sarcastically, blowing him another kiss. "I adore you, my dear friend. Until we meet again!"

By now, the fog that was rolling in from the sea began to envelope them as it moved towards the shore. Constantine lost sight of the angry French pirates but not before he heard Dureau's voice one last time.

"It shall be sooner than you think!"

Constantine knew that was probably true. Dureau's ships were probably inland at this point but he could move them out to sea quickly if he wanted to. The only saving grace at this point was the fog. For once, it would be their friend as it discouraged the French from pursuing them in it. But from this point on, Constantine knew he would have to be more careful of the French than usual.

The dirty game between them would get dirtier.

Such was the life of the commander of Poseidon's Legion.

Chapter One

Bristol Channel, several months later

THE CHANNEL WAS choppy, the sea a gray-green color after the passing of the most recent storm. Constantine's vessel *The Breath of Gaia,* or simply the *Gaia,* was returning from a journey up the River Severn and a visit to the town of Frampton, just south of Gloucester. There were three other vessels with him, smaller caravels that carried about thirty men each – the *Persephone,* the *Melinoe,* and the *Orpheus* – smaller ships that could move down river when the bottom became too shallow for the *Gaia.*

As Constantine stood on the poop deck, a light breeze lifted his shaggy blond hair. He could see his smaller ships flanking the larger vessel as they headed out of the mouth of the Severn and into the Bristol Channel. His home base was along the Cornwall coast to the south, and they would be there by morning. As he stood there looking over the side, trying to gauge just how much of the sandy bottom the storm had moved about and if his ship would run aground on it, a very large man with gold-tinted eyes walked up behind him.

"The denizens of Frampton were quite generous, my lord," he said. "In fact, it was all we could do to catch the valuables they were throwing at us."

Constantine turned to look at his First Mate; *Lucifer*, they called him. An ex-priest who had been with Constantine so long that he could hardly remember a day when Lucifer hadn't been by his side, his intimidating and ominous presence frightening the dog-water out of every man, woman, and child he came across. He was the best assassin in the fleet, surprisingly, and Constantine had seen the man do many a thing that would assure him a place at Satan's right hand.

But Lucifer wasn't much for aimless conversation, and he only spoke when he had something important to say. But he spoke in a voice that was as dark and raspy as one would imagine the devil's voice to be. Now, that voice had a hint of humor in it and Constantine merely shook his head.

"They were not throwing valuables at us to be generous," he said, turning his attention back to the channel. "They were doing it because you were standing at the mouth of the main avenue with a sword as long as a man is tall. No one wanted to be cut down by that thing."

A flicker of a smile creased Lucifer's lips. "I would like to think it is my pleasing personality that causes men to do as I wish."

Constantine snorted. "It is, my friend, it is," he assured him sarcastically. "Besides, as far as men of our sort go, we are generally very amenable when it comes to harvesting the towns."

Harvesting was a term Constantine used rather than the word he really meant – raiding and stealing. Things that pirates were known for. But Lucifer knew exactly what he meant.

"We are far more amenable than some of the others that gather along these coasts," he muttered, leaning on the rail as the sea breeze lifted his dark, curly hair. "The French, for example. At least we do not cut off the feet of our captives so they cannot run away."

Constantine grunted in agreement. "I will never understand the need for that kind of brutality," he said, watching the southern coast of Wales in the distance. "When we were in Perranporth last month, a man came to town telling tales of the French going as far as the coast of

Ireland. They evidently raided a small fishing village and captured several men to row one of the new vessels they confiscated from the Portuguese. Those who did not have their feet cut off were chained to the cannons. It was a horrific tale, to say the least."

Lucifer had heard the story. "It was Nicolas Van Rompay, I heard," he said quietly. "He's amassing a fleet, Con. You know he wants to punish you for what you did to his brother but, more than that, he wants to challenge us for supremacy over these waters. He will challenge Shaw's Devils as well."

Constantine didn't seem worried. "The day Nicolas Van Rompay can best me and Shaw MacDougall is the day we no longer deserve this great empire that we have acquired," he said. "Henry, our great king, and all of his fleets cannot defeat me in his own waters, so what makes the French think they can?"

Lucifer shrugged. "They are arrogant bastards, Con. They have more pride than common sense."

Constantine knew that and, true to form, was unruffled by the thought of a French threat, even after what had happened with Dureau those months back. "I am certain Shaw can hold off Nicolas," he said. "He hates the man, you know. But he hates the Spaniards more."

That was the truth.

Shaw "Savage" MacDougall was an ally of Constantine's, a Highlander from Scotland and the prince of all pirates along the shores of western England, Wales, and Scotland. It was well-known that the Spanish were his particular nemesis, but Shaw and Constantine had formed a powerful bond over the years, a bond that had been the result of a series of violent actions.

The first had been when Shaw had attacked the merchant vessel that Constantine had been sailing on, a vessel owned by his adoptive father. That had been years ago, when both of them were young men, but it was something Constantine had never forgotten. He'd sworn his vengeance upon the Scottish pirate and in their second encounter, it had been Constantine who had nearly robbed Shaw of not only his vessel, but of his life.

It had all been over a woman, of course. A woman had misled Constantine with her wicked wiles, blaming Shaw for something that had never occurred. But when the moment came to slit Shaw's throat, something strange occurred – Constantine had realized not only the lies of the woman, but the error of his ways. His apology to Shaw had been the seed of trust between them and in a world where men were brutal and deceitful, an honest man in the midst of such things was a rare jewel, indeed. Shaw had understood that, as had Constantine, and an unlikely alliance was born.

Joining forces with their substantial fleets, they called themselves the Pirates of Britannia and ruled the stretch of coastline from Scarba all the way to Plymouth. It was a valuable and vast stretch of coast, and most coveted by their enemies. And with death on the line, both Shaw and Constantine knew they could depend on each other no matter what.

Such was the strength of their honor.

Lucifer knew all of this, of course. He knew of the hated Spanish, the wicked French, and everything in between. He looked out to sea as he pondered the Scottish pirate prince, a man he respected a great deal.

"Shaw hates the Spanish and Santiago Fernandez is the recipient of most of that animosity," he finally muttered. "Even though the feeling is mutual, Santiago has plenty of hate for you also. You know he is repairing that man o' war he acquired a few months ago in the battle against the Dutch fleet."

"I know."

"Rumor says he intends to bring it into our territory once it is fully operational."

Constantine turned to the man, smiling because Lucifer was. "And we shall be ready for him," he said. "If Santiago and his dogs think they can damage my coast, I will ensure it is more painful for them than it is for me. They would do well to stay away."

"But you are hoping they come, anyway."

Constantine laughed, clapping him on the shoulder. "Of course I am," he said. "How else can I prove my superiority? Besides – I will bombard them from the shore with my cannons and Shaw will bring his fleet in from the north to box them in. We will sink them to the bottom of the ocean. What a joyful day that will be."

Lucifer chuckled softly because, in truth, he knew Constantine meant it. The man would be positively ecstatic should he be able to destroy the arrogant Spanish fleet. As the two of them shared the mental image of such a bloody victory, they were joined by Augustin.

Having just come up from the hold where he had been inventorying the harvest from Frampton, Augustin drew in a deep breath as the salty sea air hit his nostrils. Oddly enough, the quartermaster for Constantine's fleet was prone to sea sickness. Augustin's position as quartermaster was a new one, in fact, having only received the title after Constantine's long-time quartermaster had been captured by Nicolas Van Rompay two years earlier, strapped to the bow of the ship, and left to die in torment. Augustin, serving as Constantine's lead swordsman at the time, had fought valiantly to recover the old quartermaster, but he could not be saved.

It was that kind of loyalty that Constantine respected and, in spite of his sea-sickness, Augustin was one of the fiercest pirates Constantine had ever seen. He could, and would, complete his duties no matter how badly he felt, now as the man who literally controlled the wealth and men of Constantine's ships. Nearly throwing himself over the rail, Augustin breathed deeply.

As the man tried to calm his nervous stomach, Remy de Moray came up beside him. Remy was muscular and rather young, a handsome rake of a man who shared Constantine's philosophy about women. Often, they shared women, something that Augustin and Lucifer refrained from. Augustin was married and Lucifer was the celibate type, but Constantine and Remy more than made up for it.

"It should be smooth sailing all the way home," Remy said, shielding his dark eyes from the sun as he gazed up at the main sail. "The storm that blew through here this morning has drifted off to sea, fortunately."

Constantine nodded, seeing the black clouds from the earlier storm off to the west. "It is bombarding Ireland now," he said before turning to Remy and Augustin. "Is everything secured below deck?"

Remy nodded because Augustin couldn't seem to pull himself away from the rail yet. As Constantine's second mate aboard the *Gaia*, he was efficient and dependable.

"It is," he said. "We have goats and horses in the hold along with enough supplies to see us through the next few months. Plus, there are some lovely women's garments that a certain young woman in Perranporth might appreciate. She might very well demonstrate that appreciation and I should be happy to receive it."

He lifted his dark eyebrows rather lasciviously as Augustin stood up from the rail. "Those are for my wife," he said in a tone that Remy was afraid to refute. "She spends enough time alone at Perran Castle, waiting for me to return. The least I can do is reward the woman for her loyalty."

As Augustin glared threateningly at Remy as if daring the man to argue with him, Lucifer scratched his chin. "What about Margam Abbey, Con?" he asked thoughtfully. "We shall be passing close to it and they have never shown us any resistance. Why not stop and ask for a... donation to our cause from a rather wealthy abbey?"

Before Constantine could answer, Remy spoke. "They will not want to see us so soon after what happened the last time we were there," he said, stifling laughter. "Do you recall? We forced the nuns to drink and when they were drunk enough, the men forced them to strip off their clothing."

He was off in a fit of giggles as Lucifer shook his head with great disgust. "Upon your death, there will be a special place in hell designated especially for you," he said. "I still do not understand why you encouraged such a thing."

Remy couldn't stop laughing and, in fact, Constantine and Augustin were joining him because it had been rather humorous, if not rather dastardly.

"No one was harmed," Constantine pointed out. "I did not let the men ravage the women. In fact, some of the nuns seemed rather eager to remove those cloying habits. You see? It was not as bad as you seem to think it was."

Lucifer didn't think it was at all humorous. "You were throwing money at them," he pointed out angrily. "Of course they took their clothing off. You were throwing gold coins at them!"

Remy was chuckling uncontrollably as Augustin pushed him aside, away from Lucifer before the man became truly enraged. Ever the calming influence, Augustin held up a quelling hand.

"It was wrong to get the nuns drunk, I agree," he said. "But Con is right; they were not harmed other than their modesty. But I must say that stripping nuns is something I never thought I would see."

Disgusted by the entire conversation, Lucifer simply shook his head and turned away. "As I said," he muttered, "there will be a special place in hell for those of you who forced the nuns to disrobe."

Constantine was fighting off a grin simply because Remy was so far gone with laughter. In remembering the incident, it had been rather funny because the drunk nuns truly hadn't been distressed by any of it. At least, not at the time. Afterwards, when the drink wore off, was another matter entirely, but Constantine's men had plied the women with drink purely as entertainment. Simply another sin in a long line of sins for men who were rife with them. To be certain, he was going to hell anyway as Lucifer pointed out, and one more mark against him wouldn't matter in the long run. In any case, he sought to ease Lucifer just as Augustin had meant to.

"No more drunken nuns, I swear it," he said. "In fact, I intend that we should return to Perran Castle for a long rest. We have been quite occupied as of late and I think I should like to return home, just for a time. I might even go and see my sister, who has just given birth to her first child. A trip south to St. Ives to visit her and her husband might be in order."

The mood of the men seemed to ease at that point and Remy's incessant giggling ceased at the thought of returning home for a time. "It would be good to spend time with my wife," Augustin said, somewhat wistfully as he thought of the fair Merryn. "It has been a while since I have spent any length of time with her."

Thoughts immediately turned to their home base of Perran Castle along the western Cornwall coast, which was Constantine's main stronghold. He had two other castles as well – Holywell Castle to the north of Perran, and Mithian Castle further inland, which had belonged to the le Brecque family for many decades. It had passed to him when his adoptive father had passed away years ago and his sister used to live there before she married and moved south to St. Ives. Although returning home was always a pleasant thought, Constantine found himself restless if he stayed on dry land for too long. He had more enemies there than he did at sea, and he was much more comfortable dealing with the enemies at sea.

Still, he'd promised the men a rest and he could hear the longing in Augustin's voice as he spoke of his wife. They were in the month of October now and soon, the Christmas season would be upon them. Perhaps they would remain on land until the Christmas season passed providing the French and Spanish behaved themselves. But that was his last calm thought before the distant sounds of thunder boomed across the gray waters of the channel. Since there were no clouds in the sky, Constantine knew it wasn't thunder.

It was the sound of a cannon volley.

"Down!" he bellowed to his men. "Everyone down!"

Men began falling to the deck, a reflex reaction to Constantine's booming command. Only Lucifer and Augustin didn't fall to the deck; they began screaming at the other men further down the deck, near the forecastle, who might not have heard the command. There were men up on the mizzenmast, laying out the blackened pirate sails, and those men were like sitting ducks as a volley a cannon fire shot across the decks, tearing up everything in its path.

Wood splintered, spraying out over the men like shards of glass. More than one man was pierced by the wood. Great projectiles of iron balls ripped through the foremast and the shrouds, the rope ladders that were attached to the masts. Men who had been up on the sails were now either plummeting into the ocean or spilling down onto the deck. Once the cannonballs had sailed passed the ship and out to sea on the opposite side, Lucifer and Augustin began screaming at the men to man the cannons.

It was time to fight back.

Constantine raced to the port side of the ship, facing south at this point, in time to see a large French warship pulling out of a small inlet. The French were well into the Bristol Channel, which was Constantine's territory. Remy was suddenly beside him, handing him a spyglass so he could get a better look. The spyglass had come with a horde of treasure they'd stolen from Grecian pirates off the coast of Spain, something they'd never seen before, and Constantine used it constantly. With it, he could see the emerging French warship, a vessel he'd seen before. Disgust – and some apprehension – filled him.

"Damn," he hissed. "It is Dureau's vessel, the *Ganymede*. It looks as if the man has surprised us."

Remy nodded seriously. "Do you see any other vessels with him?"

Constantine shook his head. "With that beast, he does not need any other support," he said. "Send our other ships onward; I do not want them caught up in a battle of the bigger ships. Dureau's eighteen cannons can devastate the smaller ships, so tell them to go. They are not to stand and fight."

Remy was off, preparing to signal the smaller vessels, as Lucifer joined Constantine on the poop deck.

"They must have been following us," he hissed. "They stayed out of range just enough to watch us go up the Severn and then wait for us to emerge, loaded with goods."

Constantine was annoyed to say the least. "It is the *Ganymede*," he said. "Dureau is in my waters now. Are the port side cannons ready?"

"Aye."

"He is heading in our direction, so it would be useless to return fire at a slimmer profile," he said, his mind working quickly. "Turn the vessel south so we can come alongside him. Even loaded down as we are, the *Gaia* is more maneuverable than that behemoth, so bring us into position, Lucifer. *Quickly.* The man has caught us at a disadvantage and we must gain the upper hand."

Lucifer was off, bellowing orders to the helmsman to turn the rudder hard a-port, quickly turning the *Gaia* and giving her a much smaller profile to shoot at. Now, they were heading right for the *Ganymede* and Constantine's men were rushing to their posts even as some of them were removing the wounded to below deck. The big, black flag with the red serpent-like dragon on it, signifying Poseidon's Legion, was raised on the mainmast. Now, the French would know exactly who they were dealing with.

And the Legion was out for blood.

"Minimal damage, Con," Augustin said as he clambered up the ladder towards Constantine's position. "Those bastards could not hit anything if they tried. Women must be manning the cannons this day."

Constantine flashed a grin. "Fortunate for us," he said. He snorted. "They caught us off-guard, Gus. It was sheer luck that they did not do more damage. We have the deck cannon on the bow?"

"Aye."

"Use it. We are heading straight for them; one good shot at their foremast and we can weaken them significantly. Do it to them before they do it to us."

Augustin nodded shortly. "We are already taking aim," he said. "Look; see Lucifer up with the cannon?"

Constantine had to peer through the dangling ropes and pierced sails to see what Augustin was talking about. He could, indeed, see the man using timber wedges to control the barrel's elevation, moving it into position. Given the movement of the ship, and the constantly changing angle, it was no mean feat, but Lucifer was skilled that way. Constantine grasped Augustin by the arm.

"Fire at their foremast," he said. "When we come alongside, give them all port cannons and take out their rudder. But after that, we continue home as quickly as we can. The *Gaia* only has twelve guns and that beautiful Flemish warship of mine is still at Perranporth and all of her twenty-two guns. We need that ship to have superiority over Dureau and he knows it, so hit him as much as we can and then we run. Hopefully we can damage him enough not to follow us."

Augustin was off, going to relay orders to the gun crews and to Lucifer. Constantine maintained his position on the poop deck to the rear, his eyes on every aspect of the operations of his vessel. It was his intention to make it home in one piece, with the least loss of life, so strategy would come into play at this point. Dureau had tried to ambush him but the man was going to suffer in return.

The French weren't going to have him; not this time.

He would live to fight another day.

Lucifer's aim was true that day; he managed to destroy the fore-mast, knocking the entire thing down into the sea, and the seven guns on the port side did a good deal of damage as they passed the ship, including damaging the rudder, as Constantine had hoped.

But Dureau had time to prepare for their pass and he'd countered with a blast from nine cannons, most of them chewing up the port side deck and into the gun crews on the port side. Constantine was able to flee home much faster than Dureau was, leaving the French ship in the channel to limp away, but Constantine's boat wasn't without loss. It had been a costly encounter in that he'd lost four men, with twelve wounded, and seriously damaged the *Gaia*. Without significant repairs, she wasn't going anywhere.

The sight of Perran Castle at dawn the next day was a welcome sight for all.

Chapter Two

Village of Perranporth
One-Eyed Whale Tavern

I T WAS SMOKY and dark, even as daylight broke over the wilds of Cornwall. The windows of the tavern were small and didn't do much to allow light or ventilation into the common room of the establishment.

It was a room that was strewn with the bodies of those who had spent the night in the small hovel of safety in a part of England that was said to be the most mysterious and dangerous of all. No one wanted to sleep outside in Cornwall, so the inns and taverns were usually full of both locals and travelers. Men were on the floor, on tables, but all of them waking as the tavern keeper and two wenches moved through the room, rousing men and demanding they either pay for a morning meal or leave immediately. There was no mercy in a place like this. It was pay or get out.

Out into the sunrise of a new day.

But there were three people who hadn't slept on the floor or on the tables the previous night. They'd been some of the fortunate few who had rooms to sleep in, on dirty beds that were crawling with vermin. In fact, the woman hadn't slept on her rented bed at all. The floor, although cold and hard, had been preferable. Her body was achy as a result on this dreary morning but that didn't matter; she wasn't here to seek comfort.

She was here because she had no choice.

Sitting on the hard bench, she clutched a cup of warmed wine in her hand, sipping at it. The tavern keeper had brought it around to her and her companions, and there was a chipped wooden pitcher on the table containing the cheap, steaming drink. There was also stale bread, left over from the previous night, and chunks of white cheese that had blue mold on it. She simply picked off the mold and ate the cheese, unsure when her next meal would be.

The day ahead was filled with uncertainty.

One of her two male companions sat at the table with her but he didn't speak. He simply sat there, drinking his wine, looking to the door of the tavern expectantly. He was, in fact, expecting the third person in their party to come through that door at any moment, and as the room around them become more alive with coughing, farting men as they rose from a night's sleep, the door to the tavern finally lurched open and a young warrior, clad in leather and heavy wool, came through. He headed straight for his companions, his foggy breath hanging in the cold air of the chilly tavern.

"It is as we have hoped," he whispered loudly, claiming a seat next to the woman and nearly spilling her wine in his haste. "The ships have been sighted this morning, coming into the cove. The entire village is talking about it; le Brecque has been sighted!"

He spoke to the older man, the one who had been staring at the door in silence. When the older man heard the news, he heaved a sigh of relief.

"Finally," he muttered. "We have been waiting for almost a week in this hellish place for the man to make an appearance. At last, he has come home."

"I saw the ships myself!"

The older man sighed faintly, great satisfaction in that gesture. "Le Brecque will receive the lady's missive when he goes to the castle," he said. "He must come to the tavern to seek her after that."

With that, both men turned to the woman, who seemed uncomfortable with their attention. In fact, she wouldn't look at them, turning away as if cringing from their expectant gazes.

"I left the message at Perran Castle, as you instructed," she said. "I asked le Brecque to meet me here."

"And you mentioned why?" the older man demanded. "You told his men everything?"

The woman nodded. "I did," she said. Then, she dared to look at them. "But it all depends on whether or not the information you gave me is correct. Your nautical commanders have paid money for information on Constantine le Brecque, so let us see if what they paid for is true, Lord Wembury. It all depends on that."

Thomas Sherford, Lord Wembury, gazed steadily at the woman. She was, in truth, a lass of astonishing beauty with high cheekbones and big, blue eyes, but she was also a woman with a somewhat bold tongue. That wasn't something he appreciated, not when she was such a key player in a plot that ran all the way to the halls of London and beyond.

There were very powerful men who had entrusted him with this scheme…

So much hinged on this one lone woman and Wembury didn't like her sassy manner. It irritated him. Reaching out, he grabbed her by the wrist, squeezing hard enough so that she understood the seriousness of the situation.

"The information is correct," he hissed. "Understand me, woman; our king has been trying for years to capture Constantine le Brecque. He has used my fleet in his efforts only to see great destruction of my vessels, and lives and money lost. But his pursuit of Constantine is not because the man controls the seas without regard to the King of England. Constantine is a pirate, pure and simple. He is a man who steals and kills. He is a murderer."

The woman had heard all of this before and she didn't like the fact that Wembury was hurting her wrist. "Everyone knows what he is," she said. "Every child in this part of England has heard the rhyme – *Up the hill, over the dale, along the seashore still; among the waves, the Sea-God lives, a thirst for blood and kill.*"

It was a song that most children along the western shores of England and Wales had learned from their parents, warning them to stay away from the beaches for fear that the dreaded pirate le Brecque, often called the Sea-God, would rise out of the water and gobble them up. It worked, for the most part, but to the younger generation, it had given Constantine le Brecque a rather legendary status. There was something dangerous but admirable about the man.

And it was that legend Wembury intended to kill.

"He is no Sea-God," Wembury grumbled, "and our move against him has little to do with his piracy. There is a much more serious reason – it is because Constantine is a viable threat to the one who will assume the throne of England when Henry has been removed."

The woman had heard this, too. "I know," she said impatiently, trying to pull her hand away from his grasp. "It is Edward, Earl of March, who seeks Constantine's demise because of his claim to the throne. You have told me all of this."

Wembury wouldn't let her go. Her attitude seemed callous to the seriousness of the situation and that inflamed him.

"Listen to me, you simple girl, and listen well," he muttered. "It is Edward who will succeed the throne, not the king's bastard half-brother who calls himself a pirate and rules the seas as if they were his own private domain. Constantine le Brecque was born of Henry V's loins, a liaison between him and a young noblewoman from the House of le Brecque. Although the woman was sent away to bear her child in secret, those loyal to Henry knew of his bastard son and told him. Constantine, therefore, fostered in the finest homes and was even given the title Duke of Cornwall for a time until Henry's legitimate son was born and the title was given to him. Even so, le Brecque holds the title Earl of

West Wales. Did you know that?"

The woman did; she'd heard it from her brother several times, the same man who was sitting next to Wembury and allowing the man to pull on her.

"I did know that," she said through clenched teeth. "And let go of me. You are hurting me."

Wembury held on to her a moment longer, giving her a hard squeeze before finally letting her go.

"You may know it, but you show little respect for your role in all of this," he said, eyeing her with great disdain. "Le Brecque has more enemies than he can possibly comprehend. Not only has he made enemies in his piracy, but those who want his half-brother, Henry, removed from the throne also want le Brecque eliminated because his claim to the throne, to some, may be stronger than Edward's. As the half-brother of the legitimate king, there is a faction loyal to Henry V that could put Constantine upon the throne and that must never happen."

The woman sighed heavily as she rubbed her wrist. "This information has been repeated to me many times," she said quietly. "It has been beaten into me, inked into my brain until I can think of nothing else. I know what I am to do and I know what I am to tell him; I am the daughter of the quartermaster who served under him, a man who died two years ago at the hands of the French pirates. Using that story, I am to bring him to Three Crosses Abbey in Wales where Edward's men will be waiting for him. I know all of this and I will accomplish my task. You needn't worry."

Wembury's gaze lingered on her a moment before sitting back in his seat as if finally satisfied she understood the seriousness of what they were about to undertake. Months, even years, of planning had all come down to this one perfect plan. Edward was to be the only successor to Henry's throne, but that meant removing a man who was a very serious threat.

A bastard prince posing as a pirate.

"Excellent, Lady Gregoria," Wembury finally said. Then, he looked to the woman's brother, sitting next to him. "You have ensured she will be well-rewarded, have you not?"

Olin de Moyon nodded slowly, his gaze traveling to his stubborn, sometimes difficult younger sister. As Baron Buckland, a title he had inherited from a father who had been mentally ill for a very long time but had refused to die until only recently, he had a good deal of money and military might at his disposal and was determined to use it for the Earl of March's claim to the throne. A politically ambitious man, he needed his sister's help because he very much wanted to show his loyalty to Edward and he wanted to be in the man's debt.

That was where lovely, virginal Gregoria became a pawn in her brother's plans.

"I have promised her a home of her own and a garden," Olin said. "That is all she wants. But she will not get it until she delivers le Brecque to Three Crosses Abbey. I have a beautiful little manse waiting for her near the sea, so the sooner she accomplishes this task, the better. She is well aware of what will happen if she does not see this through."

Wembury looked at him with interest. "Tell me."

Olin glanced at his sister as if to level off a threat he'd used against her on more than one occasion. "She will be exiled from my home without a penny. She will be destitute."

Wembury smiled, a delightfully nasty gesture. "As she should be," he said, returning his attention to Gregoria. "Do you hear? And I shall make it so that no good family will take you in. Do this task for us and be rewarded. Fail, and it shall mean your doom."

Gregoria wasn't thrilled with the threats, mostly because she knew these men meant them. She was fearful of being tossed out into the world without a cent to her name. She wasn't an ambitious woman, and she'd never had any greater goals other than to live in peace with her dogs and her flowers. But the thought of being homeless and hungry genuinely frightened her. She knew she had no choice in any of this so it was best to simply see it through. For a woman with no political leanings, she didn't see this as the destruction of a man. She simply saw it as her salvation.

"I will not fail," she said steadily. "I will do as I have been instructed."

Wembury cocked a bushy eyebrow. "You'd better," he said, a hint of threat in his tone. "Now, your brother and I will retreat to another part of this room. You will sit here, alone, presumably waiting for le Brecque's response to your message. If he does not come by nightfall, then you will go to Perran Castle and demand to see him. Is that clear?"

Gregoria nodded, tired of being bullied by the man. "It is," she said. "You had better leave. You do not want to be seen with me."

That was true. Even though a roomful of simpletons had seen the three together, Wembury was fairly confident that no one would talk. There was no reason that they should and, soon enough, Gregoria would be out of the tavern and well on her way to accomplishing her task.

Gathering the possessions he'd set at his feet, including an expensive broadsword, Wembury stood up.

"Remember your duty," he muttered, collecting everything into his arms as Olin stood up next to him. "Remember your house by the sea. It shall all be yours if you succeed."

Gregoria simply nodded, averting her gaze and hoping both men would get the hint and leave her alone. She was relieved when they wandered away, heading out of her line of sight to some other part of the common room. That was all she cared about; that they leave her alone.

Then, the anxiety came.

It had all come down to this, a terrible plot at this very moment. God, she had no idea how she found herself in this situation. She was a simple woman, after all, but she was the maiden sister of a baron who had become quite politically motivated as of late. That was her only crime, being related to a man who wanted the favor of the Earl of March, and now she was involved in his scheme.

God help her.

As the morning deepened, Gregoria sat at the table near the door, sipping on watered wine, waiting for the moment that Constantine le Brecque would come through the door so she could get on with her brother's plans. Having grown up near Exmoor, she had heard of le Brecque and of his pirates. In fact, they'd even raided the coast near her home from time to time, although they'd never made it to Dunster Castle, where she lived. All she knew of le Brecque was the man's reputation for pillage and plunder, so she reasoned that perhaps it wasn't such a bad thing to betray a man like that to his enemies. He was wicked, this le Brecque, a man with a dangerous reputation. Aye... perhaps she was really doing England a service in helping her brother and Lord Wembury.

At least, she kept telling herself that.

By dusk, however, Constantine le Brecque hadn't made an appearance and Gregoria found herself taking the small road out of town, heading to the great bastion on the cliffs overlooking the ocean in her quest to meet with the great pirate who ruled these waters.

She had a task to complete and there was no time to waste, not even to wait for an errant pirate prince. She had to catch him before he sailed out to sea once again, perhaps not to return for months and months.

Therefore, she had to take the lead.

To trap a pirate.

Chapter Three

"DO YOU KNOW what I hate?"

"Nay – what?"

Constantine had asked the question as he lay on his back, staring up at the ceiling of his vaulted solar. The ceiling was a masterpiece of Norman vaulting, with arches bisecting arches, and blue stars painting on the stone. He was laying on a velvet couch, something he'd stolen off of a fine Spanish merchant ship last year along with the merchant's two very big dogs, who now lay happily at his feet. Henry and Edward, named after the fools who were vying for the throne of England, were his great companions when he was home. He never took them to sea for fear one of them might fall off the deck, or worse, become injured. Constantine had a soft spot for his dogs. He petted Henry's broad back as he rolled his head in Lucifer's direction.

"I hate laying on a bed that is not being gently rocked by the sea," he said. "I can still feel the motion of the water, yet I am on land. I hate that it is only dirt beneath my feet."

Lucifer gave Constantine a smirk as he poured himself a cup of wine. Everything at Perran Castle was the very finest money could buy, including the wine from Spain and the cups of fine Welsh pewter. He took a healthy drink of it as his dirty boots walked the fine rugs of

Constantine's solar, rugs that had come all the way from the Holy Land, made by beautiful women who covered their faces with silken scarves. At least, that was what they'd been told when they'd confiscated the rugs from an Italian merchant. Lucifer paused by a particularly elaborate tapestry, cup in hand as he gazed up at the intricate scene of an army marching on a castle.

"I do not have the sea in my blood as you do," he said after a moment. "I am very happy on land. In fact, I do believe I am happier here than anywhere."

Constantine lifted his head, his brow furrowed with worry. "You are not about to tell me that you are giving up the sea, are you?" he asked. When Lucifer turned to look at him, Constantine sat up on his velvet couch. "You cannot leave me. I was planning on giving you the *Leucosia* when we are finished with her refit. Someone has to command that mammoth warship, Lucifer. Why not you?"

He was speaking of the warship that was docked a few miles to the north, the one with twenty-two guns that they were so proud of. Lucifer was mildly surprised by the suggestion.

"You've not mentioned this before," he said.

Constantine shook his head. "I have not and, for that, I do apologize," he said. "I have been wanting to tell you and I thought to, mayhap, make a grand surprise out of it, but now you know. I want you to helm the *Leucosia* when she is fit for the sea again."

Lucifer's gaze lingered on him a moment. In truth, he was very pleased. The Flemish beauty was a great prize, but she also had a rather slippery history. She was such a prize that she'd been stolen a few times over and that was the main reason she was now up the river, in dock, so that no one could see her and consequently steal her. Once she put to sea, the odds of her being stolen would increase dramatically. Lucifer knew that very well. Scratching his chin, he wandered in Constantine's direction.

"The *Leucosia*," he said slowly, as if mulling over her name. "A ship that was originally built by the Dutch and christened the *Bruges*. Not a year later, Santiago Fernandez and his *Los Demonios de Mar* were able to damage her enough in battle so that his men boarded her, murdered the crew, and renamed her the *Astorga*. Fernandez's second-in-command, Amaro de Soto, then became her captain."

Constantine nodded as Lucifer recited the history of the grand vessel. "The man known as *Diabolito*," he said, rising to his feet and going to collect his own cup of wine. "He was, indeed, a fearsome bastard until we cornered the *Astorga* near Arcachon and battered her so badly that we were able to board her. *Diabolito* was not so powerful then; the ship became mine."

Lucifer shook his head as if disapproving of the situation. "You should have killed de Soto rather than set him and what men he had left adrift," he said. "Now, he's out for your blood. It would have been one less man out to kill you, Con."

Constantine took a long drink of the sweet red wine. He smacked his lips. "You are not thinking clearly," he said quietly. "Had I killed de Soto, Fernandez would have gone mad with vengeance. By not killing his 'Little Devil', I showed mercy, which means the next time any of my men are at the mercy of Fernandez, he may more than likely spare them. What I did was calculated, Lucifer. I never do anything without a reason."

Lucifer simply lifted his eyebrows, as if Constantine's merciful reason had just occurred to him. "You are a man with vision," he said. "Once you show mercy to Fernandez's men, he must return the favor."

"Exactly."

"And if I am caught with the *Leucosia*, he will more than likely not kill me and my crew."

Constantine tapped his skull. "It is the code of the pirates," he said. "Honor among thieves. If he kills you after I showed his crew mercy, then it shall go very badly for him. Fernandez is just arrogant enough that something such as a pirate's honor matters to him. Now you understand, my friend."

Lucifer did, indeed. "I fear that I have underestimated you. Forgive me." Then, he lifted his cup. "If you want me to command the *Leucosia*, then I shall. It will be an honor. But you know she will be a target to every pirate in these waters."

Constantine nodded. "That is why my best commander must be in charge of her," he said. "But tell me it is enough to keep you at my side. It frightens me when you speak of your love of the land over the sea."

Lucifer wouldn't look at him. He was a man of great introspect, and a man of great mystery. No one really knew anything about him other than he had once been a priest, but something had happened that had caused him to forsake his vows. He'd never spoken of it to Constantine, and they had been close friends for over ten years. Constantine figured that when the man was ready to speak of his past, he would. But upon the seas, a man's background didn't matter. Only his love of glory and his loyalty to his fellow pirate were of interest.

"My love of the land," Lucifer finally murmured as if lost in thought. "I *do* love the land. I never put to sea until those years ago when we first met, so the land has always been my first love."

Constantine drained his wine cup and poured himself more. "For me, I have been to sea from my earliest memories," he said. "You will recall that my adoptive father was a merchant."

"I do."

"He had an entire fleet of ships," Constantine continued. "Ships that would sail all the way to the Holy Land, down to Africa, or up to the north where the Northmen live. I have been everywhere on those ships with my father. I have always felt at home on the sea."

Lucifer listened to the fondness in the man's voice as he spoke. "It is said that you were borne of the waves and lifted up by the gods of the sea as their most prized possession," he said, a twinkle in his eye. "Everyone believes that you are a god, you know."

Constantine shook his head, grinning that easy smile he had. "I am *not* a god," he said. "But I will let men believe what they would. I would rather be borne of the waves than borne of a woman who was the mistress of a king, a bastard who was conceived in lust. There is something dishonorable about that. Even so, it makes me a man of royal blood and, even now, there is a kingdom ruled by a pious fool that should belong to me."

Lucifer pondered that for a moment. It was no secret that Constantine was the bastard son of Henry V, a man who should have been given his royal due but who was denied it because of his illegitimate birth. Constantine rarely spoke of it, however, so moments like this were few and far between. It was usually when he drank, which he rarely did, so the quickly-consumed cup of red wine was already having an effect. He was weary; they were all weary. Sometimes, exhaustion had a way of loosening a man's tongue.

"If it belongs to you, then press your claim," Lucifer said. "With your money, you could raise such an army that neither Henry nor Edward would be able to stop it."

Constantine shrugged. "That is of no interest to me," he said. Then, he grinned. "I could not have nearly the fun that I have now should I be forced to live on land and deal with men's petty squabbles. Nay, my friend, I am better off where I am. It is where I belong."

Lucifer held up his cup, clanking it against Constantine's in a gesture of cheer and goodwill. "And this is where I belong," he said with some warmth in his tone. "I am not going anywhere, Con. I was merely reflecting on my love of the land and the days of my youth. They were happy days in the north."

"North?" Constantine asked casually, interested that Lucifer should actually speak of his past. "North where? You have never told me where you are from, you know. I am coming to think you were born nowhere. You simply appeared one day."

Lucifer laughed softly. "I was, indeed, born," he said. "In Northumberland."

Constantine lifted his eyebrows as if he'd just been told something amazing. "Northumberland?" he repeated. "I do not believe it. Will you tell me more?"

Lucifer shrugged. "There is not much to tell," he said. "I was born, I fostered and trained as a knight. But instead of becoming a knight, I became a priest and then I found you one day when you were raiding a priory near Caernarvon. Do you recall?"

Constantine nodded, gulping more of the sweet wine. It was delicious, and warm, and very comforting. "Of course I do," he said. "You told me to repent. Then, you grabbed a broadsword and tried to force me to confess my sins."

"I only joined your band of pirates to save your soul, you know. A man like you should not be relegated to hell."

Constantine laughed. "You told me and Remy and Gus only yesterday that there was a special place in hell waiting for us."

Lucifer fought off a grin. "For them, aye. But you still have a chance to be saved."

Constantine slapped him on the shoulder. "If my men are not to be saved, then I do not wish to be saved. I will gladly go to hell with them."

"Then you are well on your way."

Constantine laughed heartily. "You would know, my friend," he said. Then, he sobered as he realized that his wine was almost gone. He cast Lucifer a side glance as he went to pour more. "Tell me something."

"What?"

"Is your real name Lucifer?"

Lucifer didn't say anything for a moment. Then, with a smile playing on his lips, he shook his head. "It is not. My mother did not hate me so much to name me that."

"Will you ever tell me your real name, then?"

"Mayhap someday."

It was as close as Constantine had ever come to nearly wresting something personal out of the very private man. But he didn't push; he knew not to. Laughing again, he put a hand on Lucifer's shoulder in a brotherly gesture as Kerk le Sander suddenly appeared in the solar doorway.

"My lord," he said. "There is a woman at the gates, asking to see you."

Constantine looked at him. "A woman?" he repeated. "What woman?"

The man gestured with his hands; very big hands that were rough with the life he'd lived. "The same woman who came several days ago, asking to leave you a message," he said. "Do you recall, my lord? Upon your return, when you asked the men for a report on the situation since your departure, they told you that a woman had come to see you. She said she bore a most urgent message and would await you in town at the One-Eyed Whale."

Constantine began nodding even before Kerk was finished. "Aye, I recall now," he said. "But I will be truthful when I say that I did not think anything of it. But she is here again, you say?"

Kerk nodded. "At the gatehouse. She has asked to see you again."

"Is she pretty?"

That caused the man to grin, displaying a mouthful of straight, white teeth. He was a very handsome man, someone that Constantine considered strong competition for female attention.

"Most beautiful, my lord," he said. "I am rather sorry that she asked for you and not me."

Constantine slammed his cup down swiftly and headed for the door; there was no way he'd let Kerk get to a beautiful woman before he did. "Then let us not keep the lady waiting," he said, weaving a bit because of the two cups of wine he'd ingested. "Did she give a name?"

Kerk shook his head. "She did not."

"It does not matter. If she is beautiful, then beauty is the only name she needs."

Slightly drunk, Constantine left Lucifer behind as he quit his solar with Kerk and headed out into the dusk. The sun was nearly gone on the horizon to the west, leaving a sky blanketed in stars and a soft sea breeze blowing in from the water.

As Constantine headed for the gatehouse, he managed to look at the mighty castle that he'd built. As the Earl of West Wales, he had lands and money at his disposal, and using pale Cornwall stone, he'd hired craftsmen and stonemasons from as far away as Italy to build his masterpiece. It took three years to construct, and had only been finished a mere five years before, but already Perran Castle was legendary in the annals of Cornwall history.

Perched on a cliff overlooking the sea, Perran was built down into the very cliff itself, dug in deep, with two enormous towers that faced the ocean, manned with eight nine-pounder cannons each, on different levels, that gave the towers a full range of fire over the ocean for miles in all directions. There were two more towers on the land side, each of them manned with six four-pounder cannons each, and there were four-pounder cannons on the battlements surrounding the castle was well. As far as fortified castles went, Perran was the envy of every warlord on land or on sea. Only a fool and his army would try to breach the seat of England's fiercest pirate.

And Constantine was well aware of it. He was as proud of Perran as one would have been over a son. It was manned by a mercenary land army he paid extremely well and they were fiercely loyal to their liege. They were different from the pirates that put to sea with him; the army at Perran was comprised strictly of land-lovers.

It was these land-lovers who acknowledged Constantine as he approached the gatehouse, a two-portcullis monstrosity that was a marvel of architecture unto itself. The first portcullis, the one nearest the bailey, was lifted but the second portcullis was closed, as were the gates beyond. Only the small, fortified mangate built into the southern gate was open and there were men lingering near it. When they glanced up and saw Constantine approach, they backed off, clearing the path so he could see just what had them so interested.

It was, indeed, a woman.

The first things Constantine saw were bright blue eyes of the most beautiful shape. The woman was finely dressed, clutching a big satchel against her, and wearing a heavy cloak with fur lining in this damp, cold weather. But all he could see were her eyes because she had the hood of her cloak pulled down, partially covering the right side and lower portion of her face. Intrigued simply by the beauty he was witnessing, Constantine went up to the portcullis.

"Who are you, lady?" he asked. "I understand you are asking for Constantine le Brecque."

The woman nodded eagerly. "I am, my lord."

"What business do you have with him?"

"I will only tell the earl."

The earl. That wasn't something Constantine heard very much but, clearly, this woman knew it was his official title. Truthfully, that made him a little suspicious. His eagerness to get close to her beauty dampened a little; assassins could be in beautiful garb, as well. He'd seen that before.

"I am Constantine le Brecque," he said, making sure there was enough of a distance between them that she couldn't thrust a dagger at him between the iron bars and make contact. "Who are you and what do you want?"

I am Constantine le Brecque...

It was those words that marked the beginning of the end. For them both, or only for him, only time would tell.

Now, the game was afoot.

Chapter Four

I T WAS THE MOMENT she'd been waiting for.

Gregoria's eyes widened when she realized who she was speaking to. After a week of waiting for the man to return from sea, and an entire day of sitting around a smelly tavern waiting for him to make an appearance, Constantine le Brecque was finally in front of her, in the flesh.

But he wasn't what she'd expected.

Gregoria was startled to realize this very big, very handsome man was the feared pirate le Brecque. In truth, she didn't know *what* she'd expected, but an attractive blond with sun-kissed skin hadn't been among her thoughts. A gnarled, old sea-rat had been more like it. But with his square jaw, full lips, and eyes of hazel that appeared golden in the weak light, she'd never seen anything so glorious. He was younger than she thought he might have been, given a reputation that seemed to have been around for years – but he wasn't too young, perhaps having seen thirty years or so. He had a seasoned look about him, as a man in his prime would.

God… was it was really him?

"Is… is it true, my lord?" she asked, sounding hesitant. "Are you le Brecque?"

Constantine looked at the men standing around him. "Well?" he demanded. "Answer the woman. Am I le Brecque?"

A host of heads bobbed up and down, looking as if a brisk wind had just sailed through the gatehouse and blown everybody's heads around like leaves in a breeze. There was no doubt that their answer was in the affirmative. Constantine turned back to the woman.

"That should satisfy you," he said. "Now, tell me who you are and what you want. I will not ask you again, so it would be best if you simply answer me."

Gregoria blinked nervously. "I… I would very much like to tell you, my lord, but I should like to do it in private. Please, my lord… it is important. I have come a very long way to speak with you."

Constantine frowned. He wasn't used to a woman not immediately doing his bidding, so the resistance and hesitation this one was showing did not please him. Turning around, he snapped his fingers at his men, gesturing for them to leave the gatehouse, and they did, being herded out by Kerk.

Constantine watched them wander off, shifting shadows cast against the walls by two heavily-smoking torches that were lodged into iron wall sconces. When his men were out of earshot, Constantine returned his attention to the woman.

"Now," he said. "You have your privacy. Tell me why you have come and tell me quickly. I am losing my patience."

Gregoria swallowed hard, pulling her cloak more tightly about her. It was cold in the gatehouse, with the sea wind whistling through, causing the torches to dance about in the darkness. In this damp and dark atmosphere, it was time to begin her tale.

Do not fail!

"My… my father told me that I could always come to you in times of trouble," she said quietly. "Tenby was his name. Do you remember my father? He used to serve you."

That brought a reaction from Constantine. Now, it was his turn to look surprised. "Tenby was your father?" he repeated. "Miles Tenby?"

"Aye, my lord. He was your quartermaster, I believe. He was killed two years ago. Murdered, I was told."

Suddenly, Constantine was whistling to his men, commanding them to lift the portcullis, and the great iron teeth began to crank open. When it was barely above the woman's head, Constantine was grasping her by the wrist and pulling her into the gatehouse. Soon enough, he was dragging her out into the bailey, heading for the keep.

"Miles Tenby," Constantine repeated as he walked briskly across the ward, pulling her beside him. "We tried to find his family after he died but no one seemed to know if he had one. We finally gave up."

Gregoria knew this. She could hear the surprise and, perhaps, even joy in his voice as he spoke. The story of the old quartermaster who had been killed by the French had come to her brother and Lord Wembury by way of a man who happened to be in Perranporth two years ago when Constantine had come ashore after the big battle with the French, looking for the families of the men he'd lost. The old quartermaster seemed to be the only one without any kin, which had given Wembury his grand idea. It was how he'd intended for Gregoria to get close to Constantine, with the story of being the long-lost daughter of the quartermaster.

It was part of the information she'd had beaten into her ever since she'd become part of Wembury's plot. Already, she could see that the mention of old Tenby was working its magic. Constantine was very interested. Gregoria tried not to appear nervous as she continued with her story because she wasn't very good at lying.

This time, however, she would have to be.

"My father was simply a man who kept to himself," she said. "He… he never spoke of his family, my lord?"

They were nearing the keep as Constantine shook his head. "Nay, he did not," he said. "We assumed he had no family although, in my profession, it is not unusual for men to keep their past lives a secret."

Gregoria had asked the question for a reason; she wanted to make sure that Constantine knew absolutely nothing of the quartermaster who had once served him.

"I suppose that is reasonable," she said, tripping over a stone in the bailey as he pulled her along. When she stumbled, he slowed his pace. "But he must not have told you where he came from or where to find his family if you were unable to find us... did he?"

Again, Constantine shook his head, unaware he was being probed. "Not a word," he said. "Although at one time, he mentioned having lived in Weymouth. Is that where you have come from?"

Weymouth. Gregoria's mind worked quickly, incorporating that town into her story. "Nay," she said. "Not Weymouth. My... my mother and I left Weymouth a year ago, after word of my father's passing reached us. A man who knew of him and had heard of his death came to tell us."

It was all perfectly plausible and Constantine had no cause to doubt her. By this time, they'd entered the keep of Perran Castle, a rather large, long structure that was built into the interior of the bailey, away from the walls that were so heavily fortified. The solar, being on the entry level, was Constantine's destination and he took Gregoria into the lavish chamber.

Lavish was an understatement. Gregoria had never seen anything like it; fine furniture everywhere, furs and carpets on the floor, and several large and fine tapestries hanging on the walls. Awestruck, she stood just inside the door, gaping at her surroundings, as Constantine went to a table that contained wine and cups and other things. As he moved to pour wine, two of the biggest dogs Gregoria had ever seen came up to her, looking at her curiously. She recoiled when she saw them, terrified they were going to eat her.

"They will not harm you," Constantine said as he came away from the table with two full cups of wine in his hands. "They are simply curious with visitors. Henry is the blond dog and Edward is the darker one."

He extended a cup of wine to her and Gregoria eyed the dogs as she accepted it. "Henry and Edward?" she repeated. "Interesting names for… dogs."

Constantine smirked. "They are named for England's king and the Earl of March, make no mistake," he said. Then, he turned to the dogs. "Sit down, you beasts. Sit!"

Promptly, the dogs planted their hindquarters on the floor. Constantine pointed at them. "Lay down, you mongrels. Lay down and be silent."

The dogs complied, laying down, but continuing to look at Constantine with their big doggy eyes. He grinned at them, patting each dog on the head.

"You see?" he said to Gregoria. "I can command Henry and Edward to do my bidding. No matter what I tell them, they will obey. That is the way it should be."

Gregoria had to admit, she found it rather humorous that Constantine should take such delight in bullying two dogs with the names of men that were in control of England. One man in particular who wanted to see Constantine dead. But she didn't smile, even though she felt like it, and sipped at the sweet, fine wine instead.

"They are very nice dogs, my lord," she said. "And… and your home is very nice, too."

Constantine turned to her. In the light of the room, her porcelain, high-cheekboned face was even more intriguing. He gestured at her cloak.

"Remove your wrap and set down your bag," he said. "Come over to the fire. It is warmer there, and you and I must speak."

Quickly, Gregoria did as she was told. She removed her cape, putting it on a fine-cushioned chair, and set her heavy satchel down next to it. Then, she made her way to the hearth that was taller than she was, radiating copious amounts of heat.

"Thank you for agreeing to speak with me, my lord," she said gratefully. "I realize I have come unannounced, but my father said you were a man who could be depended on and… I… I have a serious problem. I need your help."

Constantine's eyes drifted over her now that she was uncloaked and what he saw did not displease him; she was tall in height, round of body in the right places. Her beauty could only be described as astonishing; along with those bright blue eyes and high cheekbones, she had brown hair that glistened with red highlights in the firelight. It was wavy, gathered back into a braid, with wispy tendrils around her face. In truth, the entire vision was heavenly. Constantine could feel his interest in her growing.

"Now," he said. "I know your father's name but I still do not know your name. Will you tell me or must it remain a mystery?"

She smiled faintly, big dimples in both cheeks that had Constantine instantly enchanted. "My name is Gregoria Tenby Meyrick," she lied. "Lady Meyrick, in fact. My family calls me Gregg informally and since you are a friend of my father's, I would be pleased if you should call me that also."

Constantine smiled in return. "Lady Meyrick," he repeated quietly, realizing that she was married and it disappointed him greatly. "I should be honored to call you Gregg, with your permission. Now, tell me of this problem you have and why you need my help."

The time had come. Everything Gregoria had been waiting for. She had Constantine's attention and she knew she would only have one chance to make her story believable to him.

Men like Constantine were naturally suspicious so she knew she had to be credible, and she had to use what little information he already knew and incorporate it. The rest of the story she'd memorized could be blended into the village of Weymouth. The original town she was to use had been Southampton, so it was of little difference. They were not too far apart. She could adapt. Struggling not to appear nervous, she took a drink of her wine and turned to the nearest chair.

"It is difficult to know where to start, so I will start from the beginning," she said, planting her bottom in the chair and gazing up at him with an expression that suggested submission and resignation. "My husband was a merchant based in Weymouth. He was not the most scrupulous man, my lord. Often times he dealt with stolen items and he had dealings with pirates from time to time. Mayhap you knew him? His name was Oddo Meyrick."

Constantine shook his head. "I do not know him."

That had been a calculated question on Gregoria's part, something to make her entire story seem more authentic. Of course, Constantine wouldn't know of a fictional husband. But in asking the question, she more or less put her fictional husband's existence in Constantine's hands. He didn't know him? It was of little matter. Simply by asking the question, it seemed to Constantine that the man existed. Gregoria continued.

"Six months ago, our lives took a turn for the worse," she said. "You see, Oddo was from Wales. His family is from Gowerton and they were landowners and patrons of Three Crosses Abbey, just north of Gowerton. When Oddo was a young boy, a holy relic was stolen from Three Crosses Abbey, something that was so valuable the entire land seemed to go dark once it was stolen. Oddo said that he remembered this time very well. It was more than a blight; it was as if the devil himself had taken over the land. There was starvation and there was disease, and Oddo's own mother perished of disease during this time. As she lay dying, she made Oddo promise to find this relic, wherever it was, and return it to Three Crosses Abbey. She said that the devil would continue to reign over the land until the relic was returned."

Constantine listened with moderate interest. He was far more interested in watching her beautiful lips form words. "Why have you come to me?" he asked. "Does your husband wish to know if I have heard of this relic?"

Gregoria shook her head. "My husband is dead, my lord," she said, pretending as if she were grieved over the event and hoping she was convincing. "Oddo never thought he would be able to fulfill his mother's dying wish. But six months ago, he came upon a man who said he knew where the relic was. He told my husband that the French pirates out of Carantec had this relic and that they were willing to sell it for a price. I shall not go into the details of how my husband came into possession of the relic, for he never told me how it happened. All he told me was that he'd stolen the relic from the French pirates and that they were after him because of it. They are ruthless, as you may know."

Constantine nodded faintly. "I know."

It wasn't much of a reaction but Gregoria continued, hoping she was making an impact. "One night, they managed to chase him to our home and stab him," she said. "Oddo made it inside and gave over the relic to me, telling me that I had to take it to Three Crosses Abbey for him. I fled before the French pirates could kill me, too, but I am fairly certain they have followed me. My lord, I know of no one else who can keep me alive to return this relic to Three Crosses Abbey. My father said you were the most trustworthy man he ever knew. I beseech you for your help, my lord. An escort to Three Crosses Abbey is all I ask. I can pay you handsomely for the privilege."

Now, the gist of the situation had come forth and Constantine had to admit that he hadn't been expecting the request. But he also had to admit that he was more than interested in it because now that Gregoria was a widow, there was no husband standing in his way. She wanted him to escort her to Wales so she could deliver this object, offering her his protection from the French pirates he knew so well. Certainly, they were after him. They were always after him. But the appearance of Dureau's frigate in the Bristol Channel had been surprising; they'd been caught off guard by it. Constantine assumed the man had been there to ambush him, but could they be in the channel for another reason?

To prevent a woman from returning a holy relic to Wales?

It made a great deal of sense, more than Constantine cared to admit. Three Crosses Abbey wasn't far off the southern coast of Wales; he knew where it was because he knew most of the landmarks in Southern Wales. Undoubtedly, the French knew where it was, too, especially if they were chasing a woman trying to reach it. Lost in thought, he turned away from the hearth.

"That is quite a story," he said, sipping at the wine he'd already had too much of. "You made it all the way from Weymouth to Cornwall by yourself?"

Gregoria nodded. "It was easier to travel alone and undetected," she said. "To bring men with me would have made me a target. Men can be seen; one lone woman can often go unnoticed."

"And you had no contact with the French at all?"

She shook her head. "Not directly," she said. "But when I came to the town of Exmouth, I heard rumor that French pirates were in the town. I fled."

"But you believe they followed you?"

She shrugged. "It is possible," she said. "I have been in Perranporth for a week and have not seen nor heard of them, but that is not to say they are not somewhere, lurking about."

Lurking in channels with eighteen-gun warships, Constantine thought ironically. He looked up from his wine, gazing at the lovely vision of Gregoria as she sat perched on the edge of the chair, looking at him with a great deal of hope.

Bloody Beard, he couldn't resist such an expression. And the thought of spending a few days with the woman did not distress him in the least. It was the most attractive part of the proposal, to be sure. A quick trip into Wales and he might very well find himself with a woman he couldn't do without. He'd never had a regular mistress, but in gazing at Gregoria, he just might consider such a thing. There was something about her that drew him in.

But there was more to his willingness to accept her request. Her father had been gruesomely murdered and there hadn't been anything he could do about it. There was some guilt there, guilt that would undoubtedly propel him into acquiescing to the lady's request. How could he deny her when her father's death had been his responsibility? He couldn't, of course, and he knew it. The woman's beauty and his own lust for it aside, for old Miles Tenby, he couldn't refuse her.

My father told me I could always come to you in times of trouble.

He couldn't let Miles down again, not when the man's daughter was in need of him.

"The French are always lurking about," he said with some disgust. "These are my waters, yet they appear uninvited and without permission. But did you stop to realize that once you have me as your escort, it will make you an even bigger target for the French? They hate me, you know. Desperately. They would like nothing more than to destroy me and you right along with me."

Gregoria nodded reluctantly. "I am sure that is true, but you are the only one with enough weapons and men to resist them," she said. "I took a chance coming all the way from Weymouth alone. But should I try to go into Wales alone, I may not be so fortunate."

That was true. Constantine drained his cup, knowing he was going to do as she wished no matter if he pretended he was still thinking it over. He set the cup down and made his way over to her, sitting on the chair next to hers, studying her fine features in the firelight.

"What is this relic that the entire country of Wales is dependent upon it to keep the devil away?" he asked.

Gregoria could feel the pull from his gaze; the man was excruciatingly handsome with his tanned skin and sun-blond hair that dipped down over one eye. Simply looking at him made her heart beat faster and her breathing quicken. Abruptly, she stood up, trying to put some distance between them because his sheer presence was unnerving. She went to the satchel she'd brought with her, the heavy thing. It was heavy for good reason.

Digging inside of the bag, she pulled forth two rather large leather sacks and took them over to Constantine.

"Here," she said, dropping them in his lap. "This is what I can pay you to take me to Wales. It is a good deal of money so I hope it is enough."

Before Constantine could reply, she turned back to her satchel. He eyed her curiously for a moment before opening the pouches to see the heavy gold coins inside. There were dozens of them, perhaps even hundreds of them between the two pouches. He held them up in his hands, weighing them, as she continued to dig around in her bag.

"This is a good deal of money," he said. "You actually traveled with this money, alone, all the way from Weymouth?"

"I did."

He wriggled his eyebrows as he looked back to the pouches. "Then you are either incredibly brave or incredibly stupid."

"Or incredibly desperate."

He grinned at the comment, noticing she was coming back over to him with something in her hands. It was an old wooden box, perhaps eight inches in diameter, and Gregoria pulled off the lid, revealing what lay within.

It was a wooden cup, small, and fairly unspectacular as far as cups went. There was a lining around the top of it, metal of some kind that had been riveted to it. But on the whole, it was quite normal-looking, if not too terribly scuffed up and worn. Certainly not something that looked as if it could keep Satan at bay. He peered at it curiously.

"A cup?" he said. "That's it? I expected to see Gabriel's horn or Michael's sword, at the very least."

Gregoria looked at the "relic"; it was an old cup that Lord Wembury had found in Exeter and he'd had a silversmith put the metal ring around the rim. Then, he'd thrown it out in the pigsty of his fine home for a while, enough for the pigs to kick it around and get it very, very dirty. All he did was brush it off and put it in a velvet-lined box to call it a relic.

She wondered if Constantine would know any differently.

"It is made from wood from the true cross," she insisted. "At least, that is what the legend says. The priests at Three Crosses swear that it has healing powers, that if someone sick drinks from the cup, then they shall be miraculously healed. Those divine powers are why it has been able to keep the devil away from Gowerton. But it has been gone for many years and the land suffers. I could not help but carry out my husband's dying wish by returning it."

Constantine had no reason not to believe her. In fact, she'd been very convincing with the entire story except for the fact that she'd seemed unreasonably nervous. He attributed that to the fact that she was basking in his presence, because all women were giddy in his presence, but had he not been so attracted to the woman, he might have been suspicious of her twitching. As it was, all he could see was her beauty and the fact that she was a widow.

That was all he cared about.

A widow had experience in the marital bed and would undoubtedly know how to please a man. At least, that's what he intended to find out. It was unfortunate that Constantine sometimes let his lust overwhelm his common sense where a woman was concerned, but it was of little matter to him. He knew he could handle whatever came his way. He had confidence borne from a man who had faced death many times and lived to tell the tale.

"Very well, my lady," he said. "When did you wish to depart?"

"Immediately, my lord. Tomorrow, if possible."

Constantine didn't have anything pressing on land that would prevent him from leaving on the morrow. "Then if it is an escort you need, then an escort you shall have," he said. "You will dine with my men and me tonight and we shall discuss this venture into Wales on the morrow."

Her eyes widened in astonishment. "We… we *will*?"

"We will."

Gregoria was filled with relief as well as disbelief. Was it possible he believed everything she told him? Was this really going to be so easy? Closing the lid on the box, she struggled not to show her depth of relief in his consent. All she wanted him to see was her gratitude.

"Thank you, my lord," she said sincerely. "You cannot know how appreciative I am."

"For Miles Tenby's daughter, I am always willing to do what I can."

"And I am most appreciative," she said. "My father spoke most highly of you and I can see that he was correct; you *are* a man to turn to in times of trouble."

Blinded by his attraction to the woman, Constantine smiled rather seductively. "Of course I am," he said. "I owe your father a great deal, so it will be my pleasure to help you finish this quest."

With shaking hands, hands shaking with the realization that all of the planning and scheming for the past several months would finally come to fruition, Gregoria put the box back into her satchel.

"I am grateful," she said. It was the truth. "So very grateful."

That was exactly what Constantine wanted to hear. Grateful women would often demonstrate that gratitude. Many things ran through his mind at that moment, not the least of which was the fact that he'd be spending the next few days with the woman in their travels to Three Crosses Abbey. Perhaps he could even arrange for a delay or two. So very many things to think about.

At sup that evening, not surprisingly, his men were not as enthusiastic about a trip into Wales as he was.

Chapter Five

"I DO NOT like it."

The statement came from Augustin as he and several other men sat in a small chamber at the entry of Perran's keep, a guard room that had been turned into an armory. There were all kinds of weapons in the chamber, organized on wooden racks, and Augustin, Lucifer, Remy, Kerk, and a few other men were wandering through the racks, ensuring that weapons were properly repaired and maintained. Most of the weapons had been brought off the ships, so it was important they be kept clean and at the ready.

As quartermaster, it was Augustin's job to maintain the fitness of the weapons used by the men. He did it with great efficiency. But he was also a man with opinions this morning, a result of their meal with Constantine the night before and a woman who identified herself as Miles Tenby's daughter. The woman seemed meek and polite enough, but no one was thrilled with what she'd requested of Constantine – a journey into Wales to return a holy relic to some abbey in Gowerton. The story was rather complicated, but Constantine seemed certain it was something he needed to do.

As Augustin grumbled, the men around him were quiet with uncertainty. Lucifer stood on Augustin's left, inspecting some long swords, but he wasn't going to discuss the situation in front of some of Constantine's lesser men. A few were still in the chamber, racking up weapons. When Augustin opened his mouth again, Lucifer elbowed him.

"Quiet," he muttered. "Not now."

He was leaning his head in the direction of the men who weren't in Constantine's inner circle. There were four of them, setting up the last of the trigger-action crossbows, and Augustin begrudgingly remained silent until those men quit the chamber. But once they were gone, he started up again.

"Surely I cannot be the only one who is upset by all of this," he said as he pulled a short sword from a rack to inspect the blade. "Do you all agree with this – this folly?"

Remy didn't say anything. He tended to side with Constantine no matter what his personal opinion, so he kept his head down as he sat on a stool to use a pumice stone against a scratch on a dagger's blade. But Kerk, who was fussing with a broken leather strap on a sheath, spoke up.

"The woman paid him a good deal of money," he said. "Who cares if she is Miles Tenby's daughter or not? She is paying us for a task and the money she has paid him will trickle down into our pockets."

Augustin sighed sharply. "You do not see anything odd with this?" he asked. "She simply appeared out of nowhere and demanded Con escort her to Wales on the morrow. Has Con even thought to check out her story? He's been led astray by a woman before, you know."

"How do *you* know?"

"Because that is what made him a pirate in the first place!"

Kerk piped down after that. He didn't have an argument. But Lucifer did; he was looking at a big, beautiful long sword they'd confiscated in a fight against a small band of Spanish pirates a couple of months before. He knew exactly what Augustin was referring to.

"It was a good thing for you that Con embarked in this business," he said. "Swearing allegiance to Shaw MacDougall and becoming part of the pirates of Britannia has made it so you are a very wealthy man."

Augustin couldn't believe that the others didn't see the strangeness of this situation; perhaps they didn't realize how Constantine became involved in piracy in the first place and sought to educate them.

"I am not complaining," he said. "All I am saying is that it was a woman's lies that brought him to ally with Shaw MacDougall. Con was a naïve young man when the woman he loved told him lies, telling him that MacDougall had killed her brother and asking Con to avenge her. Con believed her, tried to kill Shaw, and then they both discovered the woman had lied. Con's merchant father disowned him after that, which is how he came to be a pirate. Has Con learned nothing from women who prey upon his weakness for them?"

Lucifer turned to him. "For a married man, you are very suspicious of women," he pointed out. "Do you believe so badly about your own wife?"

Augustin backed down, but only slightly. "My wife is a good woman," he muttered, turning back to the blade in his hand. "She would never do such things."

"And how do you know Miles Tenby's daughter would do such things?"

"We do not even know if she *is* Tenby's daughter. He never told us he had a daughter. He never told us anything at all."

"I have never told you anything, either. That is not unusual with men in this line of work."

He had a point and Augustin could see that his arguments were not being supported. There was no point in continuing if no one agreed with him, but he still couldn't help himself.

"He wants to depart on the morrow," he muttered. "I thought we were going to have time ashore. He promised us."

Lucifer shrugged. "Stay here with your wife if you wish," he said. "It is your fault you married her in the first place, knowing you would be out to sea frequently. You cannot blame Con for that."

Augustin shut his mouth after that. He could see that his comrades didn't agree with him, so he simply stopped talking. But over in the corner, Kerk spoke up.

"Still," he said thoughtfully, "the woman appeared right after Dureau's warship caught us off-guard in the channel. Now, she wants us to take her right back to the area where we last saw that warship."

Lucifer looked at him. "What are you saying?"

"That it is a trap set by the French," Augustin couldn't keep silent. "She comes to Con with a sad story of a blighted land, a holy relic, and wants Con to escort her right back through the channel where we last saw Dureau. It is possible he is still there, waiting for us. Did anyone ever think of that?"

Lucifer would have liked to have blown it off as paranoid speculation, but he found he couldn't. In this line of work, men who disregarded clues often ended up dead. Suspicion was their nature but, in this case, Lucifer wasn't so sure the suspicion was warranted.

Still... given what had happened as of late, with Constantine stealing most of Dureau's wealth and the fact that Dureau had sworn vengeance upon him, it couldn't be completely discounted.

"To me, the woman did not seem the type that Dureau would send," he finally said. "Did you look at her? She is beautiful, cultured, and did not have the look of a decoy."

"Then where did she get all of that money?" Augustin demanded. "I shall tell you where – the French gave it to her!"

More and more, Lucifer was starting to see their point. He was starting to feel the pangs of doubt. Still, he couldn't let on. Constantine didn't take kindly to men who doubted or disagreed with him, and most especially his inner circle. Constantine's control was absolute and his commanders had to display that unwavering loyalty to him because when dealing with pirates, one hint of doubt with a commander could send the entire crew into chaos. The only thing that held Constantine's crew together was Constantine's sense of absolutely control over everything. He was the captain – and the captain was beyond reproach.

Especially on the sea.

"I would suggest you keep your opinion to yourself," Lucifer turned to the men, his voice low and threatening. "If the crew gets wind of your doubt in the validity of this task, then we may have trouble on our hands. You know that as well as I do."

Augustin did, indeed, know that. He was well aware of the blind obedience given to Constantine. After a moment, he sighed heavily and put the blade aside, standing up from the stool.

"I will say no more," he said, sounding disgruntled. "But if we are to depart again, then I shall seek out my wife and spend what time I have left with her."

Lucifer let him go. He knew that Augustin had been looking forward to spending more than just a few days with his wife. Remy, feeling uncertain with the talk of French traps, left the room with a mumbled excuse. Now, it was just Kerk and Lucifer left in the chamber, and pregnant silence filled the air. Kerk finally spoke what they were both thinking.

"I am frankly surprised that Con has not considered Lady Meyrick's true motivation," Kerk said quietly, rubbing at the blade of a small dagger with a cloth. "Given the trouble with the French as of late, it is very possible she *is* a decoy."

Lucifer shrugged. "And it is equally possible that she is not," he said. He glanced at Kerk and saw that the man wasn't entirely convinced of that, so he sighed. "Still... mayhap it would be wise to seek help in this matter. If Constantine will not protect himself, then mayhap we must take that initiative."

Kerk was interested. "What do you intend to do?"

Lucifer set the blade in his hand down, appearing thoughtful as he did so. "The last we heard, Shaw was sailing south from Scarba," he said. "That was a few weeks ago, and we know that at this time of year, he anchors off the coast of Bardsey Island and goes hunting inland. He does it every year around this time."

Kerk was increasingly interested in what Lucifer was leading to. "And?" he said. "Do you intend to let Shaw know what has happened?"

Lucifer looked rather guilty as he glanced at Kerk. "Mayhap it is nothing," he said. "But mayhap this is a French trap, as has been suggested. If it is, then we will need Shaw's assistance. Con will need it if he is going to go into this blindly."

Kerk had to admit that he was rather relieved by what he was hearing. "Con can be single-minded when it comes to a woman."

Lucifer nodded. "That is true," he said quietly, "but we all have our weaknesses. Constantine le Brecque is the finest battle commander I have ever seen, but when it comes to women…"

Kerk held up a hand. "Say no more," he said. "This will be our secret. We must do this to protect him."

"Agreed."

"When will you send the missive?"

"This morning," Lucifer said. "Will you make sure the *Ligeia* is manned with a small crew? She is our fastest ship. Put Felix d'Vant in charge of her. He was raised in Cornwall and knows these waters. I will write a missive for Shaw and you will tell Felix he is to make all due haste to Bardsey Island. But I will tell you this…"

"What?"

Lucifer picked the blade back up, turning it so that the steel caught the light. "I will be watching the lady," he rumbled. "If, at any time, I feel she is putting Con in unnecessary danger, I will not hesitate to slit her throat and toss her overboard. I will simply tell Con that she must have slipped and was lost at sea. He'll never find her body, I assure you."

That was the assassin talking. Lucifer had a streak of darkness in him that ran bone-deep, hence his nickname. *Lucifer.* He would slit the lady's throat and suffer no guilt in the process. It was also why most of the men avoided him, knowing that it would only take a wrong look or a misspoken word to set Lucifer's murderous instincts off. Lucifer was a man to be feared, for many reasons.

Kerk knew he meant every word.

Therefore, he simply nodded, pleased that they had a plan. But Kerk couldn't help but feel they were somehow undermining Constantine. To send word to Shaw that Constantine might be in trouble was assuming a great deal, including the fact that Constantine's judgment might be twisted by a beautiful face and a sad story. If Constantine found out, he would not be happy.

Kerk hoped he could explain it to the man before he made them all walk the plank.

Chapter Six

CONSTANTINE DIDN'T SEE the *Ligeia* depart from Perranporth mid-morning. At least, that was what Lucifer and Kerk assumed. The boat had departed from the sandy shore and the only people who saw it depart were those tending the vessels where they were anchored on the beach. Kerk gave an excuse to those men as to why the small, light ship had departed with a crew of six on the deck and ten down below, rowing steadily against the tide. No one questioned Kerk and no one cared, and by the time Constantine was ready to depart by noon, the departure of the *Ligeia* had been forgotten.

Now, the *Gaia* and the *Persephone* were quickly being prepared for sea again and the last of the provisions had been loaded on, including enough gunpowder to ensure they would be ready for whatever they encountered along the coast. With Kerk and Augustin on the *Persephone*, Constantine boarded the *Gaia* with Lucifer and Remy.

There was a great deal of shouting and moving about from the men on the sandy beach as the crews boarded their vessels. Usually, the men walked out to the waist-deep water to climb the rope ladders up to the deck but, given that they had a woman with them and also that they had horses with them, they moved the ship in as close as they could before bringing out a ramp that went right up to the deck at a fairly steep angle. Constantine was already on board, waiting for Gregoria when she came up the ramp.

The wind was whipping about and the gulls cried overhead. There was always a sense of excitement before the ships put out to sea. Once Gregoria was on the deck, Constantine took her bag in one hand and her in the other, and escorted her over to the captain's quarters beneath the poop deck where she would be lodged for the duration of the journey. All around them, men were preparing the ship, shouting instructions or commands to each other, and the sails began to lift. Down below at water level, oars went into the water.

Since the *Gaia* was modified with a gun deck in the middle of the ship and then a storage/sleeping/rowing deck below that in the bilge of the ship, an assortment of captives were brought on board and sent below deck, chained to the rowing station and supervised by the row master, a very mean man from Italy. Constantine paid him well and the man kept the captives rowing, healthy or not. He beat a cadence for the rowers while the horses that had been brought shipboard gathered near the bow of the ship, munching on the piles of grass that had been brought for them.

It was a crowded hold.

But Gregoria didn't see the captives as they were brought on board. She was more interested in everything else that was going on around her and where Constantine was taking her.

The *Gaia* was a big ship with a wide deck but the structure of the ship narrowed dramatically towards the waterline to make the boat faster. Somehow, Constantine's dogs had made it on board, and Henry and Edward rushed past her as they neared the captain's quarters, charging through the door and into the chamber beyond.

Given what Gregoria had seen of not only Constantine's solar but of the great hall the previous night when they had supped with the other men, she wasn't surprised to see how luxurious the quarters were – there was a beautiful wooden bed, carved with goddesses and gods of mythology, silken bed coverlets, fine crystal decanters, and comfortable chairs around a very heavy, well-made table. The floor sloped slightly, as did the walls, giving the chamber a slightly vertiginous feeling, but it wasn't uncomfortable. In fact, Gregoria was fascinated by it. As the dogs jumped onto the beautiful bed and made themselves comfortable, Gregoria turned to Constantine.

"These are your quarters, my lord?" she asked.

Constantine nodded, opening the windows at the rear of the cabin, overlooking the rudder. A cool sea breeze immediately filled the cabin.

"Indeed," he said. "Make yourself comfortable here, for this shall be your cabin until we reach Wales."

Gregoria looked around the beautiful chamber, the most beautiful chamber she had ever seen. "Thank you, my lord," she said appreciatively. Then, she focused on him. "In fact, thank you for everything. You have granted everything I have asked for, including departing so quickly, and I feel as if I can never repay you for your generosity. You have such a big ship and there are so many men upon it… I feel as if I have inconvenienced everyone, but I thank you just the same."

Constantine's hazel eyes glimmered at her. After their initial meeting yesterday and then supper later than evening where he had hardly been able to speak with her because his men had been around, he went to bed feeling more interest in the woman than he'd ever had in almost any woman he'd ever met. He wasn't entirely sure why. Certainly, she was lovely, and she had a soft, deep speaking tone that was like warm honey to his ears. But beyond the looks and her voice, was her manner in general. She appeared downtrodden somehow and that was of great curiosity to him.

There was something sad about the woman, lingering just below the surface.

Certainly, the death of a husband and a massive burden would weigh heavily upon one but, to Constantine, it seemed there was something more to it. They were about to put to sea for a few days and he had every intention of coming to know the woman and discovering why she seemed so beaten. It would be at least two or three days to the shores of Wales, to the cove of Eynon where they would drop anchor and travel inland. After that, Three Crosses Abbey, as he recalled, was about a day's travel from the shore. So, in truth, Constantine knew he would have very little time with her. He wanted to make what time he did have with her count and that would start as soon as the *Gaia* went to sea.

To say he had an ulterior motive with the lady was an understatement. She wanted something from him… and he was going to take something from her.

"You have not inconvenienced anyone," he said after a moment, his gaze lingering on her before heading towards the cabin door. "Actually, you have given me an excuse to put to sea again. I become too restless upon land and most of my men feel the same way, so you have done us a favor."

Gregoria forced a smile, wondering if it was the truth. "I am pleased to hear it," she said. "When shall we reach Wales?"

He had his hand on the elaborate bronze door latch. "In two days, with good winds and calm seas," he said. "After that, it should only take a day to reach the abbey."

"Do you know where it is?"

"I know approximately where it is. Have no fear that we shall find it."

"You do not do much traveling on land, do you?"

He grinned, flashing that white smile and big dimple in his left cheek. "It makes me ill to travel on land," he said, teasing her. "Some men become sick with the motion of the sea, but I become sick with no motion on land. It is a terrible sight."

Gregoria giggled, her smile turning real. "I hope it does not come to that, my lord."

He waved her off. "Be assured that I will not humiliate myself in front of you," he said. "Now, settle in. I must see to my men. But I shall return once we are at sea. Which reminds me… do not leave this cabin for any reason. The men that staff this vessel are killers and worse, and they may look at you as an opportunity. Is that clear?"

"It is, my lord."

"Bolt this door when I go. Open it for no one but me or Lucifer or Remy. You met them last night. Do you recall?"

"I do, my lord."

"Good. Then settle in and I shall return."

Gregoria nodded, watching him leave the chamber and quickly rushing to the door, throwing the bolt as she'd been instructed. Then, she stood there a moment, hardly believing they were actually on the ship and that le Brecque was actually on his way to Wales.

In fact, ever since her meeting with him yesterday, the situation had moved so rapidly and she was coming to feel as if this were all a dream. Never did she imagine her plea to le Brecque would have been accepted so quickly and without suspicion. The man had been more than willing to help her, all for the sake of Miles Tenby. The information that Lord Wembury had paid for had been worth the cost, many times over. The name Miles Tenby had worked like magic with le Brecque, as they hoped it would.

Now, they were going to sea. Coming away from the door, Gregoria looked over the gorgeous room, thinking that it looked very much like a woman had decorated it. Perhaps a woman had. In any case, she was here and they were on their way to Wales… where one thousand of the Earl of March's troops would be waiting for them.

Waiting for Constantine.

Gregoria hadn't cared about betraying the pirate le Brecque when she became part of Lord Wembury's plot. She still didn't particularly care. All she cared about was doing as she'd been instructed and receiving her house and garden, as her brother had promised. Constantine was bringing men with him, that was true, but they would be nothing against March's troops. Unless Constantine surrendered, it would be a slaughter. But it was the man's own fault… he'd been too trusting of her story.

Fortunately, for her.

Moving over to the bed, she timidly petted Edward's big head as he lifted it and wagged his tail. She rather liked the dogs; perhaps she could take them with her to her little house by the sea where they could frolic in the garden and forget their lives as the dogs of a pirate.

… a pirate…

There was something in her that was begging her to feel some guilt in all of this, guilt that she was about to lead a man to his doom. Such a handsome man, too. Other than their initial discussion yesterday, she hadn't much time to really talk to him. She wasn't sure she wanted to. She already thought he was wildly handsome but if she came to like him, too, then that could mean trouble. So early in the plot, she didn't need any complications. The less she knew of Constantine le Brecque, and the less she spoke to him, the better it would be.

She didn't want to like the man she was helping to kill.

Gregoria began to fight off those thoughts of guilt and betrayal as the *Gaia* finally weighed anchor and pushed away from the white, sandy beach. She was watching the ocean beyond her open windows, with the salt spray and gulls crying overhead. It was really very beautiful and the soft sway of the boat had a soothing quality. Much like being rocked in a mother's arms. The boat turned around, slowly, and she soon found herself watching the shoreline as it grew more and more distant, and the sea beneath them became a dark, crystal blue.

Given that this was the first time she'd been to sea, Gregoria found it all rather exciting. It was all so fresh and new. On the deck above, she could hear men calling out commands, or calling out to each other over the hiss of the wind and sea. She couldn't hear much but she knew there was a great deal happening on the main deck and she leaned her head out to hear more clearly what was going on. The wind drowned out the words, however, and they simply became sounds she couldn't make out, so she pulled her head back in and stood at the window, watching the sea pass beneath them. It was astonishingly peaceful, something timeless and serene about it. Now, she could understand what Constantine meant about being restless on land.

At sea, there was something that fed one's primal soul.

A knock on the door roused her from her thoughts and she quickly turned from the window, remembering what Constantine had told her. *Open it for no one except me or Lucifer or Remy.* Heart pounding with a bit of apprehension, she made her way hesitantly towards the door.

"Who comes?" she demanded.

"'Tis me, my lady," came the muffled voice. "It is Con."

Somehow, the sound of his voice and the mention of his name made her racing heart beat even faster, but for a different reason this time. Was it actually possible she might be happy to see him? Quickly, she raced to the door and yanked it open. Constantine flashed her his white-toothed smile as he pushed into the cabin, shutting the door behind him.

"If the weather remains like this, we should see Wales by late to-morrow," he said. "I've ordered top speed."

Gregoria had no way of knowing that it was a lie; he hadn't ordered top speed at all. He specifically told his men to slow the pace of the travel, all of this so he could spend more time with Gregoria. But, alas, Gregoria was oblivious to his intent. She simply smiled in return.

"Thank you, my lord," she said, realizing he was looking at her with a good deal of interest in his expression and it was something that made her nervous. She turned away. "I… I have never been to sea before. This is all very new to me."

Constantine followed her like a hunter tracking prey as she moved towards the big windows that overlooked the rudder. "I thought you said your husband was a merchant."

Gregoria reached the windows. "He was," she said. "But he purchased good from ships. He did not go to sea himself."

"He did not own vessels?"

She shook her head. "Nay," she said. "But he had men he purchased from regularly. Some of them were no better than pirates themselves, the way they sold questionable items and… oh… I did not mean to say that. Forgive me."

Constantine leaned against the open windowsill, smiling at her. "You have said nothing untrue," he said. "I've known enough merchants in my time to agree with you. In fact, my father was a merchant."

Her eyes widened, surprised. "Was he?" she said. "He was not a pirate, too?"

Constantine laughed softly. "My father was a well-to-do merchant based in Newquay," he said. "He had a fleet of many vessels and the family had been in the business of sailing and goods exchange for several generations. That is how I first came to know the sea."

Gregoria was interested. "But you did not follow the family tradition?"

His smile faded and he wriggled his eyebrows. "Regrettably, I did not," he said. "Although I'd meant to. A mistake on my part led me to quite another path in life."

"You mean that you accidentally became a pirate?"

His smile was back and he chuckled, looking out over the ocean. "Nay," he said. "I did not accidentally fall into this line of work. It was a choice, more or less. But if you must know, years ago a woman I was betrothed to told me that a pirate named Shaw MacDougall had murdered her brother and begged me to exact revenge. Of course, being young and foolish and in love, I did as she asked me. As it turned out, MacDougall did not kill her brother – she was simply trying to get me killed because she was carrying on an affair with another man. Being that we were betrothed, if I died, she would inherit money from me simply because of the contract between us. I did not kill MacDougall when I discovered the woman's plan, but I did kill her lover, the man she had forsaken me for. He was from a well-placed family and a price was put on my head, but my father wouldn't help me. In fact, he disowned me."

Gregoria was genuinely surprised to hear his tale. "That is terrible," she said. "But how did you become a pirate?"

Constantine looked at her, then, a half-smile on his lips. "Because the one person who did not disown me was the very man I'd been sent to kill," he said. "Shaw MacDougall may be the prince of all pirates, carrying on a great and dark legacy, but he is also a man of loyalty and understanding. He saw what had happened and how'd I'd been duped. I swore my oath to him and captained one of his vessels for a time. But when my father died shortly after he disowned me, I inherited all of his wealth and his merchant ships. He'd never changed his will. I became a pirate in my own right, now allied with MacDougall rather than being subservient to him. In fact, I am far richer than he could ever hope to be, much to his displeasure. But we are brothers to the bone."

It was an interesting tale, one that gave Gregoria more insight into the man, which was exactly what she hadn't wanted to do. Now, she was feeling some sympathy for him as she understood his path to a life of piracy.

"MacDougall," she murmured pensively. "I seem to have heard that name, haven't I?"

Constantine nodded. "If you have lived near the sea, or have had dealings with merchant vessels, then you have surely heard of him," he said. "He is a pirate prince, literally, adopted by the last in a long line of pirate princes, dating back hundreds of years to a man named Arthur MacAlpin. Shaw is a pirate in every sense of the word, but he and I have something most pirates lack."

She cocked her head curiously. "What is that?"

"Honor."

Gregoria's gaze lingered on the man. She was becoming increasingly enamored with him, whether or not she realized it. He had an oddly gentle way about him, completely unexpected from a man with such a reputation, and when he spoke of honor... there was no doubt in Gregoria's mind that he knew what it meant.

"That is not a word usually associated with piracy," she said, "yet you speak as if you understand it."

He lifted his eyebrows, slowly inching in her direction. In fact, he'd been inching in her direction for the past few minutes, only she hadn't noticed because she hadn't moved away. He'd been so discreet about it that she hadn't even realized he was trying to close the distance between them.

"I do understand it," he said, his voice quietly. "I was trained as a knight. I fostered in the finest houses until I was of age and then I was knighted by my master. But I never really had the opportunity to use my skills because the incident with MacDougall came shortly thereafter and I have been at sea ever since. But one does not forget honor, not even when one lives the life of a pirate."

Gregoria was coming to think that there was far more to Constantine le Brecque than met the eye, but in a good sense. This was no mindless, blood-thirsty pirate. This was a man of insight and feeling. She found herself wanting to dig deeper, to know more about him, because everything she knew about him had been relayed to her by Lord Wembury.

There were always two sides to every story, and to every reputation.

"Was your father a lord, then?" she asked. "How is it possible that you trained as a knight if your father was of the merchant class?"

There was a very good reason for that but Constantine wasn't sure he wanted to tell her. It wasn't something he spoke of. Still, it wasn't like it was a secret. His true parentage had been common knowledge among the nobility for years.

"You do not know?" he asked. "You have not heard the truth about me?"

"What is the truth?"

The corner of his mouth twitched, hinting at a smile. "That I am the bastard son of a king," he said. "I was born the year of my father's coronation and I fostered in the finest houses because that is what my real father demanded. When I spoke of my father, the merchant, I was speaking of my adoptive father. His sister was my mother and that is why I bear the name le Brecque – it was her maiden name. She died after I was born and I was given over to her brother and his wife to raise."

That was quite a bit of personal information he spoke freely of, either because he didn't care who knew or because he was truly unconcerned that such information meant nothing at all. But for Gregoria, it was the most important of information – it was the very information that had an entire faction plotting to remove him. She couldn't believe he seemed so unconcerned about something that would lead to his downfall. Was he truly so clueless to the fact? She almost wanted to shake him – *do you not understand that there are those who want to kill you because of your royal blood?*

But... *no.* She couldn't say a word. She was committed to completing her task for Wembury, and for her brother, and she was committed to her house by the sea with the garden. That was all she wanted; to retire there and live in peace. She couldn't worry about the pirate she was about to betray in order that she should receive her reward. It was what she had to do or she would never be able to live in peace.

Still... guilt was starting to make itself be known.

"'Tis a fascinating story, truly," she said. "Which king do you claim as your father?"

Constantine's grin broke through. "I am not fair like the Spanish, nor am I dark and dirty like the French," he said. "You called me an earl when you first arrived at Perran, so surely you can answer your own question."

She had asked for the earl last night. She'd forgotten that fact until he'd reminded her. She wondered if that slip wasn't going to give her away and she scrambled to answer evenly. "My... my father told me that you were an earl," she said. "I do not know your full title, but he'd mentioned it once. Did I do wrong by addressing you in such a way?"

He shrugged, lazily. "You did not," he said. "It is not something I hear very much. But enough about me; I wish to know about you. We have not had much opportunity to speak other than the conversation we had last night. All I know about you is that you are Miles Tenby's daughter and that you were married to a man named Meyrick. I wish to know more about you."

Gregoria hadn't expected that turn in conversation and she flushed, turning away from him when she realized that he was suddenly very close to her. His big body was brushing up against her right side and she took a step away, discreetly, to put distance between them, but Constantine quickly closed the gap.

"There is not much to tell," she said, feeling the heat in her cheeks at his close proximity. "I was born, I grew up, and I was married for a very short time. I live modestly with… with my mother."

She tried to move away again but Constantine snaked an arm around her waist, preventing her from moving away from him. His other hand came up, cupping her face as he gently kissed her cheek.

"Please tell me there is nothing modest about you," he rumbled. "Please tell me that you are a woman of pleasure and leisure for, truly, a woman of your beauty is meant only for such things."

She gasped when he kissed her, swiftly pulling away and ending up over by the bed. She stood there, panting, as Constantine went in pursuit. "I am not a woman of pleasure," she said breathlessly. "Are you inferring that I am a… a…?"

"A whore?" Constantine finished for her, amused. The fact that she was running from him only seemed to feed his lust. "Lady, you are clearly not a whore. But with your luscious body and sweet face, you are made for a man's pleasure. That is clear. And it seems to me that you are a lady who needs protection now that your husband is dead."

Gregoria was growing faint as she realized what he was suggesting. He made a swipe for her but she moved away, out of range.

"I am *not* made for a man's pleasure!" she gasped, outraged. "I have never… that is to say, my husband was the only man… he… no one else has ever touched me!"

It was a lie, but she was grasping at straws now, off-guard with Constantine's pursuit. He could see he had her on the run but, as far as he was concerned, it was a feminine game to feed his want for her. She was toying with him and, like a fool, he was falling for it. The more she ran from him, the more he wanted her.

"That will change," he said confidently. "My lady, you are without a husband now. I am offering you my home, my protection, and my bed. You shall never want for anything ever again, I swear it. Let us return this holy relic to Wales and start anew from there. You shall have a place of honor in my household and riches beyond your wildest dreams. Do you understand what I am offering you?"

Gregoria was shocked. Frightened, outraged, and shocked. But she was also flattered, and those emotions battled it out for supremacy as she tried to stay away from Constantine. The man had a terribly hungry look in his eye.

"I will *not* be your whore!" she said.

"I did not say whore. There are better words for it than that; some of the greatest women in the world were concubines or companions to great men."

"Concubine?" she nearly shrieked. "That is nothing but a brood mare!"

Constantine was starting to laugh; he was also starting to close the gap between them. She had backed herself into a corner of the chamber and the only way out would be to run around him.

But he wouldn't let that happen.

"Brood mares serve a purpose," he said evenly. "I can only imagine what strong sons I would have from you."

If Constantine wasn't sure if she could become any more outraged with the conversation, he was wrong. She was quickly growing furious.

"Concubines are cheap, common women," she scolded. "I am not cheap and I am not common. I resent you for suggesting it!"

He was nearly on her and when she realized that, she tried to move away but he grabbed her, shoving her back into the corner of the cabin and pinning her with his big body. One arm went around her to hold her tightly while the other hand began to roam. He buried his face in her neck, suckling at her flesh.

"I agree," he purred against her flesh. "You are not common and you are not cheap. You are a fine, beautiful woman the likes of which I have never seen before and I must have you. Do you not realize how fine you are, Gregg? If your husband never told you, then the man was a fool. You should be told daily how fine and beautiful you are."

Gregoria had never been kissed by a man like this, not ever. Constantine was holding her fast with one arm while the hand of his other held her head still, fingers intertwining in her hair as his lips moved up her neck and onto her shoulder. Hot, sweet kisses rained down on her flesh and now her heart was racing for an entirely different reason…

She liked it.

She liked his flesh against hers, his lips on her neck, her shoulder. She could feel his hot breath against her throat and it fanned flames within her that she never knew existed. Oh, God… was this what it meant to be kissed by a man? She was panting so heavily that she was growing faint with it, as if she couldn't control herself or her resistance to his sensual onslaught.

And his hands…

Those big, strong, rough hands were holding her fast. His mouth was on her shoulder, nibbling on her flesh, and all of the protests on Gregoria's tongue died right there in her throat. She couldn't get them out because, frankly, she didn't want to get them out. She couldn't, in good faith, resist the man and his touch. She'd never known anything like it. Her body was growing limp, her knees like jelly and, suddenly, he was loosening the ties on the front of her bodice.

It was so fast and so skillfully done, that she hadn't even noticed until he pulled on the bodice and her left breast sprang free. The same big hand that had been intertwined in her hair swiftly moved to that breast and his mouth along with it. He was suckling her nipple before she realized what had happened and her hands came up, slapping at his head, but it was a terribly weak gesture. Constantine released her torso and used that hand to pin her wrists above her head as he continued suckling her breast, now wet with his saliva. Using his teeth, he pulled away the rest of the bodice, freeing her right breast.

And then, he feasted.

Gregoria couldn't have fought back had she wanted to. He had her pinned as his mouth moved between her breasts, suckling furiously. She could hear soft groans, realizing that they came from her as the man made her feel all shades of passion in his sensual onslaught. But Gregoria was a maiden and if things kept going the way they were, Constantine would find that out, too. She'd been saving that virginity for her husband, if she ever married, but the way her life was progressing, she doubted that would ever happen. Her brother wasn't intent on finding her a husband; he'd never even suggested it.

She was destined to grow old alone.

But is *this* what it meant to have a husband? To be touched so tenderly, to have bolts of lightning shoot up your body when intimate parts were touched? To feel warm and safe and wanted? God, she couldn't think at the moment.

All she could do was feel.

And feel, she did.

Suddenly, Constantine dropped her wrists and he hiked up her skirts, lifting her up and wedging himself in between her legs, which he'd pulled apart to straddle his hips. Gregoria was so far gone with what he was doing to her that it took her a moment to realize the position he'd put her in. She thought it had been for more kissing, more suckling but, in fact, that wasn't what he had in mind. Before she could protest, or even think of a good excuse why this should not happen, she felt his manhood pressing on her tender woman's center. He was rubbing himself on her, bathing himself in the wetness he'd created in her, preparing himself for entry.

She knew what was coming.

Oh, God, she thought with her last shred of coherency. *It is happening!*

It happened, indeed. Constantine gripped her by the buttocks and thrust forward, deep into her tight and virginal body. A sharp, searing pain rippled through Gregoria's loins as she dropped her head, biting off her cry of pain in his shoulder, groaning softly as he thrust hard a second and a third time before being fully seated.

When he began to roll his hips, thrusting in and out of her, the sharp pain quickly evaporated, leaving a sensation that Gregoria could have never imagined in its place. Something warm, wet, and thrilling was happening now.

With Gregoria's back against the wall of the cabin, Constantine held her buttocks against him, thrusting into her tight body but doing it in a way that he was also rubbing against her, pleasuring her. Gregoria was only focused on the junction between her legs where these miraculous sensations were taking place, not even considering the fact that, in spite of her protests, Constantine le Brecque had, indeed, taken what he wanted from her. He'd made her a whore, planting his manhood in her warm, wet recesses and pleasuring himself as men did.

But she hardly cared.

"Never has this felt so good," Constantine murmured into her neck, biting at her flesh and causing her to gasp. "You were made for pleasure, lady. *My* pleasure."

Gregoria couldn't even answer him. He was sucking on her breasts again and, suddenly, the junction between her legs tightened up before she felt the release of such pleasure that she cried out with it. Stars were shooting all through her body and as she experienced her first climax, Constantine smiled faintly, kneading at her soft buttocks even as his own release rapidly approached.

"You are mine," he whispered. "Do you understand me? Now, you are mine. Mayhap my seed shall find its mark and a strong, intelligent son shall be born from your body. Tell me you shall bear me a son."

Gregoria was nearly incoherent. He was still moving in her body even as she tried to understand what had just happened, a spasm of the most amazing pleasure. Did he ask her a question?

"A… a…?" she stammered.

Constantine's mouth came down on hers, kissing her deeply, his tongue filling her mouth and licking at her. Gregoria had no idea how to respond other than to let him do as he wished, because everything he'd done to her had given her the utmost pleasure for the most part. Like a fool, she simply let the man have his way in spite of her earlier protests. But as he kissed her passionately, he thrust hard into her and emitted a soft grunt, and she could feel his male member throbbing inside of her body. It was enough stimulation that she, too, experienced a second and lesser release, her entire body ripe with passion and excitement.

But Constantine continued to thrust into her, slowly now that the passion had died down, but there was still a wildfire blazing between them. Gregoria could feel it every time their bodies came together. There was heat between them that was beyond imagination.

"A son," he whispered even as he kissed her. "A lad from your beautiful body. Tell me you shall bear my son."

At this point, Gregoria was close to swooning. Her arms ended up around his neck, holding him for dear life because she was certain that if she did not hold on to him, she would slither to the floor and be lost forever. She held him tightly even as he moved away from the wall, still attached to her, and chased the dogs off the bed so he could lay her down. When he finally put her on the feather-stuffed mattress, he ended up beside her, holding her close as the ship rocked gently beneath them.

As they lay there in the languid midday, Constantine found himself reliving the past few minutes. He'd never before asked a woman to bear his son, so why now? There were strange forces at work, forces that had him more attracted to Gregoria than he'd ever been attracted to a woman in recent memory. His physical attraction to her was undeniable, but his emotional attraction… well, that scared him. He'd never asked a woman to bear his son before. There was a hint of permanence in that request, as if he'd finally found someone he thought worthy of such a thing.

Aye, that scared him a great deal.

He didn't even know the woman, in truth. He'd had two conversations with her and, already, he'd bedded her. But it had been such an overwhelming need that it had been impossible for him to resist. He'd given in to it, just like he gave in to all of his whims.

But he was coming to wonder if she wasn't a whim.

It was a strange situation, indeed.

Beside him, Gregoria began to snore softly and he realized the woman had fallen asleep. That was good because he really had no idea what to say to her. Usually, he had no problem with after-sex conversation but, this time, he was a bit tongue-tied. Something about this act had been... different. He didn't know quite how, but it was. Therefore, he thought it best to leave her alone to sleep while he headed up to the deck.

He had a lot of thinking to do.

Carefully, he disengaged himself from her and rolled off the bed, standing up to secure his breeches. But he happened to look down as he did so and saw blood on his manhood. When he turned to the bed and carefully lifted her skirt, he could see that the blood was coming from her. It wasn't particularly alarming – either she was on her woman's cycle, or there was another answer that he found particularly curious.

She was a virgin.

Having clearly told him she had been married, it didn't seem likely that she was a virgin. Unless she'd been lying, of course. And if she'd lied about that, what else had she lied about? Constantine wasn't a fool; he knew he'd given in to her request easily. *Too* easily. He knew his men weren't happy about it, but they had the sense not to confront him. He knew they worried for his safety, considering how many men would have loved to have seen Constantine le Brecque dead. But if Gregoria had been sent by his enemies, then they knew where to hit him where he was the weakest – with a beautiful woman.

And he'd fallen for it.

There was a good deal on Constantine's mind when he left the cabin and quietly shut the door.

Chapter Seven

Off the coast of Bardsey Island, Wales
Late the next day

OH, BUT IT was a feast!

Boiled crab that had been harvested in big nets off the coast of Bardsey Island made a tremendous meal, and Shaw MacDougall was sucking up every last morsel he could get his lips on.

It was the evening after a day of hunting for Shaw and his men. Aboard his mighty vessel, *Savage of the Sea*, Shaw and his crew were enjoying a rare moment of peace and leisure. That didn't often happen in their line of work.

Having come down from the north on the Isle of Scarba where his castle was situated, a safe haven for him and his men amongst the rocky island in the wind-swept sea, their destination had been Bardsey Island for the fine hunting and fishing it had this time of year. The small crabs were abundant, as was the wildlife on the island itself. His men had hunted boar all day, along with the crab, and even now his cook was below deck, salting the butchered boar.

But in the captain's cabin where Shaw and his men had gathered to feast, there was a good deal of food on the table and only two men to eat it. Shaw and his first mate, a massive Viking-looking man appropriately named Thor, seemed to have the table to themselves for the moment because the other men in Shaw's chain of command were on shore finishing up with those who had been doing the actual fishing and hunting.

Nets needed to be brought in and the last of the hunt was being butchered on the shore before being brought onto the ship. This was some of their fun, and recreation, and it only happened one time a year. Shaw thought that it was the very best time of year. He'd been doing this kind of thing since he'd been a wee lad and it was in his blood. It reminded him of happier and more carefree days.

"If we dunna hurry, there will be something left for Kelly and Lachlan," Thor said, his mouth full. "Do ye truly intend to share this with them?"

Shaw finished sucking the meat out of a claw. "I canna eat any faster," he said. "I have eaten at least ten more than ye have. When did ye start eating like a woman?"

Thor frowned, his blond brows angled. "This is my second meal of crab today," he pointed out. "I ate nearly an entire pot earlier today when they were first brought aboard. I had tae make sure they were edible, ye know."

"God, ye're a glutton."

"Ye have no idea."

Shaw snorted as he broke open another boiled crab and began to feast on it. "Do ye recall last year when we invited Con and his men tae feast with us?" he asked. "I've never seen such a feeding frenzy in my life."

Thor grinned, crabmeat on his lips. "I notice ye dinna ask them tae join us again this year."

Shaw shook his head, his long black hair wagging back and forth. "Why would I? Those Sassenach are worse than a pack of dogs. I canna abide by such selfishness."

"Ye mean ye are afraid they would eat everything and there would be nothing left for ye."

Shaw eyed him. "Lucifer can have all he wants because no one would dare tell the man otherwise, but Gus and Remy...." He shook his head as if appalled by their behavior. "They ate most of the crab and then lied about it. Tried tae blame it on me, telling me that I had eaten it all when I was drunk."

"In their defense, ye *did* have a good deal to drink."

"Not enough that I wouldna remember eating an entire pot of crab!"

The events of last year still rightly upset him and Thor fought off a grin at the man's indignity. "I canna abide men who dunna take responsibility for their actions."

"Nor do I. The bastards."

Thor's grin broke through; he couldn't help it. "Well," he said, "then that is the last time we invite that rabble tae our table tae sup."

Shaw nodded his head firmly as he sucked on another claw. "Rabble, indeed," he said. "At least Con has some manners. I love the man. But his men..."

A shout from the deck outside his cabin cut him off, and both Shaw and Thor turned to see a great deal of commotion through the open door. It seemed fairly serious and by the time Thor and Shaw set the crab aside and made their way out onto the deck, there was a ship close by, approaching swiftly under increasing swells.

It was dark this night, with a sliver moon, which meant that it was difficult to see much upon the water until objects were fairly close. But Shaw could see that the vessel was flying the red dragon of Constantine le Brecque, as it was illuminated on the bow by a fatted torch in an iron cage. Immediately, he went to the rail of the ship.

"Ahoy!" he called.

Someone was waving at him from the vessel. "Ahoy!" came the response. "Permission to board!"

"Who are ye?"

"Felix d'Vant, my lord. I have been sent by Lucifer!"

Sent by Lucifer and not by Constantine. That gave Shaw a stab of concern as well as confusion, but he waved the ship onward, issuing orders to his men to bring the vessel alongside. He maintained his post on the rail, watching as the ship drew close but not too close. With the increased swells, they didn't want the ships hitting each other. Someone lowered a skiff from the other vessel and three men got on board, two to row and one who simply stood at the bow. Once the skiff came close to the *Savage of the Sea*, the man on the bow leapt from the skiff and caught the rope ladder that had been lowered for him. Deftly, he climbed it.

Shaw was waiting for him. He immediately recognized the man as one of Constantine's senior sailors; he'd seen the man before. *Felix d'Vant*, he'd said. The man dipped his head politely in greeting.

"My lord," Felix said. "Pardon my intrusion, but I have come bearing a message from Lucifer. May I deliver it to you in private?"

Shaw could sense that something was wrong; d'Vant had an urgent manner about him, and he immediately thought the worst.

"What has happened?" he asked. "Is Con well?"

D'Vant nodded. "Constantine is well, my lord," he said. "But Lucifer wishes for me to deliver a missive to you."

"Con dinna send ye with a missive?"

"Nay, my lord."

The situation was becoming increasingly perplexing. Without another word, Shaw motioned for the man to follow him. He led Felix back into the captain's quarters where a big table with a half-eaten pot of crab sat on the surface. There were crab carcasses everywhere, in piles and on the floor. Once they were inside, however, Shaw came to a halt and turned to d'Vant.

"What is it?" he asked, his voice low. "Why have ye come at Lucifer's request?"

D'Vant, a tall, blond, and handsome young man, scratched his head rather nervously. "What I tell you has come directly from Lucifer, you understand," he said. "I am simply the messenger."

"I understand. Get on with it."

D'Vant did. "Three days ago, a woman came to Perran Castle," he said. "She claimed to be the daughter of Miles Tenby. If you recall, Miles Tenby was the quartermaster who was heinously murdered by the French two years ago. Do you recall the incident, my lord?"

Shaw did; he had a sharp memory. "Aye," he said. "Go on."

D'Vant nodded. "The woman told Constantine that her now-dead husband had stolen a holy relic from The Water Bearers and that now they had come for her," he said. "She told him that she was being chased by the French but that she was determined to fulfill her dead husband's wish of restoring the stolen object back where it belonged – to Three Crosses Abbey in Wales. She has requested that Constantine escort her to Wales, as a favor to her dead father, and Constantine has agreed."

Shaw didn't see what the trouble was. "*And?*"

D'Vant cocked an eyebrow. "And, Lucifer is not entirely sure this is not a trap by the French," he said quietly. "He is afraid that something is amiss. He begs you to come to Eynon Bay, my lord, and provide support to Constantine on this mission."

Shaw scratched his head at the odd story. Now, it was starting to make some sense and he could see why Lucifer was concerned. "I recall when Tenby was murdered," he muttered. "I was there. Con tried tae save the man but there was nothing he could do. Now, ye say that Tenby's daughter has come tae Con with this... this *story*?"

"Aye, my lord."

"And Con is tae help the woman return something her husband stole from the French pirates?"

"Aye, my lord."

Shaw stared at him a moment before scowling. "And Con doesna suspect this may be a trap?"

D'Vant sighed heavily. "It is possible, but he is willing to help her just the same," he said. "The woman... she is quite beautiful, my lord. She... she seems to have used her charms on Constantine."

Shaw understood a great deal in that halting explanation. "The man is a slave tae a beautiful face," he muttered. "My guess is that he has been blinded by her."

"That is Lucifer's guess, also."

"And Con has shown no suspicion at all?"

D'Vant shook his head. "I do not know, my lord," he said. "All I know is that Lucifer has asked for your help. It is possible that Constantine is heading to his doom, lured by a beautiful woman and, if that is the case, then your assistance would be appreciated."

Shaw shook his head in a gesture of disappointment; not that he wouldn't have done the same thing should a beautiful woman have come to him for help. But he was surprised that Constantine hadn't been more careful of the situation. The Constantine le Brecque he'd known for years was shrewd and cunning. Moreover, he'd had trouble with women lying to him before... had he forgotten?

"The man knows better," Shaw said after a moment. "He knows dangers abound for him as well as for me. We must be very careful who we trust. Has he not learned that yet?"

D'Vant didn't have an answer. "I am honored to serve Constantine le Brecque," he said resolutely. "In battle, there is none finer."

Shaw held up a hand to ease the man's offense at his comment. "It is true," he said. "In battle, there is none finer than Constantine. I would trust the man with my life a thousand times over. But he has a weakness for beautiful women and everyone knows it, including his enemies. Where is Three Crosses Abbey?"

"Off Eynon Bay," d'Vant said. "Do you know where that is?"

Shaw nodded. "I do," he replied. Then, he sighed faintly. "If Lucifer has sent ye, then it means he must truly be worried. The man doesna panic without reason."

D'Vant nodded, his expression filled with hope. "Then you will come?"

Shaw nodded faintly. "I will," he said. "But this isna some dastardly scheme tae get my crab, is it?"

D'Vant cocked his head, puzzled. "My lord?"

Shaw eyed him. "Ye knew where tae find me, did ye not? This is my hunting grounds this time of year."

D'Vant was still puzzled. "Lucifer knew, my lord."

"And he did not tell ye tae steal my crab?"

"Steal... *crab*?"

Shaw knew the young man wouldn't understand the inference. Fighting off a grin, he waved him off. "Never ye mind," he said. "The crabs stay with me, no matter what Lucifer told ye tae do. Go back tae yer ship, d'Vant. We'll weigh anchor at dawn."

D'Vant emitted a sigh of relief. "Thank you, my lord," he said. "We will be ready to sail with you."

With that, he turned and headed for his vessel, making haste down the rope ladder. Shaw watched the man go, pondering all he'd been told. It was possible that Constantine wasn't in any trouble at all, but Shaw wasn't willing to take the chance. If Constantine needed help, then Shaw wanted to be on hand to give it, especially against those bastard French. As he stood there, lost in thought, Thor entered the cabin. Looking at Shaw, his expression was full of curiosity.

"Well?" he asked. "What has happened?"

Shaw shook his head in a weary gesture. "Ye wouldna believe it," he said as he headed back over to the table. "It seems that Con may be in a bit of trouble. Lucifer has asked for our help."

Thor's appeared concerned. "*Lucifer* asked? Why not Con?"

"Because Con has apparently been seduced by a woman and canna see the danger of it."

Thor considered that possibility. "Is it serious, then?"

Shaw shrugged as he took his seat, resuming where he'd left off with the crab. "It could be," he said. "Ye know that Con has named all of his ships after the sirens of myth? It seems that one of those sirens in the flesh is trying tae lure the man tae his doom."

Thor lifted his blond eyebrows at the possibility. "Then we will help him?"

Shaw pointed to the seat that Thor had occupied earlier. "We will, indeed," he said. "Sit and I will tell ye what Con's man just told me."

Lured by a beautiful woman. When Shaw was finished explaining, Thor had to say that he wasn't surprised. But, then again, history was full of men who had been lured to their deaths by a beautiful face. Only this time, the Devils of the Deep had an opportunity to prevent it from happening to one of their own.

Before dawn the next morning, a fierce squall rolled up from the west and the ships anchored at Bardsey Island found themselves struggling against the elements. With time of the essence, Shaw wasn't happy that the storm would delay their arrival.

He hoped the sirens would not win, after all.

Chapter Eight

H E'D BEEN AVOIDING HER for an entire day.

Literally, half of the day before and most of this day as well. For a man who had wanted to greedily soak up every possibly moment with Gregoria, he wasn't acting like it now.

He was confused.

But that wasn't like Constantine at all. The man was always supremely confident, always knowing the right thing to say or do and then completely comfortable with those decisions. He'd gone through life knowing he could handle any situation, and that included anything that happened with women. He controlled his destiny, and everything else around him, so when something occurred that he wasn't entirely in control of, Constantine found himself confused more than anything.

Bedding the woman hadn't been merely bedding her; perhaps that was the most confusing thing to him. Something about the act had gone beyond the mere physicality of it. Now, he was feeling something, although he wasn't sure what it was. All he knew was that Gregoria lingered in his mind, her soft body and sweet voice, and he couldn't seem to shake her.

Gregoria…

Gregg.

He hadn't slept at all the night before. He'd stayed up all night, on watch, up on the poop deck as the *Gaia* glided effortlessly over the sea. They were heading north, nearly parallel with the Devon coast. He knew that simply by the position of the stars, which had been bright against the nearly moonless night.

Off to the right, buried in a forest that lined the edge of the coast, was Baiadepaura Castle, a massive and dark structure that had been built upon the ruins of an old Roman fort. Legend said that a ghostly Roman legion haunted the place. Further up the coast and off to the left would see Lundy Island and, beyond that, the Bristol Channel. Eynon Bay would be on the other side of the channel and then, finally, Three Crosses Abbey. In about two days, his time with her would be at an end. As much as he wanted to keep his distance from her, there was a large part of him that wanted to resume where he'd left off with her.

If Lucifer and Remy had noticed Constantine behaving oddly, they didn't say anything. In fact, everything had been normal when he emerged onto the deck after his romp with Gregoria up until this very moment. Lucifer had even remained on watch with him last night and they spoke of the stars, of the French, and of the coming winter. Many subjects bounced around but not one of them had been about the lady in Constantine's cabin.

It was a good thing, too – Constantine didn't want to discuss it, not even with himself.

"Ship off the port bow!"

The cry came from the crow's nest and Constantine moved to the port railing, straining to see what the lookout saw. The wind was picking up, blowing east, and they were moving against that wind. They were having to use a maneuver called *tacking*, which meant they were zig-zagging over the waves in order to make headway against the wind. Even so, the captives rowing below were still having to strain against the current and it had been slow going the past several hours because of it. But the ship that finally came into view was heading in their direction, quite swiftly, and Lucifer came up behind Constantine, handing him his spyglass. Constantine peered through it.

"A merchant vessel," he finally muttered. "They must be coming from either Wexford or Dungarvan. The sails are white with blue... a blue outline of something. Wait... I see it now. A horse."

He handed the spyglass over to Lucifer, who took a good look at the incoming ship. "That is Efford out of Plymouth," he said. "That fat idiot who has the fleet of those new ships from Copenhagen. Remember? We met up with him last year when he presented a Letter of Marque from Henry, giving him permission to destroy pirates like us."

Constantine nodded and took back the spyglass, taking another look. "I remember," he said. "He thought he was clever, calling himself a privateer, when he was simply a merchant whose pride exceeded his common sense. As I recall, we sank one ship out from underneath him when he tried and damaged two others."

Lucifer cast him a long look, an amused twinkle in his eye. "Then he is a fool to travel these waters, alone."

Constantine had to agree. "As I said, his pride exceeds his common sense," he said. "But he is also richer than Midas himself. If he is coming from Ireland, then he must have a heavily-laden vessel, rich for the taking."

Lucifer could smell a battle in the air. "That is true, but he is usually armed," he said. "Do we take the chance of an engagement with a lady on board?"

Constantine looked at him as if the man had lost his mind. "Why would we *not*?" he asked harshly. He thought perhaps that Lucifer had been reading his tumultuous thoughts and he didn't want the man knowing how confused he was over the lady. But when he saw Lucifer's startled expression as he snapped, he forced a mischievous grin, trying not to look like a fool. "What I mean to say is that we cannot pass up such an opportunity. If Efford is armed, then all the better. We will take his goods *and* his ship if he angers me enough. Relay the orders to the men and raise the red banners."

Lucifer was on the move, bellowing orders as the men beat to quarters. They weren't a big crew, but they were very efficient, each man worth his weight in a fight. Constantine didn't tolerate lazy or fearful men, so every man on the ship was running for his weapon and his position. Overhead, the red le Brecque standards were raised on the yardarm of the mainmast.

The red standards had a purpose; they were cut to look like dragon's wings to match the flag that few on the top of mainmast, so in the wind, the banners snapped and writhed like massive wings. Since the figurehead on the *Gaia* was the head of a dragon, the winged banners gave it the illusion of a serpent flying over the water. Every sailing man from the Mediterranean to the North Sea knew the sight of Constantine le Brecque's red-wing banners and his dragon ship.

Beside the *Gaia*, the *Persephone* also raised wing-like banners, snapping briskly in the wind, and followed the *Gaia* on a parallel course towards the very large merchant ship, which had clearly sighted them. They began to turn due south, showing the *Gaia* and the *Persephone* its broadside, and Constantine's ships adjusted course accordingly. It wasn't long before the four-pounder cannonballs began to fly.

Cannon fire could be heard, echoing across the water, but they were warning shots. Constantine's ships weren't close enough to hit, so it was a waste of ammunition on the part of the merchant ship but it was meant to send a message. Of course, Constantine ignored the warning shots. With his men positioned at the bow of each of his ships with two four-pounder cannons, he was about to send a message of his own.

But he was smarter than the captain of the merchant vessel. He waited until they were in range and took aim at the mainmast, lobbing off two shots in short time. The first one barely missed the mainmast but the second one plowed into it, causing the thing to list dangerously. Over on the *Persephone*, Augustin and Kerk came around the rear of the merchant vessel and with seven cannon bursts, shot out the rudder.

Very quickly, the large merchant vessel was dead in the water.

Dead, but not out. They managed to load their portside cannons and blast out at the *Gaia*, hitting her twice on the gun deck while the other five skipped over the main deck or simply brushed past and out to sea.

At that point, however, the *Gaia* was in too close for them to accurately reload without damaging their vessel further, and Constantine had his men throw out grappling hooks, pulling the vessels closer so they could board the floundering merchant ship. The *Persephone* closed in on the ship's starboard side, effectively boxing the vessel in.

After that, it was pandemonium.

IN CONSTANTINE'S CABIN, Gregoria was well-aware that something terrible and frightening was going on.

And it had all happened rather quickly. Ever since setting sail yesterday morning, the seas had been calm and the trip had been smooth as far as trips went. But, much like Constantine, she was still grappling with what had happened between them the day before. Every time she thought of it, she had to fan herself, swept away by the memories of heat and lust as Constantine had backed her into a corner and had his way with her.

She couldn't decide if she was more embarrassed at her lack of resistance or more angry that Constantine had pushed himself on her. Truthfully, he didn't *exactly* push himself on her. Gregoria was convinced that she could have repelled him had she truly taken a stand, but she hadn't. She'd melted like butter at his touch, becoming boneless and spineless and foolish. Her maidenhood, which she had maintained these twenty-two years, had been lost all in a swift, passionate moment. For dignity's sake, she knew she had to show Constantine that she was outraged by his conduct and that she would never again tolerate him taking advantage of her but, secretly, she was hoping he would come back to his cabin and kiss her again.

He had such wonderful kisses.

It was, therefore, a strange game she played for the rest of the day and into the night, torn between embarrassment, anger, and hope. She'd vowed not to let herself become interested in or otherwise attached to Constantine, but given what had happened between them, that was now impossible. She already felt a great deal of interest in him, like it or not, and when Constantine didn't join her for the evening meal, she had been vastly disappointed. One of his men, the one named Remy, had brought her supper, carried upon silver trays by two fairly well-dressed seamen. Gregoria noticed that all of Constantine's men were well-fed and well-dressed, the evidence of a prosperous pirate.

In fact, the serving utensils and plate that she was served with were fine and expensive. The plate was pewter, inlaid with semi-precious stones, and the knife and spoon were solid silver and heavy. The food was some kind of fresh fish, cooked over a flame, with a sauce of mushrooms. It had been delicious, accompanied by a fine wine, and Gregoria ate until she could eat no more. Upon a silver plate that one of the seamen had left on the table were battered apple slices, fried, and then coated with honey. Full as she was, Gregoria still managed to stuff apples into her mouth.

After a meal like that, with sweets and wine, sleep came easily. She collapsed on the fine bed, swathed in silks, and the dogs slept next to her all night long. She only awoke because someone brought a meal to break her fast, and she rose sleepily to devour a steamed dish comprised of bread, eggs, apples, currants, and nuts. It was the second fine meal she'd had shipboard, which led her to believe that Constantine and his men ate very well when they were at sea. She had hardly eaten so well when she was on land.

The dogs slipped out when the seamen came to take her trays away and Gregoria was left alone in the cabin as the sun rose. She was coming to feel more foolish now as a new day dawned, foolish at her behavior the previous day and embarrassed because Constantine evidently had no plans to return to her. Perhaps he'd gotten what he'd wanted and there was no more reason to visit her. Disappointment turned into sorrow. Gregoria was coming to think it was justified punishment for the way she'd allowed the man to have his way with her.

She was getting no better than she deserved.

Therefore, she planted herself at the windows that overlooked the rudder and watched the sea pass by. It was a fine morning but as the day passed, it began to get windy. The sea became rough and, for the first time, she began to feel queasy. She was better when she remained by the windows with the breeze whipping in her face, so she planted herself there and didn't move. As the day progressed, she'd given up hoping that Constantine might return, so now all she could do was wait until they reached Wales. Given the way her stomach was feeling, and the sad confusion in her heart, she was hoping Wales would make an appearance sooner rather than later.

It was time for her to get back to that house and garden near the sea and forget all about Constantine le Brecque.

But then, the explosions started to come. At first, they were distant, but Gregoria could tell that the ship had taken a turn; the land that had been on the horizon all morning was now at a different angle. She could hear the faint shouts of men and, somewhere, someone was beating on a drum, a cadence she hadn't heard before. She came away from the windows and wandered the cabin in tense silence, trying to hear what was going on, when the entire ship abruptly shuddered as the cannons were fired.

With a yelp, Gregoria grabbed hold of the nearest wall, bracing herself against the concussion of the cannons. The ship was rocking from the blasts and she struggled to keep her footing as she stumbled back over to the windows to see if she could spy what was going on outside.

Smoke from the cannon fire blew back into the cabin and she coughed, waving her hands to scatter it so that she could breathe. Sticking her head out the window, she could see the bow of another ship alongside. But that was about all she could see because of the smoke; still, the ships were very close together and she could again hear the faint shouts of men. Suddenly, it occurred to her what was happening.

"We're being boarded!" she gasped.

Terrified she was about to become a spoil of war, Gregoria raced about the room, looking for something to defend herself with. There were two closets in the room and she yanked the first one open, only finding things like silver cups and other treasures, which weren't of any interest to her unless she planned to beat somebody over the head with a fine cup. But the second closet contained two swords, shoved into the back, and she grabbed one of them, nearly tripping over it when she realized how heavy it was. It was long, too, but she didn't care. It would be better to protect herself with a long, sharp sword than a short dagger. Someone could get too close to her if she only had a little blade for protection. But with this sword, she could hold off a man at a good distance.

Then, she waited.

Sounds of battle were all around her. The door to the cabin was bolted because Constantine had told her to lock it, so she had. She'd only opened it for the men who brought her food, but she promptly threw the bolt again when they left the cabin. Too frightened to open the door and peek out to see what was happening, she simply stood back by the windows, the sword in hand, listening to the chaos going on around her and waiting for the bolted door to be kicked down. Surely, if thieving men were on the ship, they would want what in the captain's cabin.

She was in the captain's cabin.

It seemed like forever as she listened to the shouts and cries of battle. Gregoria had never heard such things before and her mind began to race. God's Bones... she'd lived a quiet life, hadn't she? A good life? She'd been kind to her mother and did as she was told. She'd even let her brother put her in this position, thinking she was being an obedient girl. Not that she'd had much choice, but still... she'd been a good girl, hadn't she?

God, please do not let me be killed in this madness!

More banging, more yelling. The sea was becoming rougher and a quick glance from the window showed black clouds moving in from the west. A storm was coming. And then she heard the screams; it sounded like women screaming.

In fact, she could hear the screams above everything else, the crash of the sea and the roar of the wind. It was horrifically unnerving, all of it, and suddenly the screaming was on the other side of the chamber door. There was yelling and fighting and screaming, and the door was being bumped against. Terrified that a woman was being killed on the other side of the door and she wasn't doing anything about it, Gregoria summoned her courage and went to the door, unbolting it and yanking it open.

A figure in silks and ruffles came spilling in through the door, all kicking feet and swinging fists as she landed on her backside. Astonished, Gregoria looked up to see Constantine and Lucifer standing in the open door, with chaos on the main deck beyond.

It was all that she had feared, and then some. It was as if someone had just opened the door to hell.

Chapter Nine

CONSTANTINE WASN'T SURPRISED to see Gregoria standing in the doorway with a sword in her hand.

Cooped up in the captain's cabin without any knowledge of the madness going on around her, it would make sense that the woman wanted to arm herself. Surely she must have thought the entire world was crashing down around her and, for a brief second, his heart leapt at the sight of her. It was such a joyous leap, something he'd never experienced before, as if the mere sight of her brought him contentment.

But that brief, warm moment was swiftly dashed when the woman who had literally fallen backward into the cabin leapt to her feet and began swinging her fists.

"Beasts!" she howled. "Where is my sister?"

The woman was a short little thing, with dark silky hair that was now a mess all over her head and shoulders, but she wasn't giving up without a fight against two significantly larger men. When she took a swing at Lucifer, he put a hand on her forehead and gave a strong push, causing her to crash back onto her buttocks again. Constantine gave her a push with his booted foot for good measure, pushing her further inside the chamber and away from the door.

"Keep her in here," he told Gregoria. "Bolt the door and do not let her leave."

Gregoria's mouth fell open with shock. "But…!"

He cut her off. "No questions," he demanded. "Bolt this door and do not leave. That is not a request."

His tone was cutting, harsh. Startled by the command and his controlled manner, Gregoria simply nodded her head as Constantine grabbed the door latch and yanked the panel closed. But the little woman was on her feet again, rushing for the door, and Gregoria intercepted her.

"Nay!" she said, trying to pull the woman away. "It is not safe out there. Did you hear him? You must stay here where you will not come to harm!"

Furious and frightened, the dark-haired woman slapped her right across the face. Startled, Gregoria slapped her back. Clearly, the dark-haired woman wasn't used to being touched or resisted, because she swung at Gregoria's face again and Gregoria ducked, giving the woman a shove back and sending her stumbling.

"You'll not hit me again, do you hear?" Gregoria said angrily. "Try it and I shall slug you right in the nose!"

The dark-haired woman came to an unsteady halt, holding on to the wall for balance as the ship rocked about. "Are you in this with him?" she demanded. "If you are, then I will fight you to the death!"

Gregoria scowled. "Of course I am not a pirate!"

"Then why are you here?"

That was a good question, one with an answer that would make it seem as if she were, indeed, in collusion with Constantine. She didn't want a battle on her hands with this terrified woman so she struggled to calm down, hoping her demeanor would encourage the frightened woman to calm as well.

"I am here on another matter," she said evenly. "But I assure you, I am not a pirate. And those men are putting you into this room with me to keep you safe. There is a battle going on out there and you will be hurt if you leave this cabin."

The woman pushed her long hair out of her eyes, revealing a rather lovely face. She had dark, flashing eyes and rosebud lips, but her expression was set and hard.

"They put me in here to keep me a prisoner," she said flatly. "Are you a prisoner, too?"

Gregoria wasn't sure she should answer that because the woman wouldn't appreciate the truth. It was rather complicated, so she sought to change the subject.

"Why would you be a prisoner?" she asked. "Did your ship not attack this ship?"

The woman's face darkened. "We fired only to protect ourselves," she said. "I know who commands this ship; it is Constantine le Brecque, the most wicked pirate in these waters. He is taking my father's ship as a prize!"

"Who is your father?"

"He is a merchant!"

Gregoria learned a lot in that agitated explanation. Given Constantine's vocation, she was quite certain she couldn't deny the woman's charge.

"If you fired upon him first, mayhap you angered him," she said, trying to search for an explanation. "Where is your captain? Surely he knows it is not safe to fire on a pirate ship."

The woman growled. "He is dead," she said, suddenly appearing as if she were about to cry. "I saw him killed with my own eyes. One of le Brecque's men speared him through the heart."

At that, she turned away, clearly upset with the turn of events. Once the sheer panic eased, all that was left was terror and sorrow. In truth, Gregoria felt a little sorry for her.

"My name is Gregoria," she said, trying to ease the situation a little. "Everyone calls me Gregg. What is your name?"

The woman had her back to Gregoria, dabbing at her eyes. "Genevieve," she said. "I am Genevieve Efford."

"Where do you live, Genevieve?"

Genevieve eyed her. "Why would you ask such a question?" she demanded, becoming agitated again. "This is not time for idle conversation. We must find a way to get out of here!"

Gregoria didn't know what to say about that other than repeat what she'd already told her. "It is too dangerous," she said. "You are much safer in here."

Genevieve didn't like that answer. "But my sister is out there," she said. "I must go and save her!"

Gregoria had a feeling the woman was going to charge the door, so she moved to put herself in between the door and Genevieve. "Constantine and his men will make sure she is safe," she said, hoping it was true. "If you go out there, you'll only get hurt. I am not sure how many times I can tell you that."

"But I must save Vivienne!"

"At the cost of your own life? What will happen to her if you die?"

That slowed Genevieve somewhat. She backed down but her movements were full of angst. Realizing that she was essentially helpless in all of this, she turned around, wandering aimlessly for the open windows. Smoke from the cannons was still wafting in but she didn't seem to notice. Her mind was wandering to the chain of events and the predicament she now found herself in. Even though she'd quieted, she still had a wild-eyed, shocked look about her.

"Sweet Mary," she breathed. "What I would not give to simply go back to Ireland."

"Ireland?" Gregoria said. "Is that where you live?"

Genevieve didn't say anything for a moment, her gaze on the storm that was blowing in over their heads. "I have for the past year," she said. "My father has property there."

Gregoria was relieved to see that the woman seemed to be calming. "I have never been to Ireland," she said. "What is it like?"

Genevieve shrugged. "Like England," she said. "The land is green, the people fair, only Ireland seems much more ancient to me. There are great mounds built by men thousands of years ago, and great stone monuments. I have a horse and I would go riding every day. I... I just want to go back."

Gregoria could hear the wistfulness in her tone. "I am sure you will be able to, someday."

Genevieve turned to her sharply. "As the prisoner of a pirate?" she snapped. "Somehow, I do not think they will let me go back to Ireland. They will probably sell me off to the highest bidder."

Gregoria wasn't sure if that was a possibility or not, so she simply kept her mouth shut. She was coming to the end of being able to comfort the woman and, soon enough, her real purpose for being here might come out. That would start the anger all over again. Just as she pondered what more to say to the woman, there was a loud bang against the cabin door. Rushing to the door, Gregoria put her hand on the bolt.

"Who comes?" she yelled.

"Open the door."

It was Constantine. Passing a glance at Genevieve, wondering if the woman was going to rush the door anew, she threw the bolt and the door lurched open. It seemed at that moment as if everything in the world abruptly spilled into the cabin; Henry and Edward, the dogs, rushed in, barking and agitated, while Remy came in behind them holding three gray, scruffy-looking puppies in his arms. As he headed over to the bed to set the puppies down, a young woman was forcibly escorted into the cabin by Lucifer.

The woman was crying at the top of her lungs, wailing, and Genevieve rushed to the woman, trying to pull her away from Lucifer as she pounded on the man's arm.

"Release her, you beast!" she howled. "Let my sister go!"

Lucifer released the woman, but only when he was ready to. Genevieve tried to charge him again, to kick him, and he reached out a long leg and blocked her kick, shoving her back in the same motion. She ended up on her knees near the table where the meals had been served and, because of the violent roll of the ship, there were items on the floor – a spoon, a tray, and a cup. She picked up the cup and hurled it at Lucifer's head.

"You monster!" she cried, picking up the spoon and blindly throwing it at him. "You are a brutal, vile monster!"

The cup missed Lucifer, although barely, while the spoon hit him on the arm. All he did was frown at the woman and shake his head with great disapproval as he headed out of the cabin. Meanwhile, the woman's sister was weeping hysterically. Genevieve scrambled off of the floor and went to her sister, throwing her arms around the woman.

"Are you well, Vivi?" she demanded. "They did not injure you, did they?"

Vivienne Efford, tiny and thin and dark-haired like her sister, shook her head. Genevieve kissed her and led her over to the bed where the puppies were starting to move around, sniffing everything.

"Look," Genevieve said with gentleness no one had yet heard from her. "Look at your dogs; they are fine. You must take care of them."

Sobbing, quivering, Vivienne sat on the bed and began to hug her puppies as Gregoria stood back and watched the scene. The sisters weren't injured but they were both frightened out of their minds. Even though Lucifer had quit the cabin, Constantine was still standing near the door and when Gregoria looked at him, she was somewhat startled to see that he was staring at her. He just stood there and looked at her for a moment as Vivienne wept and Genevieve tried to soothe her. With the noise of sorrow in the background, Gregoria made her way over to Constantine.

"Are they really your prisoners?" she whispered. "What do you intend to do with them?"

His gaze lingered on her. "That should be of no concern to you."

She looked at him seriously. "Forgive me, but it is," she said. "I am very concerned for them. Please do not harm them. They are just young women and they are so very frightened."

Constantine heard the concern in her voice. Although she understood the theory of piracy, the practice of it was something quite different. She had no idea how such situations were handled or how such deeds were carried out. But the questions didn't bother him because he could see that she was genuinely concerned – not demanding, or bullying – but concerned for other human beings. That kind of compassion was rare in Constantine's line of work unless it was from his fellow pirates with regards to each other. But seeing it from Gregoria towards women he only saw as part of the treasures of the merchant ship – somehow, it touched him.

"I am not going to harm them," he said quietly. "But you must let me decide their fates."

Her brow furrowed. "Fates?" she repeated. "Genevieve told me that all she wishes to do is return to Ireland. Can you not simply return them to Ireland? It would be the compassionate thing to do."

Constantine wasn't a man who took kindly to being questioned. All of his men knew that. But he was being amazingly patient with Gregoria's questioning, mainly because he knew she wasn't questioning his authority. Simply his intentions. Moreover, coming from her… it was different somehow. He realized that he didn't want to upset or offend her.

"I want you to do something for me," he said softly.

"What is it?"

Reaching up, he cupped her chin briefly. "Ease the ladies," he said, dropping his hand. "There is drink in the cabinets. Give them some. There is also water in the corner, a barrel anchored to the deck with a lid on it. Give Henry and Edward some water to drink. Tend to every creature in this cabin and I shall return when my tasks are complete."

His touch. God, even that slight touch to her chin sent bolts of excitement racing through her body. The man had the ability to turn her knees to liquid with merely a touch, and his voice… it had been gentle. Kind, even. In the midst of a battle, he was calm and cool and patient with her. It was all quite disorienting but all quite wonderful. When she spoke, there was a quiver in her voice.

"I will," she said. "Did... did you really attack her father's ship? Genevieve, I mean. She said you attacked her father's ship."

Constantine thought he needed to make things clear. His business was his business, and it was no concern of hers. She was curious, frightened about what was happening and concerned for the young women, but now her questions were bordering on disapproval and he didn't like it.

He didn't like seeing disapproval in her eyes, especially when it pertained to him.

"What I do is my own affair," he said, rather defensively. "Just because I am escorting you to Wales does not mean that my business stops. You, on the other hand, will do as you are told. Nothing I do concerns you and you would do well to remember that."

Reprimanded, Gregoria lowered her gaze, her cheeks warm with embarrassment. Constantine was immediately sorry but he couldn't bring himself to apologize or even ease his stance. She had to know her place and he wouldn't tolerate her interference.

Even if her intentions were altruistic. Altruism and piracy didn't go hand-in-hand.

... did they?

Leaving Gregoria in the cabin with the young women, Constantine fled and slammed the door behind him. Bloody Beard, whoever heard of an altruistic pirate? He'd be the laughing stock. He'd spent so much of his life going after wealth and making a name for himself that it was all he knew. Merchant ships like this – they were his life's blood. The spoils from this ship would pay his men and be used for trade. It was necessary. In Perranporth, it was plunder like this that kept the local economy going when his men visited villages in the area and spent their money there. Gregoria just didn't understand that it was more than stealing or looting – it was necessary to the economy of Cornwall, for the most part. It wasn't as if Constantine derived some sick pleasure from his way of life. It was simply a means to an end – money to support him, his men, and his way of life.

Out on the main deck, the fight was dying down for the most part. His men had secured the merchant ship and were now bringing over the goods that had been stored in the hull. There was heavy smoke from a fire at the bow of the ship and Constantine moved to get a better look at it. It was quickly consuming the front of the ship and he could see Lucifer and Remy as they bellowed to the men to move fast and remove all they could before the ship burned up and sank.

Still more of his men were moving the surviving crew of the merchant ship onto the *Gaia*, taking them below where the captives were kept. There was also a beautiful black stallion that had been secured to the stern of the ship and his men had rigged a cradle to move the horse over to the *Gaia*, but the horse was frightened so Constantine jumped in to help.

As the flames began to consume the merchant vessel, Constantine managed to cover up the eyes of the stallion and hold the animal steady as his men rigged the rope cradle and heaved the horse between the ships, landing it gently on the deck of the *Gaia* where there were men waiting to tend it. By this time, the merchant ship was listing dangerously by the bow and Constantine made his way back to the *Gaia* to survey their take. Remy was there to meet him.

"Well?" Constantine said. "Have we cleared everything from the merchant ship?"

Remy nodded. "Mostly," he said. Then, he pointed to the bow of the crippled ship and Constantine turned to see Kerk in the water, swimming towards the *Gaia* with four goats in tow. "Kerk was able to free the animals in the front of the hold."

Constantine snapped at his men to rush and help Kerk pull the goats from the water. They did so, heaving the animals out by their necks. They were wet, but unharmed. "No more livestock on board?" he asked.

Remy shook his head. "There were more goats, but we transferred them to the *Persephone*," he said. "In fact, what do you want to do about all of this? We have quite a bit of merchandise and most of it on the *Gaia*. Will you carry all of this to Wales?"

Constantine shook his head. "Nay," he replied. "Move the *Persephone* alongside and we'll transfer everything over to her. You can then take the *Persephone* back to Perranporth while the *Gaia* will continue to Wales. I cannot, and will not, take a heavily-laden vessel any further than I have to. It is safer to return the goods home as soon as we can."

"Aye, my lord."

"Go and make the necessary preparations."

As Remy headed off to move everything over to the *Persephone*, Constantine wanted to get a better look at the black stallion. It was a magnificent animal with a shiny coat and furry fetlocks, quite big and muscular. He had a weakness for fine horses and knew this one would make an excellent addition to his collection. He petted the beast, inspecting the legs, making sure the animal hadn't suffered in the chaos. It seemed fine except that it was still quite excited, so he instructed his men to keep the animal's eyes covered. He also wanted someone with the animal constantly to see to its wellbeing, and a sailor with a great fondness for horses was assigned.

With the last of the cargo being transferred to the *Gaia*, the merchant ship went through its death throes as the burning wreckage slipped beneath the sea. Heavy smoke covered the area and Constantine had the *Gaia* moved away from the smoldering ruins to keep his ship protected.

The conquest of the merchant ship had been an unexpected benefit to this trip, making the entire undertaking well worth his while. Perhaps now his men wouldn't look upon this venture so unfavorably. They thought he didn't know of their concerns, but he did. Constantine wasn't a fool. He knew what his men were thinking better than they did at times. He knew this haul would ease some of that disapproval. Disapproval that their leader, a man great enough to lead titans, was letting a woman influence his decisions.

But that was far from the case. At least, Constantine kept telling himself that.

Muddled in thought, he went to the poop deck of the *Gaia* and surveyed the activity as all of the goods on the decks of the *Gaia* were moved over to the *Persephone*. It was an extremely rich haul and Constantine specifically assigned Kerk the duty of taking the *Persephone* back to Perranporth and then inventorying the entire haul. He trusted Kerk and knew the man would keep everything protected until his return to Perran Castle.

But thoughts of Gregoria were heavy on Constantine's mind, even as he went about his duties. Try as he might, he couldn't seem to shake her. Specifically, he was dreading the moment when he would send his men into his cabin to remove the two captive women to take back to Perran Castle. Gregoria had asked him what he intended to do with the women and the answer was obvious; it was the same thing he did every time he captured women as part of a haul or conquest – he would auction them off to his men as wives or concubines. He might even award them to men who performed admirably in battle. Women were possessions, like that beautiful black horse or the trunk of fine silks they'd come across. They were items for a man to do with as he pleased.

… weren't they?

He had a feeling Gregoria wouldn't think so.

Therefore, Constantine was a coward in the end. When it came time to move the captive women to the *Persephone*, he sent Lucifer and Remy and Augustin to do it. He pretended to be busy with other things, but he could hear the screams of the women as they were removed from his cabin and taken aboard the *Persephone*. They were screams of terror and of pain, the cries of women whose future was now uncertain. They were cries that had never bothered him before in all the years he'd been at sea but, this time, it was different. The cries cut into him.

… what if those cries had belonged to Gregoria?

God, what was *happening* to him! That woman, that *silly* woman who had come to him with tales of a holy relic and had convinced him to help her return it was under his skin more than he wanted to admit. Had she bewitched him somehow? Had those big blue eyes and sensual body hooked him more than he had realized? He should be angry about it; so very angry but, instead, he found himself wanting to go and see her. She was in the cabin below his feet, undoubtedly upset about the captive women being moved to the *Persephone*, and he'd stayed away like a weakling. He hadn't wanted to face her.

He was going to have to face her sometime.

Once the captive women had been taken below deck on the *Persephone*, Constantine summoned his courage. Heading down to his cabin, he could see that the door was wide open. The deck was fairly devoid of men at this point, most of them working on securing the *Persephone* for her return, so he made his way into the cabin, prepared for a tongue lashing. He wasn't sure what he was going to find or what mood Gregoria would be in, and he wondered why he even cared. But he did care.

That was his problem.

"What did you do with those women?"

He had barely entered the open door than Gregoria was firing the question at him. He lifted a blond eyebrow at her.

"I am not sure I care for your tone," he said. "I told you that what I do is none of your affair."

Gregoria was standing back by the windows, arms crossed angrily. "Then why did you come back in here?" she asked. "You knew I was going to ask you. Do you know that Lucifer and one of your other men dragged those women out of here, kicking and screaming?"

He was struggling not to show any remorse because she made something he was immune to sound so terrible. "If they were kicking and screaming, then that is their fault," he said evenly. "They could have gone peacefully. They chose not to."

Gregoria wasn't surprised by the answer, but she was disappointed. She was so angry, so upset, that she was trembling. All of those soft, warm feelings she'd developed for Constantine were in danger of fizzling out, like water dousing a flame. But, in truth, she was only lying to herself if she thought that was really the case. Whatever she felt for the man was beginning to anchor itself deep. But to see how his men had treated those women – at Constantine's direction – hurt her deeply.

"What kind of man are you?" she finally hissed. "I thought you were kind and helpful. And now… now…!"

"Now *what*?" he said, losing the battle against his patience. "What did you really think I am when you came to seek my help, Gregoria? Some fine, noble knight, a gentle man that lives a genteel life? You knew better than that. I never put on any illusion of being anything other than what I am – a thief and a man of business. That is all."

His words were like a slap in the face. Gregoria stared at him and her lower lip began to tremble. Disillusioned, she averted her gaze and turned away from him.

"Then put me off this ship," she hissed. "I will go back to Perran Castle with the rest of the cargo. I want off!"

His jaw ticked as he watched her stiff back. "What about this relic you want to deliver to Wales?" he asked. "You were quite determined that I escort you, fearful of the French as you were."

"I would rather face them!" she suddenly shouted, whirling to look at him. "Surely they cannot be any worse than what you are!"

His jaw flexed. "Is that what you think?" he said. "Then you really are a fool. Shall I tell you how I differ from the French? If you have been told anything about them at all, then you know that they cut the feet off of their captives so they cannot run away. Did you know that? At least I do not maim my captives."

Gregoria hadn't heard that and she gasped with shock, trying to cover it but not doing a very good job. "That… that is horrible!"

He nodded. "Indeed, it is," he said. "Do you know what else the French do, especially to women captives? They will chain you to a bed shipboard so that you cannot escape – chaining your hands to the head of the bed – and then any man who feels the need to sate his lustful needs in the soft folds of your body has the opportunity to do so. Considering how many men they carry shipboard, anywhere from thirty to fifty, you could find yourself violated thirty to fifty times a day.

Even if you become with child, they do not remove you from that bed. Men will continue to relieve themselves in your body until you give birth to that child, which they will then throw overboard the moment it is born. The blood and guts from childbirth will barely be out of your body before another man is putting his seed in you. Now – do you still believe I am not any worse than the French?"

By the time he was finished, she was looking at him with tears in her eyes and a hand over her mouth.

"Dear... God...," she breathed through splayed fingers. "Tell me that is not true."

"Of course it is true. I would not lie to you."

She blinked and tears spattered on her cheeks, which she quickly wiped away. "You... you will not do that to Genevieve or Vivienne, will you?" she asked hoarsely. "The women you captured, I mean. The women that were just here. You will not be cruel to them like that, will you?"

"Why do you care so much about them? You do not even know them."

She sighed faintly, shaking her head. "I do not *need* to know them," she said softly, pleadingly. "All I know is that they are young women who do not deserve to be punished simply because they were on a ship that you wanted. Is it possible for you to show some compassion for their plight?"

"Why?"

"Because it would be the right thing to do. Does it not ever occur to you to simply do what is right and good, for once?"

It didn't, not ever. *Chattel!* He thought. *Those women are simply chattel!* But it was clear Gregoria didn't think so. Constantine's plan had been to auction them off to his men, but looking at Gregoria's pale face, he wasn't sure he could do that any longer. She cared too much about what happened to them and, God help him, he cared what she thought. He was beginning to feel foolish and weak, angry at himself that Gregoria's opinion meant so much to him. She brought an element of compassion to his view of the world that hadn't been there before.

He hated it.

But there was no use in arguing with her. She simply didn't understand. Worse still, she was making him second guess things he'd been doing ever since he took to sea. *Do what is right and good.* He didn't even know what that meant.

"I do not live my life by doing the right thing, Lady Meyrick," he finally said. "I live my life by what is best for me and my men. Your father lived the same way, I might add, so do not judge me so harshly lest you judge your father as well."

Gregoria had nearly forgotten about Miles Tenby. She'd been so wrapped up in her budding feelings for Constantine, and now this, that she'd completely forgotten about the man she'd claimed as her father. With a shake of her head, one of disappointment, she lowered herself into the nearest fine chair.

"My father said you were a man to come to in times of trouble," she muttered. "I suppose I did not realize that also meant you had no moral compass. I do not know what I expected, but it was not what I have experienced. I want no part of it."

Constantine was hurt by that and he had no idea why. Perhaps it was because he was coming to respect Gregoria just the slightest; along with her obvious beauty and determination, she had a deep heart. Most men considered that a weakness, but Constantine was coming to think that it wasn't a weakness at all. He envied someone who could feel as deeply as she did and, in spite of what she'd said – that she wanted off the ship – he wasn't going to let her go.

Increasingly, he realized that he couldn't let her go.

He started to move in her direction when he caught sight of Henry and Edward, sleeping on the bed where they shouldn't be, cuddled up with three gray puppies. He'd seen the puppies brought on board but had no idea they hadn't made it on to the *Persephone*. All five dogs were sleeping like the dead and, as a man with a softness for dogs, he went to the bed and bent over, petting one of the sleeping puppies. It occurred to him that he was showing the dogs more compassion than those two women and, with that thought, he was coming to understand what she'd meant. Would he have auctioned the dogs off or have treated them so poorly? Probably not. They were weaker creatures, dependent upon men.

So were women.

Heavily, he sighed.

"Then what would you have me do?" he asked her. "With those women, I mean. What do you want me to do?"

Gregoria was surprised by the question. Not that she believed he was truly seeking her advice, but she gave it, anyway. "Genevieve wanted to return to Ireland," she said. "Could you simply return them to Ireland?"

He shook his head. "I will not," he said. "But I will take them home. I believe their father is based in Plymouth."

Gregoria was looking at him with increasing hope. "Truly?" she said. "You would do that?"

He shrugged, petted the puppy one last time, and turned for the door. "Do you still want off the ship?"

Gregoria watched him walk to the door. "Do you want me off the ship?"

He came to an unsteady halt right by the door, refusing to turn and look at her. "That was not the question," he said quietly. "Do you want off the ship?"

She stood up from the chair, her gaze riveted to him. All of the hurt and confusion was draining away, leaving behind the warm feelings she'd developed for the man. Somehow, she knew there was something good in him underneath all of that piracy and plunder. She didn't know how she knew, only that she did.

Something in her heart told her so.

"I will get off in Wales, if that is acceptable," she said, making her way towards him, wishing he would look at her. "I... I did not mean to cause you any trouble, my lord. It is simply that this is my first experience with… well, with whatever it is you do. I am not accustomed to such things."

"I know."

"How much further to Wales?"

He could hear her coming up behind him and it was as if his entire body ignited. He finally turned to look at her, gazing into those big blue eyes, but no words would come to mind. All he knew was that he wanted to touch her, and he did. He reached out, cupping her face between his two big hands, and kissing her deeply on the lips.

Gregoria collapsed against him, responding to his kiss, her knees weakening to the point where she could barely stand. His kisses grew more forceful, his arms going around her, and she simply let the man have his way with her. She'd only known him a matter of days, but she couldn't remember when he hadn't been around her. When he hadn't been embedded in her heart somehow.

"Even if it was years to Wales, it would be too soon," he breathed against her mouth. "You inflame me, Gregg, as I have never been inflamed before. The feel of you, the scent of you… it is fuel for my soul."

Gregoria wrapped her arms around his neck, holding him tightly. "Must Wales be the end?" she whispered. "When you leave me, will I ever see you again?"

His frenzied kisses slowed, his hands now rubbing her back, almost in a comforting gesture. "Do you ask because you wish to see me again?"

It seemed to Gregoria that he had let his guard down. Because of that, she let hers down, also. "I… I do," she said, hoping it wasn't the wrong thing to say. "What happened yesterday… I thought mayhap… that mayhap you did, also."

He was silent a moment, his forehead against hers, feeling her soft heat against him. She felt so very good wrapped up in his arms, better than any woman he'd ever experienced. His thoughts of keeping her as a permanent mistress had only grown stronger.

"I do," he admitted. "You shall not leave me, Gregg. I want you to remain with me."

Gregoria's heart had wings; it was soaring in a way she'd never known, full of the joy of his words. "I will."

"Swear it?"

"I do."

He kissed her on the forehead, on the nose, and then put a finger under her chin, tipping it up so he could kiss her lips. Their eyes met for a moment and Gregoria could see something undulating in his dark gold depths. It was turmoil and emotion, everything all rolled up into one. As if he had no idea what he was truly feeling; all he knew was what he needed.

He needed *her*.

Without another word, he left the cabin, shutting the door quietly behind him. He didn't even tell her to bolt it; he simply slipped out. Gregoria stood there, eyes on the door, wondering what she had just committed herself to. Responding to his question – her desire for him – had been truthful. She did, indeed, want to stay with him. But the fact remained that she was taking him to Wales for a specific purpose, a purpose that would see his end. The Earl of March and one thousand men were waiting for Constantine le Brecque at Three Crosses Abbey, and it was her task to take him there. She hadn't cared in the least before, but now... she cared.

She cared a great deal.

But there was terrible fear in telling him the truth. It would ruin everything between them, everything that was developing. Feelings so precious and true that they were surely a gift from God. But Lord Wembury wouldn't understand that, nor would her brother or the Earl of March. So much was dependent upon her.

And what had she done? She had failed. She had become attached to a man who stole and killed for a living. She'd just witnessed the man pillaging a ship and stealing the cargo, and cruelly treating two young women. Could a man like that change? Probably not. She was a fool for having let herself fall for the man.

But she couldn't help herself.

Greatly torn, Gregoria found herself in tears as she returned to the chair near the window, searching her soul to determine which was the correct thing to do. Stay with Constantine because she was infatuated with him, and he with her? What happened when that infatuation wore off? He would cast her aside, she would be an enemy of her brother and of Lord Wembury, and the quiet house by the sea with its garden would be a bitter memory. She would have nothing but the memories of an affair with a great pirate.

A man she could quite easily sell her soul to.

... would it be worth it?

By evening, the storm that had rolled in during the battle was blowing full-force, reflecting the deep and trouble state of Gregoria's soul.

Chapter Ten

Parrog Bay, Southern Wales

IT WAS AS bad a storm as Shaw had seen in a very long time. The good news was that the wind was blowing in from the northeast to the southwest, which meant he had made astonishing time from Bardsey Island. He was already in southern Wales and he hadn't expected to see this land until tomorrow morning. If the winds kept up, he would be at Eynon Bay by the morrow.

But the bad news was that his vessel was taking a beating. They had a cracked mizzenmast and he wasn't entirely sure the foremast wasn't cracked, either. The winds had been brutal. Given that a broken mast would slow him down for a couple of days at the very least until it could be repaired, he made the decision to seek shelter so the crack in the mast could be reinforced before it snapped. That choice drove him straight into Parrog Bay.

Parrog Bay was a smaller cove in southern Wales, but it provided enough shelter so that his ship wouldn't get pummeled. The ship's carpenters remained on board to reinforce the mast but Shaw and most of his men disembarked the ship and headed into the small fishing village of Parrog for some warmth and shelter. After a day and a night of that terrible storm, they were all eager to be on level ground and protected from the winds.

It had been a while since Shaw had been in this part of Wales, mostly because this was Constantine's territory and also because he really didn't give a hang about Wales in general, other than to eat its seasonal crab. But he had been to Parrog in the past and he and his men headed for the big tavern on the edge of town, one called The Hungry Dogfish. As they approached the establishment through the rain and wind, they could see the glowing lights in the cracks of the shuttered windows and the smell of smoke was heavy in the air, indicating a big fire.

And it was the warmth from the fire that slapped them in the face when they opened the front door, a blast of stale heat that was both revolting and welcoming. The common room was crowded with people, men and women having come in out of the elements to ride out the storm, but Shaw wasn't interested in the patrons or in being polite. He wanted a table to himself and his men wanted food. When it was clear the customers of the tavern had no intention of giving up their tables for him and his men, Shaw gave a quick nod to Thor.

It was time to make room.

Soon enough, tables were being overturned and men were scrambling to get away from the gang of pirates that had just entered the tavern. Rather that deal with the cutthroats, men and women were rushing from the tavern, out into the rain they'd been so comfortably avoiding. Now, it was pandemonium as Shaw and his men took over about half of the tavern. Those brave enough to remain were crowded in to the opposite side of the room, as far away from the pirates as they could get.

The common room smelled of rotten wood, old food, and the smoke from the big hearth. Shaw claimed a chair at one of the six tables his men had confiscated and sat down, pulling at a loaf of bread that had been left behind when the previous diner had fled. It was good bread, with rye grain in it, and he chewed heartily as the fearful tavern owner and a couple of older serving wenches inched their way in his direction.

Already, his men were calling for food and drink, and the wenches scattered as the owner continued towards Shaw, who was clearly the leader of the group. He was giving commands and his men were following without question. The tavern owner stood near Shaw, nervously.

"A meal, m'lord?" he asked. "I have boiled beef tonight. 'Tis very good."

Shaw nodded. "Bring it all," he said. "My men are hungry. And do ye have something better than watered ale?"

The man nodded. "I have a sweet Malmsey at a good price."

"Bring it."

The man scooted off, leaving Shaw and the others to begin removing their wet outer clothing. They were close enough to the hearth that men were laying out their cloaks on the stone and watching the steam rise. As wet clothing was set out and the men returned to their table for the drink that was being brought out, the other patrons of the tavern seemed to relax. Realizing the pirates weren't there to kill them and burn out the place, but simply to eat, they began to resume their tables and their conversation, which was now in whispers.

A tentative peace settled.

"I canna remember such a gale," Thor said as a serving wench handed him a cup of wine. He drank heartily from it. "It must be something fierce further tae the north. Came in over Ireland, I would think."

Shaw nodded as he, too, accepted his cup of wine. He took a big drink, smacking his lips at the heavy sweetness of the liquor. "'Tis blowing down from the north, 'tis for certain," he said. "If the men can get the crack in the mast repaired tonight, we can continue on in the morning. If these winds keep up, we'll be at Eynon Bay tomorrow sometime."

Thor nodded, pondering the deep red wine in his cup. "I have been thinking…"

"What?"

"Have ye thought on what tae tell Constantine when we arrive? I suspect that Lucifer dinna tell him he summoned us."

Shaw sighed thoughtfully. "That was my impression as well," he said. "I suppose we simply tell Con that we were trolling his waters for victims."

Thor grinned. "He'll be angry if ye tell him that," he said. "These are his waters. The victims would be his."

Shaw chuckled. "I know it," he said. "But 'tis better than telling him that Lucifer sent for us because he's afraid the man is in danger. Under no circumstances do we tell Con who sent us word, do ye hear?"

Thor nodded. "I know," he agreed. "The more I think on it, the more concerned I am for Con. Lucifer has never sent us word like this, not ever."

Shaw sobered dramatically. "I canna imagine that Con doesna know what he is doing," he said. "I've never known the man tae make a bad decision. Rash, aye. Bad, no."

"Then what do we tell Con when we see him?"

"I'll think of something."

With that, they retreated into their drink as the tavern keeper and the wenches brought out big bowls of steaming boiled meat and a pea potage. As the men began to dig in, like a feeding frenzy, a very drunken old man wandered over to their table.

It was an old man who frequented the tavern, bothering the customers and drinking all he could get his hands on. He thought nothing of approaching the pirates who had just settled in.

"Ahoy!" the old man said, grinning and weaving about. "I know who you are, *bachgen*. I saw your ship in the cove. 'Tis a fine vessel, it is."

He was near Shaw, who soundly ignored him as he delved into his food. The tavern owner tried to chase the old man away, but he wouldn't go. He simply went to Shaw's other side, watching as the men wolfed down the food.

"I used to live at sea myself," the old man continued. "I was a fisherman and my father before me. Do you know there is good fishing off of Ramsey Island this time of year? Fish as big as a man!"

Shaw shoved meat into his mouth but, at this point, he turned to look at the old drunk. He looked the man up and down before returning to his food.

"I eat my share of crab," he said, mouth full. "Bardsey is the best place for that."

The old man was thrilled that he'd gotten a response. "Anglesey, *bachgen*," he insisted. "That is where you will find the best crab. Do you ever fish there?"

Bachgen was an affectionate slang term for boy, or son. Much like men in Scotland called each other *laddie*. Shaw shook his head to the question.

"I havena," he said. "We just left Bardsey."

The old man took another swig of the cheap ale in his hand. "Then you're coming too far south for good crab," he said. "But just two weeks ago, I was in Swansea. They were pulling fish out of the sea that were twice the size of a man, big silver fish they were cutting up and selling for a fortune."

Shaw had a soft spot for old men who told tall fish tales. His own father had been such a man and he glanced at Thor, winking at the man as if to pull him in on the joke.

"Fish twice the size of a man, eh?" he said to the old man. "Were ye the great catcher of those fish, then?"

The old man snorted, taking another drink of his ale only to realize it was empty. Seeing this, Shaw picked up the pitcher of the Malmsey and poured it into the old man's cup, much to his delight.

"Thank you, m'lord," he said gratefully, licking his lips of the very sweet wine. "Now, to answer your question. You think you are jesting with me, but the truth is that I've caught bigger fish in my life. *Much* bigger fish."

"Is that so?"

"Aye, 'tis!" the old man insisted. He took a long gulp of the Malmsey before continuing. "As big as a boat!"

Now, Shaw was fighting off a grin at the exaggerating old man. "Well, now," he said, "ye're something of a hero, are ye? Bringing in fish as big as a boat? I would have liked tae have seen it."

The old man was now being very friendly with Shaw, his new best friend. He put a gnarled old hand on Shaw's shoulder.

"If you'll take me on your ship, I'll show you where the best places are to find big fish," he said. "I… I know I'm just an old fool, but I could be of some use to you."

Shaw turned to look at the old man. "Ye're not an old fool," he said. "Ye're an old liar, but ye're not an old fool."

Those at the table who had heard the insult erupted in soft laughter, including the old man. "Mayhap I am an old liar at that," he agreed, somewhat embarrassed. "But… but I'm sharp. I see things. And I know things. I can tell you where the danger is so you and your men can avoid it."

Shaw pretended to be interested. "I see," he said. "And just where is there danger around here?"

The old man took a giant swallow of his wine, nearly draining the cup. Already, it was making him drunker than he had been, mixing the sweet wine with the cheap ale as he was.

"Down south," he said. "Down towards Swansea. There is a *Saesneg* army outside of Swansea. You would do well to stay away from a village called Three Crosses."

Three Crosses. Hadn't he heard that name before? Shaw's humor vanished. "An English army near Three Crosses…?" He trailed off, realizing with horror where he'd heard the name. Wasn't that what Lucifer's messenger had told him? "Three Crosses – the abbey?"

The old man nodded, rather unsteadily. "Remember I told you that I was just in Swansea, visiting my son, in fact," he said. "I… I don't have my boat any longer, so I must travel on land. 'Tis an embarrassment for an old sailor like me."

Shaw didn't want to hear of the embarrassment. He wanted to hear of the army. "And so it is," he said. "But this army… ye're certain it was at Three Crosses?"

The old man nodded. "Aye," he said. "When I was returning home to Parrog, I had to hide from the army. It was dug in at Three Crosses. So you must not go there!"

As Shaw clarified what the old man was saying, Thor spoke up. "Three Crosses Abbey," he hissed at Shaw. "Isna that's where Con is supposed to go?"

Indeed it was, with an English army sitting there, waiting for him. Suddenly, the awareness of the situation all came barreling down on Shaw in a big rush and he slammed his cup to the table, turning to Thor as if he could hardly believe what he was hearing. Grasping at the situation, like pieces to a great puzzle, he began to fit those pieces together.

"Ballocks," he muttered. "A *Sassenach* army is in the same place Con is going?"

Thor's expression reflected the same shock that Shaw was feeling. "It seems so," he said. "But mayhap they're no longer there. That was several days ago, at least."

Shaw's head snapped to the old man. "How long ago was this?"

The old man couldn't help but notice that his new pirate friends didn't seem so pleased with the information. "About nine days ago, I recall," he said. "Why does that surprise you? *Saesneg* are all over southern Wales."

"Did the army show any signs of leaving?"

"'Tis hard to tell. I avoided them mostly. But they seemed camped there."

The pieces of the puzzle were fitting together in a most distressing way. Shaw finally returned his attention to Thor. "Nine days ago," he said ominously. "If they're still there, Con will run right into them."

Thor was as astonished as Shaw was. "But do ye suppose the Sassenach army already knows that?"

An expression of horror crossed Shaw's face as he shook his head, sickened by the reality of the situation. "*Know* it?" he repeated, aghast. "I'd be willing tae wager that they're waiting for him. That woman Lucifer spoke of is leading Con straight to them. It wasna the French we had to worry about, but the damnable English!"

Thor's eyes widened. "An ambush!" he hissed. "Constantine le Brecque would make a fine trophy for Henry. Ye know he's been trying tae capture him for years!"

There was no more time for talk. The shock of the situation propelled them to their feet, bellowing to their men to do the same. Confused, but never ones to question an order, Shaw's men were quickly on their feet, some of them with food still in-hand as they rushed from the tavern with Shaw and Thor leading the way. No one had any idea what was going on until they reached the ship, tossing about in the cove during the storm, and Thor explained to the crew what was happening.

An ambush.

The *Savage of the Sea* set sail for Eynon Bay in a tempest because there was no time to waste. Constantine and his men were walking into a trap, and Shaw could only pray they intercepted the man before that happened.

Chapter Eleven

Southern Coast of Wales

BY SUNRISE, THE WEATHER hadn't improved in the least. Constantine thought it might have even gotten worse. The spray was vicious and the ship was being buffeted mercilessly but, just after sunrise, the coast of Wales came in to view on the horizon.

Constantine had to admit that he was glad.

But it was a struggle to reach the shore because they were heading into the wind. They'd been using the tacking zig-zag maneuver since last night and had somehow made headway, but it had been a good deal of hard work. Even now, his men were exhausted as they continued to strain, trying to keep the ship in one piece as it rolled and shuddered against the sea. The *Gaia* was a strong, seaworthy vessel, but Constantine had to admit that he'd be glad to put the ship into the cove and find her some protection. Like most strong women, she could only take so much.

And that included Gregoria.

The woman had been sick all night and this morning, she was still deathly ill from the violent sea. Constantine had gone in to check on her throughout the night and she'd been in bed with the five dogs, unable to rise for her sickness. Constantine knew they had to reach land quickly, if only for her sake, but he also kept an eye on Augustin, who hadn't returned to Perranporth with Kerk and the *Persephone*. He'd elected to travel on with Constantine. The man was carrying out his duties flawlessly, as always, but Constantine had seen him hanging over the railing on occasion. For Augustin's sake, it would be better to find land, too.

Therefore, they crept along the sea, heading towards the land on the horizon. Because of the nearly horizontal rain at times, everything shipboard with the exception of the captain's cabin was soaking wet, men and provisions included. They'd had a difficult time keeping the gunpowder dry for the cannons, and he'd eventually had most of it taken into his cabin to be stored away from the elements. The entire time they'd loaded the sacks of powder in to the cabin, he'd kept an eye on Gregoria over on the bed, but she never moved a muscle.

Now, the day was edging on towards the nooning and, luckily, the storm was starting to ease. The wind was still fierce at times, as was the rain, but there were also pockets of sunshine as the clouds were scattered about overhead.

The *Gaia*, beaten and weary from enduring the elements, closed in on Eynon Bay and when the sun appeared between the clouds again, Constantine could see the details of bright green strip of land as they began to draw nearer. If the weather continued to clear, then it would make their travel much easier. By the time they finally neared the golden, sandy shore of Eynon Bay, the rain had stopped for the most part and the sun was shining brightly in between a scattering of dark clouds.

Entering the bay was tricky because Eynon had a series of sharp rocks off to the east and west, while the sandy shore was right in the middle of them. There was a narrow sea opening for the ships to get through, one that had underwater rocks on either side, but once the *Gaia* was through the strait, they entered the large, calm bay with almost no movement to the water. They were, perhaps, an eighth of a mile or less from shore, on a soft and sandy bottom, when Constantine ordered his men to drop anchor. Happily, they did.

The tempest was finally over.

Once the anchor hit the soft-sand bottom through the murky water, stirred up by the storm, Constantine breathed a sigh of relief. He leaned against the poop deck railing and inhaled long and deep. Now, the ship was stable for the moment and his mind began to move ahead to what they needed to accomplish for the day, but he wasn't so sure Gregoria would be up to it. Given how seasick she'd been, it was possible they'd have to wait a day or two before heading off to Three Crosses.

All the more time he could spend with her.

"The ship is secured," Lucifer said, catching Constantine's attention as he came up the ladder to the poop deck. "There's a crack in the foremast but, other than that, it looks like it survived relatively unscathed, although the ship's carpenter is sounding down below for leaks."

Constantine's attention moved to the masts above, the sails tattered and some of the ropes hanging loose. "The *Gaia* is a tough old girl," he said, patting the railing affectionately. "She has weathered worse than this."

Lucifer, too, was looking up to the tattered sails. "That is true," he said, "but if this tempest had raged much longer than it had, we may have had some issues."

Constantine shrugged. "Mayhap," he said. "Just wait until you get the *Leucosia* out to sea. Now, *that's* a sturdy vessel. Remember what we had to go through to get her?"

Lucifer grinned as he recalled that particular battle and started to reply, but he was cut off when Remy and Augustin mounted the stairs to the poop deck.

"The bilge is at two feet and holding," Augustin said. "There are leaks, but the carpenter is sure he can shore them up. There are men manning the pumps all day and all night, so the *Gaia* will be fit in no time."

It was good news all around and Constantine sighed with satisfaction. "Thank the Sea Gods," he muttered. "It could have been much worse. How did the horses fare below?"

"Well enough, but they're jittery, so 'tis time to get them off this boat."

That was true, for all of them. There was nothing like stable land after a storm. Overhead, the clouds were scattering even further as a brisk breeze picked up from the east. Gulls cried overhead, looking for a meal in the wreckage of the beaten land below. Constantine watched them for a moment before his thoughts shifted to the task to come.

"And we shall," he said, leaning back against the railing. "In fact, break out the ramp and start moving the horses onto the shore. We have a trip into Wales to discuss."

His men were listening. "You never made any mention about who would go and who would remain on the ship," Lucifer said. "What are your plans?"

Constantine lifted his eyebrows thoughtfully. "The four of us will go," he said. "How many horses did we bring?"

"Ten."

"Then it will be the four of us, five of our men, and the lady," he said. "The rest of the men will remain here on board and, once we depart the ship, they will move it out into the channel and away from the shore. It will be safer that way."

Lucifer nodded. "Who will you leave in command?"

"The ship's carpenter. Aeolis has been with me a very long time and he understands what it means to command a vessel. I am sure you all agree."

They did. "It is midday now," Augustin said, looking up at the sky and the position of the sun. "Do we depart now or wait until morning?"

Constantine grinned at the man. "I have a feeling you would like to disembark now onto something that is not moving about," he said, watching Augustin sheepishly shrug. "The lady surely shares your desire, Gus. We will depart as soon as we can get the horses off the ship and gather our supplies. See to it; the faster you move, the faster we depart."

Augustin flew into action with Remy in tow. As the two of them moved off, Constantine turned to Lucifer. "You will select the land party," he said. "Make sure they are heavily armed. Then you will find Aeolis and tell him what I told you. I cannot imagine we will be more than a few days, but tell him to move further out to sea and stay vigilant for our return."

Lucifer nodded. "Aye," he replied. Then, he hesitated a moment. "And the lady? Shall I tell her to prepare?"

Constantine shook his head. "Nay," he said. "I will tell her. She has had a rough time of it. But given that she has never been to sea, I am not surprised. The rolling sea is something that takes time to grow accustomed to."

Lucifer could hear something in Constantine's voice that caught his attention; there was softness there when he spoke of the lady. *Warmth.* That wasn't like Constantine to speak of a woman in such a way and he couldn't help the doubt, confusion even, that he began to feel.

"Once we reach the abbey and the lady has completed her task, has she made arrangements for someone to escort her back to wherever she came from?" he asked.

Constantine wouldn't look at him. In fact, he didn't even respond for a moment or two. "She is not going back to wherever she came from," he finally said. "She will be remaining with me."

Lucifer wasn't surprised to hear that, not in the least. Ever since the lady had come into their midst, Constantine had been behaving oddly. It was clear that he'd lusted after the woman and no matter what he said, he hadn't escorted her to Wales purely for the sake of Miles Tenby. Lucifer was fairly certain Miles had nothing to do with it at this point; it had been an excuse on Constantine's part. He may have believed it in the beginning but, now, Miles Tenby was far from his thoughts.

It had been as Lucifer had feared from the beginning, that the woman claiming to be Miles Tenby's daughter was luring Constantine to his doom. Lucifer was waiting for Dureau's warship to come swinging around the point at any moment, cannons blazing, but Constantine wasn't showing the same concern. Either the man knew something they did not, or he was genuinely unconcerned that all of this might be a trap. For Constantine's sake, and for the sake of everyone risking their lives for the venture, Lucifer thought he should speak up.

"What does that mean, exactly?" he asked politely. "Are you to keep her as a concubine? That's not like you, Con. As long as I've known you, you've never kept a woman. What's going on?"

Constantine knew this question would come. He also knew his men were silently questioning his decision to take Gregoria to Wales. He'd known all along. But they weren't a crew to keep secrets from each other because, in their profession, it was all about trust. If Lucifer couldn't trust him, and trust that he knew what the man was thinking, then it would make their lives very difficult from that point on. Therefore, he faced Lucifer as he spoke.

"I know I have never kept a woman," he said. "But men grow up. They change. Lucifer, I am attracted to Gregg. In fact, I cannot remember when I have been so attracted to a woman. There is something about her that grips me and I cannot shake it, no matter what. In fact, I am not sure that I *want* to shake her. She intrigues me. I know that you and Gus and Remy believe me foolish for agreeing to take her to Wales, as if the woman is somehow leading me to my death, but I am not convinced that is the case. Even if it is… I cannot help my attraction to her. Mayhap, that is why you are here – to save me from myself. It would not be the first time you have had to do that."

He was grinning as he finished. Lucifer respected him a great deal to confront the issue and try to explain himself even though he didn't have to. The captain never had to explain himself to his crew but, in this case, Lucifer was glad he had. So very glad. It made the situation easier to deal with.

"Aye, we were all concerned," he finally said. "But we did not question you. We simply followed. You wanted to come to Wales, so we came with you."

Constantine put a hand on his shoulder. "I saw the *Ligeia* leave Perranporth," he said quietly. "I assume you sent her away?"

Lucifer was coming to feel foolish, thinking Constantine hadn't seen the ship depart. He thought he'd been fairly slick about it. But Constantine was a man who knew everything that was going on with his empire.

Lucifer should have known better.

"I sent Felix to find Shaw," he admitted. "If the man is not occupied, mayhap he could come to Eynon Bay, too. Just in case Dureau decides to show up."

Constantine gave him a crooked smile. "I know you too well, old friend," he said, slapping him on the shoulder before lowering his hand. "You worry like an old woman, but it does not bother me. I know that your intentions are true. When I saw the *Ligeia* sail away, I assumed that was what you had done."

"And you did not confront me?"

"Why should I?"

Lucifer shrugged. "Because it could have been viewed as undermining your command."

Constantine shook his head. "I know you better than that. You would never do such a thing."

Lucifer fell silent, thinking on the man who was his commander, his friend. A man he'd known for many years but a man he'd never let get particularly close to him. Constantine didn't know things about Lucifer that perhaps he should have known, or should have been trusted with. At this moment, Lucifer thought it was perhaps the right time to show Constantine that he trusted the man much as Constantine trusted him. Constantine had shown faith; he'd not become angry even when Lucifer had done something that could have been considered a form of betrayal.

I know you better than that…

Perhaps Constantine did know him well, but he didn't know everything. Lucifer thought that, perhaps, now was the time for total trust, and truth, between them, so that Constantine would see that there truly was a bond between them. Something unbreakable and enduring. But it was difficult to speak on things he'd kept buried all these years.

"We have known each other for many years," Lucifer said after a moment. "We do know each other well."

Constantine nodded. "As well as we can know anyone, I suppose."

"But you do not know everything about me."

"I know what I need to know."

Lucifer remained silent. When he did speak, his tone was very quiet. "You asked me if Lucifer was my real name," he said. "My given name is Rhoan de Wolfe. I was born of the great house of de Wolfe and my father is the Earl of Wolverhampton. I am his eldest."

Constantine looked at Lucifer as if he could hardly believe what he was hearing. In fact, an expression of great concern washed over his features.

"Why do you tell me this now?" he asked. "Bloody Beard, man, are you truly afraid we will not make it out of Wales alive that you feel the need to confess this to me?"

Lucifer smiled thinly. "Nay," he said, turning to look at him. "I just thought it was time for you to know."

Constantine was puzzled by the confession, something that had never been spoken between them in all of the years they had known one another. Faintly, he shook his head.

"But why?" he asked. "Keeping your name to yourself has always been your choice. I have never pressed you on it."

Lucifer nodded. "I realize that," he said. "But when you say that I worry like an old woman, you must understand that I have reason to."

"Go on."

Lucifer took a deep breath before continuing, summoning his courage. "The reason why I no longer speak to my father is because I, too, did something foolish once that drove me away from him," he said softly. "When I was very young, my first post as a knight was serving the Duke of Richmond. His wife took a liking to me and, before I realized it, I was bedding her regularly and she rewarded me richly. It went on for quite some time and she became pregnant with my child. When the lad was born, unfortunately, he looked just like me even though the duke claimed him as his own. After that, my father came to Richmond and took me away, explaining to me that the duke had requested I be removed. My father was so ashamed of me, Con... you cannot imagine how ashamed. But I think he was more angry that my firstborn son, his firstborn grandson, would inherit the dukedom of Richmond and not the earldom of Wolverhampton. In any case, my father made his disappointment known and stripped me of every-thing – money, possessions – everything. He sent me to the priory at Caernarvon as punishment and we have not spoken since."

A great deal came to light in that quiet confession and Constantine didn't take it lightly. It was rare for men in his profession to bare their souls like that and rarer still for Lucifer to speak of anything personal. Constantine felt as if he'd been entrusted with a great secret, a great story.

"Are you really a priest, then?" he asked. "I have always assumed so because I found you in the priory."

"The priesthood was simply a cover story. I am not a priest; I am a sinner of the greatest magnitude with a father who is deeply ashamed of him."

Constantine was looking the man in the face, seeing the sorrow in his eyes. "Then we have that in common," he said. "Fathers who want nothing to do with us."

Lucifer smiled wryly. "Why do you think I became attached to you?" he asked. "We have much in common, you and I. Great men, who should hold great stations in life but, because of circumstances, we find ourselves robbed of what is rightfully ours."

Constantine thought the correlation between them was rather iron-ic. "That is very true," he said. "You should inherit Wolverhampton, while I…"

He trailed off, unable to voice that which rightfully belonged to him. It was of no use, speaking of something that would never be, but Lucifer spoke for him.

"You should be the King of England instead of that idiot who now sits upon the throne," he said, watching the ironic flicker of Constantine's lips. "But I did not tell you my story to seek your pity or your understanding. I told you the story to make it clear that I was a fool for a woman once myself and it cost me everything. Therefore, if I worry about you in a situation like this… it is for good reason. I wish someone had worried so about me, too, long ago. Mayhap I would not have made such a mistake."

Constantine scratched his blond head, a smile on his lips. "Do you really think so? Given how you felt about the duchess, would you have listened to anyone else?"

Lucifer could only shrug. "Mayhap," he said. "Mayhap not. I was young and strong, and she was older and far more cunning. I was in her spell. Women weave spells, Con. They are bewitching creatures. I simply do not want to see you make a mistake."

Constantine knew that. He reached out, patting the man on the cheek. "I will not, I swear it," he said. "But with you around, you will not let me, will you?"

Lucifer chuckled softly. "I will do all I can to ensure you do not make a fool out of yourself."

"I appreciate that."

"And that you remain alive."

"You are a true and good friend, Lucifer."

Before the conversation could continue, they both heard a bang on the deck below, a door slamming. Turning their attention to the deck, they saw Henry and Edward bounding out into the sunshine followed by three hairy, gray puppies.

Soon enough, Gregoria's dark head appeared as she made her way out to the railing, inhaling deeply of the fresh sea air, as the dogs ran about her. Constantine and Lucifer were watching her, with Constantine's expression rather soft while Lucifer's was rather curious, until she turned and saw the men on the deck above her.

"When can I get off this bloody ship?" Gregoria demanded. "I swear that I am going to jump into the water at this very moment and swim to shore."

Constantine laughed softly as he came away from the rail and made his way towards her. "Not to worry," he said. "The men will be offloading the horses right away and you can follow them onto dry land."

He was chuckling as he came down the ladder from the poop deck, but Gregoria didn't think it was so funny. She was still nauseous and miserable.

"Excellent," she said, hand to her stomach. "Then I will go and change my clothing into something more suitable for travel. And these dogs – they need to run around. I believe they need to eat."

"I will have them tended to, my lady."

He was coming nearer and Gregoria forgot her misery a moment, feeling relief and joy simply to look upon his handsome face. There was a light in his eyes when he looked at her that hadn't been there before, and her unhappy stance softened, just a bit.

"Do you intend to bring them with us into Wales?" she asked.

Constantine came to a halt in front of her, although he was still standing very close. She could almost feel the heat from his body and her heart began to flutter, just a bit. He had that effect on her.

"Nay," he said. "They will remain here. We do not need the added bother of taking the dogs."

"You seem to have inherited three more since leaving Perranporth."

"I noticed."

They were talking about the three gray puppies, who seemed to be very happy to be out of the cabin. Gregoria reaching out to pet Edward when the big dog came up to her and leaned against her.

"They have made for good companions during the journey," she said. "But I believe they belong to Genevieve and Vivienne. Will you return them to the women?"

Constantine watched the puppies as they leapt around the deck, sniffing and playing. "Mayhap," he said vaguely. "I have not thought on it."

Gregoria didn't push. She hadn't talked to the man since yesterday and she didn't want the first words between them to be those of her nagging at him one way or the other. She, too, watched the dogs as they frolicked about.

"They are fine animals," she said.

He smiled. "They are spoiled," he said. "They nearly crowded you right off the bed. I saw."

It was her turn to chuckle. "They *are* a bit pushy, that is true," she said. "But they are sweet. I am glad to have had them with me."

He lowered his head so that he was closer to her, his voice barely above a whisper. "Just so you know, I will not share our bed with them," he muttered. "I shall be the only one curled against your body."

Gregoria flushed deeply. For a woman who had so vehemently swore that she would not be the man's concubine, she seemed to have drastically changed that opinion. Having developed feelings for the man had seen to that, clouding her sense of judgment in all things pertaining to him. She'd spent the entire storm confined to bed, feeling sicker than she'd ever felt in her life, and pondering the conversation she and Constantine had where he'd asked her never to leave him. No one had ever asked her that before and it made her feel wanted and needed.

Now, it was a dilemma that had overtaken her entire being.

Hanging over her like a great, dark cloud was her entire purpose for being on the ship – *betrayal*. She'd come to the conclusion that she must tell Constantine the real reason for her presence. She had to untangle the lies she'd told him and pray he could forgive her. But she was terrified the man would never trust her again, and it was that fear that kept her from confessing.

Even now, as he warmed to her, speaking of the bed they would share, she was loathed to tell him the truth. She didn't want to lose this warmth, this affection, because it was something she'd never known. She'd spent her entire life being treated with cold indifference and to finally find someone who thought she was special, who treated her with kindness and sweetness, made her realize what, exactly, she'd been missing.

It didn't matter if she became Constantine's concubine. The man had shown her more joy and warmth than anyone ever had.

She never wanted to lose it.

... God, she was a coward...

"It is something we can discuss at a later time," she said, unused to flirtatious games. "But I did like the dogs in the bed. They kept me warm."

Constantine flashed her that brilliant smile. "I shall keep you warm, I promise," he said. "This big body is exceedingly warm, so you needn't worry. Now, if you are going to change into traveling clothes, make haste. As soon as the horses and provisions are moved onto the beach, we will make our way to Three Crosses."

Three Crosses, where the Earl of March's army awaited him. That fact stuck in Gregoria's belly, bringing on a fresh wave of nausea. Unable to look at him, knowing her horrible lies were about to come to fruition, she turned away, looking over the sea.

"I... I will change in a moment," she said. "I have spent all of my time shipboard cramped in that cabin, so I just need a moment or two to breathe fresh air."

Constantine put a hand on her back, a soothing gesture. "Not too long," he said. "Breathe your fill and then gather your things. I should like to make it to Three Crosses by the morning."

She looked at him, then. "Is it that close?"

He looked out over the land, the green line that went as far as the eye could see. "I believe so," he said. "I will confer with the locals when we go ashore to confirm it."

Patting her back once more, he headed off, moving to complete his duties before he left the ship. Gregoria watched him go for a moment, his prideful swagger causing her heart to swell with adoration, before returning her focus to the water.

More and more, the realization of where this journey would take them was eating at her, so much so that she was beginning to think of ways to avoid it. If she was so fearful to tell him the truth, then why not lie about it? Could she lie to him and tell him that the cup was lost in the storm? It would be believable, of course. The storm was terrible and everything in the cabin had been tossed around. A bag thrown through one of the open windows would be lost forever.

But it would be one lie atop another, a house of lies that could collapse at some point and ruin everything she was hoping to preserve. As she wrestled with her conscience, her feelings, a shadow fell over the railing and she looked up to see the pirate known as Lucifer standing there.

He was a very big man, very tall and dark. He had eyes that were a murky hazel color and a big scar across his chin. He wasn't unhandsome, but the fact that the man had a terrifyingly ominous presence made him seem larger than life. Gregoria resisted the urge to recoil from him as he stood a few feet away from her.

"I heard that you did not fare well during the storm, my lady," Lucifer said politely.

Gregoria smiled weakly. "This is my first time at sea," she said. "I suppose I failed at becoming a good seaman."

Lucifer lifted his dark eyebrows, in agreement or in sympathy, it was difficult to know. "A man's love for the sea is not won all in a night," he said. "Or a woman's love for the sea, as it were. It takes time and practice, both of which I understand you shall have."

She cocked her head curiously. "What do you mean?"

"I mean that Constantine told me you were to be his… companion."

Gregoria was surprised Constantine had spoken of it and her

cheeks mottled a shade of red, embarrassed. She averted her gaze, turning back to the sea. It was clear that she was struggling for an answer in the face of this stranger's question.

"He... he has been very kind to me," she said.

Lucifer was studying her with those intense eyes. "Kind?" he repeated. "Is that why you have agreed to stay with him? Simply for kindness?"

Gregoria shrugged. "I think that you have asked a very personal question, my lord," she said politely. "This is something that is between Constantine and me. I am sure if he had wanted you to know more, he would have told you."

She was right, but Lucifer thought he saw defensiveness in her manner. *Guilt.* So she didn't want to be questioned? He didn't like it because it suggested to him that the woman had something to hide.

"Mayhap he will," he said coolly. "Or mayhap it is none of my affair. In any case, there is something you should know."

She looked at him. "What is it?"

He leaned forward, lowering his voice. "Know that I shall be watching you," he said, his tone a throaty growl. "If, at any time, you hurt the man or lead him to harm, I shall slit your throat and they will never find your body. Therefore, if I were you, I would watch my step. I would make sure everything you do for Con, you do with his happiness and health in mind. If you have any other motive, the last thing you see will be my blade carving into your flesh. Is this in any way unclear?"

Gregoria went pale; she could see simply by looking at the man that he meant every word. He meant to kill her if he had a mind to. But she couldn't decide if it was a purely selfish motive or because he cared for Constantine, as his commander. All Gregoria knew was that she'd just had her life threatened by a pirate and she believed him, implicitly.

"It is clear," she said, trying not to sound as if the man had frightened her to death, which he had. "You... you needn't worry."

Lucifer lifted one of those dark eyebrows, like the arch of a raven's wing. He didn't believe her but he stopped short of refuting her. He'd made his position on the matter clear enough.

"I hope not," he said. "Do not give me a reason to doubt you and we shall get along fine."

Was he toying with her? Now, Gregoria's fear was turning into anger. "Because you have threatened me?" she asked. "You have just established the relationship between us, and I will respect it. There will be no 'getting along'. Do not expect a great friend simply because you have threatened my life and I am afraid of you. I am not, you know. Not in the least."

Lucifer rather liked her reply; it was bold. The woman wasn't afraid to stand up to him or, at least, she wasn't willing to let him bully her. "Then we understand one another."

"We do."

"Then there will be no mistaking where we stand."

"None at all, my lord."

That was all he wanted to know. Turning away, he headed down to the hold of the ship where the men were starting to bring out the ramp to offload the horses. He had duties to attend to, but he'd also felt the need to make sure the lady understood his position in all of this. He didn't like the situation in the least, or the spell she seemed to have cast over Constantine, and he wanted to make sure she was aware.

He had his eye on her.

Chapter Twelve

EYNON BAY HAD a small village just off the sand where there were a few businesses before the forests of Wales closed in on them. It was a nice, cozy little village, with smoke from chimneys streaming up into the sky now that the storm was easing, pewter-colored clouds blown away by the crisp breeze.

But the village was empty. Or, at least, that's what Constantine thought as they came up the path from the sandy beach and entered the town proper. There was absolutely no one moving about in the early afternoon, but it occurred to him that they were probably all in hiding with the *Gaia* sitting out in the bay. It was a recognizable ship along this coast. They were fearful that Constantine le Brecque and his legion were coming for their women, their money, and their blood.

Pulling his silver steed to a halt as he came to the edge of the town, Constantine motioned Lucifer forward. All the while, he was looking around, concerned with the fact that everything seemed unnaturally still. The only things moving seemed to be the birds overhead and the soft lap of the waves against the shore.

"My lord?" Lucifer asked as he came alongside.

Constantine was looking over the soggy, wind-swept village. "I fear our reputation has preceded us," he said. "I was hoping for a hot meal on a table that wasn't rocking from side to side."

Lucifer was looking around because Constantine was. "I do not think anyone is open for business."

Constantine cast him a long look. "Let us see if we cannot change their minds."

With that, he charged into the town and raced up to the first establishment, a shuttered tavern with the name "The Sea Hag" carved into a piece of driftwood above the door. Clearly a tavern of some kind, Constantine kicked at one of the shuttered windows until the wood splintered. He could hear gasps of fear inside, which told him that people were, indeed, hiding from the pirates out in the bay. But he was used to dealing with such fear; the only way to combat it was to give them what they expected and then leave them in peace, causing them to feel as if they'd been spared by that which they feared. It was a cruel, if not effective, tactic.

"I want hot food and cold drink," he bellowed into the broken window. "Let me in and you shall not suffer. But if you do not unbar the door, I shall burn this place over your head. The choice is yours."

By this time, Lucifer and the others had come riding up behind him, including Gregoria. She was a little wide-eyed at Constantine's tactics, but they had the desired effect – in short order, the door to the tavern was unbarred and Constantine dismounted his horse, securing the animal before he made his way inside.

Lucifer, Gregoria, Augustin, Remy, and the men that had been selected as an escort followed. But it was a hesitant group, suspicious of what might be waiting for them inside. But when all seemed safe enough, they proceeded deeper into the structure.

The tavern was dark because the windows were shuttered, but they managed to find a table near the hearth. There was a lot of fumbling and banging going on because it was so dark. When Augustin smacked his knee on the edge of the table, he roared.

"Open the bloody windows!" he boomed, rubbing at his pained knee. "And bring us some candles before we break our necks in this place!"

In the darkness, Remy smacked into him, accidentally. He reached out quickly, grabbing Augustin's arm to steady him.

"That is probably what they are hoping for," he muttered.

Augustin cast the man an annoyed expression but he kept his mouth shut, more or less presuming that Remy was correct. He didn't want to admit that he hadn't thought of that. As they took their seats at a large, heavy table near the hearth, which was being stoked to bring forth some light into the room, an old man and his equally old wife approached the table.

"I haven't much by way of a hot meal, m'lord," the old man said nervously. "What we had this morning is almost gone and the meal for tonight is not yet finished cooking."

Constantine sat on the end of the bench, wearily, pulling Gregoria down to sit next to him. "Are you the tavern owner?"

"I am, m'lord."

"What do you have to eat that is plentiful?"

The old man, round and rather slovenly, was wringing his hands. "Bread and cheese," he said. "I have stewed apples."

"What do you have to drink?"

"Ale from Swansea."

"Bring it all. Whatever you have, we will eat it." He caught Gregoria's worried expression and had an idea why the woman was concerned. They were pirates, after all, and their intentions when it came to demanding service were never predictable. "And... we mean you no harm. We are not here to steal anything from you or roust you. Provide a good meal and I shall pay you handsomely."

The old man nodded and dashed off, back to the rear of the establishment with his wife shuffling after him. Constantine reached out and poked Remy across the table, pointing to the couple that had run off into the kitchen.

"Go with them," he said. "Make sure they do not poison whatever they plan to feed us."

Remy nodded and stood up, a dagger in one hand and the other hand on the hilt of the sword at his side. Gregoria anxiously watched him go.

"He is not going to hurt them, is he?" she asked.

Constantine shook his head. "Nay," he said. "But we want to make sure they do not try to hurt us, either. There have been times when hosts have tried to rid the world of our type of menace."

Gregoria suspected what he meant, especially since she'd heard the order he'd given to Remy. "They believe they are doing the world a service by poisoning your food and drink?"

"Aye, something like that."

Behind them, more of the shuttered windows were opened, allowing the light and breeze to infiltrate the common room. The temperatures were mild enough that the windows could be open, ventilating the otherwise smelly room. The other patrons of the tavern, who had been hiding in the shadows, crept out to resume their seating now that it had been established that Constantine and his men were only here to have a meal. Slowly, things began to return to normal as the ale and bread and cheese began to make it out to the table.

Conversation was quiet for the most part as the ale was passed around. Constantine went to pour some for himself, thought better of it, and moved to pour it for Gregoria first. It was the polite thing to do, but he was so unused to being polite around women that he had to stop and think about how to behave. He didn't want her thinking he was a barbarian. He tipped the pitcher over her cup, but she suddenly put out a hand, stopping him.

"I… I do not think I want any ale," she said.

He looked at her, realizing she seemed a little pale. "Why not?"

She swallowed, looking at him strangely. "Because ale makes my head swim," she said. "And even as I sit here, I feel as if I am still on the ship."

He noticed she was holding on to the table with one hand and he grinned. "I understand," he said. "That happens to most of us when we come onto dry land after being on the sea. Remember? I told you I did not like being on the land very much because it made me sick."

She smiled wanly. "Now, it is making me sick also."

"That is exactly how I feel every time I disembark the ship," Augustin said from across the table. He had heard their conversation. "I have been at sea for several years and, still, it makes me ill, so I know exactly how you feel."

Gregoria found some hope in that statement. "What do you do for it?"

Augustin held up a finger as if to beg her patience as he turned to the tavern owner, who was standing at the end of the table, ensuring everyone had enough to eat and drink.

"You, there," Augustin said to the man. "Do you have any peppermint or ginger? Even cloves would do, either mashed up by itself or used as an ingredient in something."

The old man considered the question seriously. "The boiled apples have cinnamon and cloves in them," he said. "And a touch of honey and onions and vinegar."

Augustin waved the man on. "Bring two big bowls," he said. "One for me and one for the lady."

As the man dashed off, Gregoria looked at Augustin with some fear. "Apples and onions?"

Augustin nodded. "Trust me," he said. "Eating them will settle your belly, especially with the cloves."

Gregoria didn't argue with him; she assumed he had much more experience in this kind of thing than she did. "How long before the world stops rocking?" she asked.

Augustin grinned. "An hour or less," he said. "Give it time. Soon enough, it will settle down."

It was encouraging to hear that because, at the moment, she was quite uncomfortable with the way everything was moving about. Underneath the table, she could feel Constantine's hand on her knee, giving her a squeeze now and then, and she couldn't even enjoy it.

"I fear that I would make a terrible seaman," she said to Constantine. "I like it much better on land."

He chuckled. "It probably would not be so bad had we not run into the storm," he said. "When the seas are smooth, there is nothing more wonderful."

Gregoria watched him as he spoke, seeing his love for the sea in his face as he did so. It was the first time she'd really noticed that, a softening of his features when he spoke of the ocean. Like a man speaking of a lover, almost.

"I can tell that it is something you love to do," she said quietly.

Underneath the table, he squeezed her knee again. "I have since I was a wee lad," he said. "My father used to take me aboard his vessels, as I told you, and we would sail the seas. It is where I am most at home."

"Have you not heard what he is called, my lady?" Augustin entered the conversation again. "It is said that Constantine was borne of the waves and lifted up by the gods of the sea as their most prized possession. Everyone believes that, you know."

Gregoria's smile turned genuine as she looked at Constantine. "Is that true?" she asked. "Is that really the story of your immaculate birth?"

He laughed softly. "Not exactly," he said. "But sometimes it feels I was borne of the sea. That is my home, more than anywhere else on the earth."

"Then mayhap you'll leave Perran Castle to me," Augustin said, winking at Constantine when the man frowned at him. "I'll have use of the castle while you spend your time in the halls of Poseidon."

Gregoria grinned as Augustin and Constantine traded mild insults after that; evidently, Augustin wasn't worthy of Perran Castle but Augustin thought differently. Gregoria had never really seen Constantine interact with his men on a casual basis, and it was a noteworthy occasion. Considering what she'd always heard of pirates – a rough, uncouth group of murderers, filthy in their habits as well as in their outlook on life – to watch Constantine and his men at this moment, one could have never guessed what their vocation was.

To Gregoria, it seemed as if they were simply normal men in the course of a normal day. But for the fact that everyone in the town of Eynon Bay seemed to be hiding from them, there was nothing different about them, as least to the casual observer. But a noble vocation was far from the truth for these men; this was Poseidon's Legion, the most feared group of English pirates in these waters, something that had been hammered into her by her brother and by Lord Wembury. But they didn't know these men like she was coming to; it was possible that everything she'd been told about them was wrong.

She wanted to believe that.

One of the things that made this situation appear so normal was the easy rapport between Constantine and his men. They taunted each other, or spoke seriously to each other, without a blade or blood drawn. Their conversation was, for the most part, quite civilized. Even the lesser-ranking men seemed civilized. Gregoria rather liked Augustin, for he spoke to her politely, but when Lucifer entered the conversation, she turned her nose up and looked away. She wasn't going to pay attention to a man who had threatened her life should she betray Constantine.

Even if he had every right to.

The reality of the situation was settling once more, biting at her now, nipping away at the angst and confusion she felt. God, was it possible Lucifer knew something of her true objective? She wasn't sure how he could know, but the way he looked at her suggested that he knew something. He didn't trust her. He had every right to threaten her but she still resented it. How could she explain she'd been sent to betray a man because others wanted him dead, not because there was anything personal? But that had been before. This was now.

There was something very personal about it now.

Foolishly, she'd brought the holy relic with her. She'd entertained the thought of throwing it overboard and telling Constantine it was lost, but she'd decided not to do it, afraid she'd be seen or somehow get caught up in yet another lie. Now, they were on land and it was less than a day to Three Crosses where the Earl of March was waiting.

… but what if she *kept* them waiting?

What if she could delay their travel enough so that the Earl of March believed they were never coming? She knew the English had already been in Wales for a couple of weeks; they were in Wales when she and her brother and Lord Wembury made it to Perranporth to seek out Constantine. That was well over a week ago. Was it possible she could delay enough so that the Earl of March would grow weary of waiting and simply leave? That would involve quite a delay on her part, perhaps faking an illness. Anything to save Constantine.

But perhaps instead of elaborate lies or plans, she should simply summon the courage to tell him what she'd done. Perhaps he would hate her but, in the end, at least she could live with herself.

Perhaps that was what this was finally about… her self-respect. The neglected, bullied woman who had hoped for a house by the sea was finally finding her self-worth in the arms of England's more feared pirate. He seemed to believe in her, misplaced as his trust was.

But perhaps that meant she could believe in herself.

More food came as Gregoria stewed in her thoughts, listening to Constantine and Augustin and Remy laugh about something. She didn't really understand much of what was being said; something about a Scottish pirate friend lusting after a woman who turned out to be a man. They seemed to find that quite hilarious.

The second pirate that had been sent into the kitchens to watch the food emerged, sitting at the table as boiled apples and onions and even porridge was put on the table. Everyone seemed to be grabbing for their own bowls of food, but Constantine and Augustin made sure Gregoria had the first serving of the apples and onions. The compote smelled heavily of cinnamon and cloves, and Gregoria sampled it timidly, soon realizing that it was delicious. Warm, spicy, sweet… it filled her belly and made her feel much better than she had in a while. Augustin had been correct; the clove and cinnamon seemed to help her nausea. By the time she finished the bowl, it was almost completely gone.

She was also able to eat some of the bread and butter that the tavern keeper's wife brought out after that. The bread was fresh and the butter salty, and she enjoyed it a great deal. The old wife seemed to be fussing over her quite a bit, making sure she received the first pick of the bread before anyone else did and bringing her boiled apple juice to drink because she didn't want the ale. She was a big woman, busty, smelling of strong perfume mixed with body odor. Every time she moved, the rather pungent scent filled the air. Had she not been so nice, Gregoria might have tried to move the woman away from her. But as it was, she was being very kind. Gregoria appreciated it. The woman was bending over the table to take away an empty bowl when Constantine suddenly stopped her.

"You," he said, pointing at her neck. "Let me see that cross you are wearing."

The woman looked down at her chest; she was wearing a few chains, one of them even bearing keys, but she singled out the necklace Constantine was referring to and held it up to the light; it was a magnificent silver cross inlaid with dark blue sapphires. The old woman seemed to be more at ease with the men than her husband was by this point and she spoke up.

"This?" she asked, watching Constantine nod. "Aye, laddie, my husband gave this to me years ago. It had belonged to his mother, the old bat, but then it became mine. It looks better on me!"

She was snorting at her own humor, causing Gregoria to laugh. She had about two teeth in her head but that didn't stop her from smiling broadly.

"It is beautiful," Gregoria said. "I have never seen such a lovely piece."

The old woman held the cross nearer so that Gregoria could get a closer look at it. "Sapphires from the orient, I'm told," she said. "My mother-in-law said the necklace was made for a queen in ancient times but, somehow, it ended up on the neck of a poor old fish wife. I don't know how she came about it, but I'm sure the Queen of Sheba didn't give it to her. She must have stolen it."

She was chuckling at her humor again as Gregoria smirked. "Well, it is quite beautiful," she said. "You must be very proud of it."

As the old woman shrugged, Constantine seized on it. She didn't seem particularly attached to the necklace but he, on the other hand, knew it was a very expensive piece. He'd seen enough jewels to know that it was a rare find. Either the old woman didn't know what she had around her neck or she didn't care. In either case, Constantine was about to do what he didn't normally do for a piece of goods – barter.

He wanted it.

"I will give you four gold crowns for the necklace," he said, watching the humor drain from the woman's face. "I'd wager that you cannot find anyone around here to pay you what that necklace is worth, but I can. Sell it to me and keep the gold. I am sure you can use the money more than you can use that necklace."

The woman was shocked. She looked at the necklace in confusion before returning her attention to Constantine.

"Four... *four* gold crowns?" she repeated. "For *this*?"

"Five."

That caused the woman to pull it right off her neck and hand it to him. Constantine took the necklace swiftly as he dug into the purse at his belt and pulled forth five gold coins with the face of Henry VI stamped on them. They were newly minted, not a mark on them, part of a larger haul he'd come away with the year before when he'd ambushed a royal treasury vessel heading for France. He handed them over to the old woman, who gleefully rushed off to show her husband the deal she'd made for the necklace. Meanwhile, Constantine turned to Gregoria.

"Here," he said, lifting the necklace over her head and settling it on her neck. "For you. For bravely enduring a terrible storm and living to tell the tale. You deserve to be rewarded."

Gregoria was greatly surprised as he put the necklace on her and she looked at it in shock, stunned by his generosity.

"I do not know what to say," she said, awe in her voice. "It is so beautiful. I have never had anything so beautiful, ever."

Constantine watched her features as she spoke. He could tell how deeply sincere she was and it gave him a good feeling, knowing he'd made her happy. As a man who had experienced a great deal in life, it gave him the most satisfying feeling he'd ever known. Mostly, all he ever gave people was a sense of terror. But to give joy... that was a better feeling altogether.

"It was made for you," he said, lowering his voice. "Not that old bird with the missing teeth. It was made for someone of your beauty and grace, the definition of a true queen."

She looked up from inspecting the cross. "Beauty and grace are the definition of a queen?"

He shrugged, rather embarrassed because not only were his men listening in, but he wasn't used to speaking flattering words that were actually true. He was a master at telling women what they wanted to hear and not meaning a word of it. But in this case, he meant everything he said and was embarrassed for it.

"Con, we have an entire vault full of jewels and finery," Remy said from across the table. "She could have had her pick of anything there."

Constantine looked at Remy, unhappy that the man had interrupted his moment with Gregoria. "And she can still have her pick," he said. "She can have it all if she wishes. But this..." he chuckled nervously. "I wanted to give her something that I actually paid for. Something that I bought just for her."

It made no sense to Remy, but it made some sense to Augustin and Lucifer. There was a difference between giving a woman something that you acquired through battle or theft and something you took the time to purchase. Items you stole had no meaning because they were mere possessions. But to buy something specifically for that woman... well, that meant something.

Lucifer passed a long glace at Augustin, who merely lifted an eyebrow and turned back to his drink. The Constantine who had departed Perranporth those days ago was not the same Constantine they saw before them. Considering the man had admitted it to Lucifer, he already knew what was going on, but Augustin was starting to realize how much had changed. Constantine was buying gifts rather than stealing them.

Times were changing, indeed.

And they had changed for Gregoria, as well. She couldn't take her eyes off the magnificent cross. When she heard arguing in the kitchen of the tavern between the owner and his wife, she knew it was over the necklace, but she didn't care. The only way they'd get it back is if they cut it off her cold, dead body. She'd never had a man give her anything at all, and certainly not a gift so special, and she held on to it, the sheer act of the gift touching her more deeply than she'd ever been touched before. It meant something. *Constantine* meant something.

Tell him he cannot go to Three Crosses!

A voice was screaming in her head. My God… the man was being kind to her, buying her gifts and, still, she was selfishly keeping silent about his fate. But the necklace had become the tipping point, toppling her right over onto the side of truth. She could keep silent no longer. Now was the moment she'd been dreading, but she had to summon her courage. Constantine's life depended on it.

As she opened her mouth to tell the man she needed to speak with him, alone, Lucifer suddenly stood up.

"Look," he said, looking around what was now a barren common room. "Everyone has left."

It was a shocking observation. Abruptly, everyone was on their feet, weapons being unsheathed. There was instant tension in the air as Constantine and his men reacted to an abruptly empty tavern.

"Where did everyone go?" Remy said, broadsword in hand. "Did anyone even see them leave? Where are the owner and his wife?"

Gregoria had been caught off guard by the sudden movement

around her, men who were now apprehensive that something was amiss. Somehow, someway, everyone in the room had slipped out while they were eating and drinking, and the usually observant men hadn't noticed a thing. They had been focused on apples and onions, or silver crosses. As she looked to Constantine to ask him what had happened, he grasped her by the arm and began to shove her down under the table.

"Get under the table," he told her. "Quickly, now. Do not come out until I tell you to."

Gregoria didn't argue. Frightened, she slipped down beneath the table, on her knees on old food and old rushes. It smelled horrible down under the table, but she crouched down, watching the feet of Constantine and his men move around the table, fanning out. She even heard Remy calling to the tavern owner and his wife, receiving no reply. Just a she heard Constantine mention that they should leave immediately, it was as if the entire world exploded.

It was a deafening sound. Wood went flying, splinters scattering all over the floor, and Gregoria shrieked as a full-scale battle suddenly waged over her head. The table was heavy, fortunately, but that didn't stop from getting it bumped around significantly. When it moved, she moved, fearful that the table was going to tip over or come down on top of her. Absolutely terrified, Gregoria covered her head with her hands and prayed.

She wasn't the only one doing the praying. Constantine and his men were outnumbered; Constantine could see that from the beginning. Men with swords and axes had come charging in through the front and the rear of the tavern, with a few even barreling in through the windows, causing the shutters to snap and wood to fly.

It seemed like an organized assault by an organized army, but Constantine very quickly realized that these weren't soldiers. Some of the men were carrying clubs or pitchforks, looking as if they'd never seen a day of battle in their life. Some of the men simply stood on the fringes, letting the men with bigger and better weapons go after the pirates who had infiltrated their town.

But those men were being cut down quickly, especially by Constantine, Lucifer, Augustin, and Remy. These were men who had trained as knights most of their lives and they knew how to fight a battle. Constantine had leapt up onto the table, the one Gregoria was huddling beneath, and he'd managed to slash, kick, or gore several men right at the onset of the fight. Unlike a knight, however, Constantine and his men didn't wear any armor or protection, which was to their disadvantage in close-quarters flighting like this. But that knightly instinct was felt in their sword as they fought off what seemed like the entire town.

"This isn't an army, Con," Lucifer said, jumping onto the table next to him. He kicked a man to the ground who charged at him. "If I had to guess, I would say the town banded together when they saw the *Gaia* in the bay. We made it easy for them to corner us by coming into the tavern."

Constantine nodded. "That was my thought, also," he said. "But the fact remains that there are more of them than us and unless we intend to kill the entire town, we had better find a way out of here."

Lucifer was surveying the scene, watching Remy and Augustin kill a pair of men who had rushed them with shovels. "Shall I tell the men to start moving out?"

Constantine barely avoided having his ankle cut into by a man with a big, broad blade. Kicking the man in the side of the head, he used his sword to gore him in the back between the shoulder blades in a clean kill.

"Aye," he said, yanking his sword from the man's body. "Have them back away and get to their horses. Tell them to head out of town and we will regroup on the road to the north."

Lucifer took his orders and began to move. It was mayhem in the little tavern as tables were kicked over and chairs broken. Somewhere over near the hearth, one of Constantine's men had shoved an opponent into the fire, and the man screamed as flames began to consume him. That had Constantine's attention until he saw someone whack Augustin on the back of the head, sending the man to his knees. Another man was coming up behind Augustin, preparing to stab him, but Constantine went flying off of the table to put himself between Augustin and his attackers.

In short order, he fought off the men with the blades, goring one and badly injuring the other. By the time he turned to Augustin, the man was struggling to his feet.

"Are you well enough?" Constantine asked, grasping him by the arm to steady him. "That was quite a hit."

Augustin's right hand was on the back of his head. "That was nothing," he muttered. "My wife hits me harder than that. But thank you for preventing those fools from using me like a pin cushion."

Constantine flashed him a sly grin. "I did it for your wife, not you," he said. "If you are killed, she would probably try to whack me in the head because of it."

Augustin grinned weakly, feeling dazed and sick but still able to fight. "Merryn is bold that way," he said. Then, he started looking around. "We would do better to get free of this confined space, Con. We are boxed in here."

Constantine wasn't hard pressed to agree. Making sure Augustin wasn't going to totter back to his knees again, he let the man go and fought his way through the group. Some of the attackers were fleeing now, confronted by men who truly did know how to fight, and the floor was littered with wounded, but none of them were Constantine's men, thankfully. He was nearly to the heavy table shielding Gregoria when something quite terrible happened.

Lucifer was fighting a very big man who had two hammers in his hands, swinging them at Lucifer and trying desperately to make contact, but Lucifer managed to stay out of the way. But the big man with the hammers somehow tripped, fell back onto the big table, and the legs snapped, sending the whole thing crashing right down on top of Gregoria.

In a panic, Constantine rushed the table and tried to shove the big man off of it, but it wasn't so easy. He was still fighting, rolling around on the slanted table like a turtle on its back, swinging those hammers violently. Constantine finally had to brain the man with the hilt of his sword simply to stop him from moving so they could pull him off the table. Once he was down on the floor, it took both Constantine and Lucifer to lift the table off of Gregoria.

The force of the table falling had knocked her cold and she lay on the floor, amidst the scraps and old rushes. Gravely concerned, Constantine rolled her onto her back to survey the damage, but there wasn't anything he could see. He wasn't going to take the time to fully inspect her, either, so he moved to gather her into his arms.

"I must remove her from this place," he told Lucifer. "Clear a path to the door for me."

Lucifer was on his feet, shoving men aside with his big arms and big weapon. Augustin and Remy, seeing the unconscious lady in Constantine's arms, moved to assist, fighting their way through the crowd and helping Constantine make his way to the door. It was blind chaos in the room, now with flames from the disturbed hearth creeping up one of the walls, and Lucifer began to bellow to the men to retreat. Everyone began moving for any opening, windows included.

Lucifer was nearly to the door when he suddenly grunted and listed sideways. He wasn't moving forward any longer and Remy and Augustin had to rush forward to see why the man wasn't moving, but they couldn't quite see what had the man hobbled. All they knew was that they had to get out of the fighting, so they each took an arm and dragged Lucifer out as Constantine, carrying Gregoria, came up behind them.

Now, they were out of the tavern and in the street. Several of Constantine's men were mounted already, trying to fight off the tide of opponents that were now spilling out of the smoking building. Constantine was greatly concerned for Gregoria but he was also greatly concerned for Lucifer, who was on his knees. When he came around the front of the man, he saw why.

A long dagger hilt was protruding out of his left side, right at the base of his ribcage.

"Damnation," Lucifer hissed as Augustin and Remy dropped to their knees to assist him. "I almost made it out before someone threw a knife at me."

Constantine took a moment to visually inspect the wound, as much as he could without actually touching anything. He was still holding Gregoria.

"Bloody hell," he muttered when he saw the size of the hilt. "The blade has to be a least the length of the hilt."

"I will remove it," Remy said, moving in to get a grip on it.

"Nay!" Constantine snapped. "There is no time to do it here. Get him back to the *Gaia*. I will take Augustin with me to Three Crosses. *Move.*"

They did. Remy slung Lucifer's right arm across his broad shoulders, practically carrying the man back to the sandy beach where the *Gaia* hopefully hadn't moved too far off shore yet. There hadn't been enough time to really move the vessel very far and that's what they were counting on. But Remy was having trouble dragging Lucifer's dead weight along with him, so another of Constantine's men came to his aid, helping him evacuate Lucifer to the beach.

Meanwhile, Constantine had to move quickly. He had to think of himself, of Gregoria, and of getting clear of the fighting. His silver steed was still tethered where he'd left it and he raced to the animal, heaving Gregoria up into the saddle as gently as he could before leaping onto the saddle himself and taking hold of Gregoria before digging his heels into the animal and tearing off out of town.

He hoped Augustin and the remainder of his men were following because he couldn't take the time to look back. His only concern at the moment was removing Gregoria from the battle and taking her someplace safe to assess her injuries. It could have been nothing more than a knock on the head when the table fell, or it could be something substantially worse. All he knew was that he had to get her to safety. He didn't even care about himself at that moment; only her.

The dark forests of Wales swallowed them up as the road disappeared into the trees.

Chapter Thirteen

S HE WAS BACK on the ship again. It was rolling. Everything was rolling.

Gregoria opened her eyes to see horse's legs beneath her and the muddy road zinging by as the horse ran. Everything was a blur. Some of the mud was flying up in her face, specs of it hitting her in the forehead. Realizing she was upside down, slung over the saddle of a horse, when her last memory had been of a fight going on around her, she panicked in thinking that she'd been abducted from the fight.

All kicking feet and swinging arms, she could feel someone trying to steady her. She thought she might have even heard a familiar voice… Constantine's voice… but she couldn't be sure. All she knew was that she wanted off the galloping horse.

Gregoria got her wish. She was fighting so much that the horse was pulled up to a stumbling halt and she managed to pitch herself off in such a way that she ended up on her feet. But she was still moving with the momentum of the swiftly-moving horse and she stumbled back, ending up on her arse in the middle of the muddy, rocky road. Feet suddenly hit the ground beside her.

"Are you well, love?" It was Constantine, grasping her by the arm and hauling her to her feet. "Did you hurt yourself?"

Gregoria's head was swimming as she held on to Constantine for support, relieved that it was him to her rescue and she wasn't in the clutches of an enemy. "I… I do not think so," she said, putting a hand to her head. "What… what happened? Where are we?"

Constantine put both hands on her because she seemed so unsteady. "Come over here," he said, leading her over to the side of the road where there was an upturned stump. "Sit down before you fall down. How do you feel?"

Gregoria wasn't entirely sure how to answer that question. Sitting on the stump, she struggled to orient herself. "My head hurts," she said, looking up to Constantine and wincing because the bright sky over his head hurt her eyes. "What happened? Where are we?"

Constantine crouched down beside her. "There was a fight back in Eynon," he said. "Do you remember that?"

She nodded. "I do," she said. "There were men all around and then… I think they broke the table I was hiding under."

Constantine grinned faintly. "They did, indeed," he said. "It was a heavy table and it must have hit you on the head when it fell. I took you out as quickly as I could and now we are on our way to Three Crosses."

Three Crosses. Suddenly, Gregoria's head wasn't hurting as badly as the stab of terror those two words gave her. Everything came to her all in a flood; her thoughts before the fight began, when she had been planning on telling Constantine everything, and then her intentions being thwarted by the battle. She began looking around in a panic.

"How long has it been since we left the town?" she asked. "How far have we come?"

Constantine could see the fear in her expression, although he didn't understand it. "Everything is well," he assured her. "We were not followed from town."

That wasn't the answer she sought. She looked at him. "How *far* have we come?"

Constantine threw a thumb at the road, in a general northerly direction. "Far enough," he said. "At this pace, we should be there in another hour or two. We are not too far away now."

That bit of news gripped Gregoria with fear. *We are not too far away.* She grabbed hold of him, looking at their surroundings, seeing mostly hills and fields with trees in the distance. There were dots of white sheep down the hill, corralled by two figures she presumed to be shepherds, but other than the sheep and the two men, she couldn't see anyone else. No army was lying in wait.

Thank God!

There was no more time to waste.

"I must speak with you privately, my lord," she said to Constantine, her pale face full of angst. "Please send your men away."

Constantine simply nodded, turning to tell Augustin to take the men up the road and he would join them later. As the men began to move, Gregoria kept her head down, watching them out of her peripheral vision, waiting until they were far enough away before she would bring forth that painful subject. Before she could speak, however, Constantine was brushing the specs of mud from her forehead.

"I must tell you something," he said.

Her hand went to her forehead to brush off the area he was picking at. "What is it?"

"You will call me Constantine. Or Con. I will answer to whatever you want to call me, Gregg. But please do not address me formally any longer."

She looked at him, wide-eyed. That sweet request had her heart racing and her courage fading. But… *no.* She couldn't lose courage, not now.

She had to save Constantine's life.

"I want you to listen to me carefully and try to reserve judgment until I am finished," she said, her voice trembling. "I have a great deal to say and not much time to say it. Will you do that? Will you listen to me?"

"I will always listen to you."

God, he was just making this harder. Frightened, full of sorrow,

Gregoria stood up from the stump and moved away from him, if only to gather her thoughts. After a few moments, she turned to him.

"I grew up in a household with my mother, my brother, and my father," she said quietly. "My mother and father died some time ago, leaving me with my brother. He is very ambitious, you see, for the Earl of March's favor. He is so desperate for it that he offered to help the earl gain a clear path to the throne and he is using me to accomplish that task."

Constantine wasn't sure what she was talking about, an unexpected subject in the midst of chaos. He stood up, his gaze upon her.

"What do you mean?" he asked. "What is he having you do?"

Gregoria could see that he wasn't understanding what she was trying to say. Heavily, she sighed. "I am not being clear," she said. "Constantine, I must be plain. I lied to you. Miles Tenby is not my father and I was never married to a man named Meyrick. I have never been married at all. The cup I told you is a holy relic is simply an old cup with no greater glory. My name is Lady Gregoria de Moyon and my brother is Olin de Moyon, Baron Buckland. His liege is Lord Wembury. If you do not know him, you should. He hates you with a vengeance. My brother and Lord Wembury, in order to be in March's good graces, have forced me to lie to you. If you go to Three Crosses, the Earl of March is waiting for you. You are a threat to the earl's claim to the throne and they want you removed. Therefore, you must turn around at this very moment and make haste back to your ship. Get out of here, Constantine. Get out of here before they find you and kill you."

By the time she was finished, there were tears brimming in her eyes. Had Constantine any less self-control, there would have been tears in his eyes, too. He felt as if he'd just been hit in the gut, feeling shock and disappointment as he'd never felt in his life. No, he hadn't seen this coming. He hadn't seen this at all. But he should have.

He felt like a fool.

"Are you serious?" he asked, stunned.

"Never more serious in my life."

If the first hit to the gut was painful, this second hit was about to take him to the ground. He was actually having trouble standing as he realized that all had not been as it seemed. Something had been going on around him that he'd been too blind to suspect or too foolish to realize.

Gregoria wasn't who she appeared to be.

She was a traitor.

"Then all of this was part of your plan," he said, trying to remain calm. "Endearing yourself to me, making me feel as if... all of it was part of your plan."

"I had to earn your trust, aye."

"It worked. Brava, my lady. Now, what do you intend to do?"

Gregoria could see the pain in his eyes as he spoke and it clawed at her, ripping her heart and soul right out of her body. She could see, in just that brief exchange, that she had badly hurt him.

"I do not plan to do anything more," she insisted. "I told you to go. You must return to your ship immediately. I... I cannot let you go to Three Crosses."

Constantine's pain-filled gaze lingered on her before looking away. "Now you become the noble hero?" he said. "You have me now. You could easily finish what you started."

Gregoria shook her head. "Nay, I cannot," she said. She was desperate to explain herself, as if that would make a difference now. "When I came to Perran Castle, I simply wanted to be done with all of this. I had been bullied into this position, promised a small house and a garden of my own should I succeed. All I wanted was my house and my garden, and to get away from my wicked brother. I am his ward, you see, and he controls everything. When he told me what I had to do, I could not refuse him. I had no choice but to go through with it. I didn't care that I was betraying you at first, a greatly feared pirate. I thought that I might even be doing the world a great service. But as we came to know one another... I came to care very much. No one has ever been as kind to me as you have been, Constantine. You changed everything."

Constantine wasn't going to be taken in again; his defenses went up. All of the soft words in the world weren't going to matter to him now. He wasn't going to fall for them.

"That was my mistake," he rumbled. "It was my terrible mistake to be kind to you, to think you were different from the other women I have known. But I see you are just like the rest. Greedy, treacherous wenches."

His words hurt her, but Gregoria knew she deserved them. "I know you must think so," she said, fighting off the tears. "I knew that by telling you the truth, we would lose everything between us. I did not have to tell you, Constantine, but I did. I love you too much to see the Earl of March get his hands on you. That is why you must take your men and flee back to your ship this very moment. I cannot even be sure the Earl of March and his men have not come down this far, thinking we might be coming into Eynon Bay. They may very well be scouring the road for you."

His eyes narrowed. "How would they know that?" he asked. "Did you manipulate that, too, somehow?"

Gregoria shook her head. "I heard my brother mention, once, that you would not dock in Swansea because there are too many people there who would either try to capture you or resist you," she said. "Everyone knows that Eynon is a port for smugglers. There are only so many bays along this coast that you could have come to."

She had a point. She also had a point in mentioning that she did not have to tell him about any of this. She could have quite easily allowed them to continue on, right into the waiting arms of the Earl of March. But she didn't. Something had stopped her from finishing her objective.

I love you too much to see the Earl of March get his hands on you...

Bloody Beard, was it true? Did she really love him?

Frustrated, and deeply hurt, he turned away from her, taking a few steps down the road, his mind mulling over what he'd been told. He was in such turmoil that it was difficult for him to grasp only one thought. All he knew was that he'd let his guard down for this woman and it had turned around to bite him in the arse. He was an idiot; he knew that now. His men had known it all along and they'd tried to warn him, but he didn't listen. He hadn't wanted to listen, thinking he knew best.

Is this what it felt like to have loved and lost? No wonder he'd never wanted any part of it.

"I thought you were different," he finally said. "A beautiful, intelligent woman who wanted to be with me. A woman who was willing to accept me for all of my faults and willing to accept who I am."

Gregoria could hear the anguish in his voice and she took a step towards him, wanting so badly to put her arms around him. This was what she had been so fearful of; losing him. Now, it was happening. She'd already lost him. All of that warmth and affection between them was gone, and the pain of it was more than she could bear.

"I am willing to accept you for who you are," she said hoarsely. "I am sorry I came to you under false pretenses; I truly am. Had I not fallen in love with you, it would not have mattered. I would have turned you over to the Earl of March and not thought anything of it. But it was my mistake to love you and everything about you. That is why I am telling you that you cannot go to Three Crosses. I will go on alone and explain to them that I was unable to bring you to them. I will think of something. But you... you must leave immediately. The longer you remain, the more chance of you being seen. Will you go, Constantine? Will you *please* go?"

He simply stood there while everything she said sank in, not moving. Had he not been so emotionally fragile, it would have been much easier to walk away from her. But one very large factor kept him from walking away – she had confessed to him before he discovered it for himself. Now, she was trying to save him, trying to prevent something terrible from happening. *She loved him.* No one had ever loved him before, at least no one he *wanted* to love him. Could he really walk away from her under these circumstances? He was afraid that if he did, he would never forgive himself.

God, he wanted to believe her.

So badly.

"If you go to Three Crosses to tell the Earl of March I have escaped you, he will not treat you kindly," he said, turning to look at her. "Look me in the eye, Gregg; tell me that there is nothing else you are withholding from me, nothing else you have lied about. Now is the moment for total truth between us or, I swear, you will be dead to me."

Hope sprouted in her heart. "I have told you everything," she said, feeling desperate and anxious. "But I must apologize; when I started this task, I was only thinking of myself. I was only thinking of the house and garden I was promised. I was not thinking of the man I had been sent to betray. I am sorry that I thought my house and garden to be more important than you in the beginning. I was wrong; so very wrong."

All he could see in her face was total, utter honesty. He could see the same pain reflecting in her eyes that he was feeling at the moment, the pain of something precious slipping away. She loved him; not only had she told him so, but he could tell simply by looking at her. If he was honest with himself, then he supposed he loved her, too. Having never been in love, there was no other way to explain the feelings in his heart. There was no other way to explain the joy he felt when he looked at her. Even now, he was feeling joy even though she'd hurt him. But she was trying to redeem herself.

If it was foolish to let her try, then he was about to be a fool. A *big* one.

"I suppose we all do things we regret," he finally said. "God knows, I've had my share. There is much I regret in life, but you are not one of them. Do not make me change my mind, Gregg. Please."

Gregoria could hardly believe it. Was he actually forgiving her? Tears filled her eyes as she gazed at him.

"I will not, I swear it," she murmured. "I am so very sorry for all of this, Constantine."

"I believe you."

"*Will* you forgive me?"

She was begging him. Unable to stand her remorseful expression, he went over to her and cupped her face in his two big hands, looking her in the eye.

"Aye, I will," he said. "But do not make me regret any of this. No more lies, ever. No matter what."

She nodded, blinking, and her tears spattered on his wrist. "I swear upon my mother's grave, no more anything," she whispered. "But you must go now. I must go to Three Crosses and face my brother and Lord Wembury and the Earl of March."

He shook his head. "You are not going anywhere," he said. "You are returning to the *Gaia* with me. You promised, you know. I will hold you to it."

"Are… are you certain?"

"Of course I am," he said. "Now, let us go find Augustin and the men and tell them we are turning back. There is no point in telling them any of this, so you will let me make excuses. They are probably not too far ahead. In fact, I want to…"

He was cut off by the sounds of thundering hooves, heading in his direction from the north. Concerned, he helped Gregoria to mount his fat steed just as his men came up and over a rise, heading in his direction at top speed. That pounding cadence of men rushing at him had Constantine leaping onto his horse in front of Gregoria, gathering the reins tightly to control the animal, who began to dance about as his men approached.

"What is it?" he called.

Augustin was in the lead. He heard the question. "Go!" he boomed. "There is an army behind us!"

Startled, Constantine turned to see a horde of armored men on horseback pursuing. They were less than a quarter-mile away, at the bottom of the rise that Augustin had just crested, and they were coming fast. Therefore, he didn't ask any questions; he dug his heels into his horse and sped off after his men.

But it was a harried flight. The road was muddy and slippery, and rocks and dirt flew up, pelting the riders and covering them with mud. Constantine could feel Gregoria holding on to him tightly as he maneuvered his horse up in front, up near Augustin.

"What happened?" he yelled over the wind.

Augustin turned his head slightly and it was then that Constantine realized the man had a bloody scratch on his face. "They were in the trees about a half-mile north," he shouted. "Dozens of them, crawling all over the area. They fired a crossbow at me and it barely missed."

That explained the scratch on his cheek, but it also underscored what Gregoria had said; *they may be scouring the road for you.* Evidently, they were. They were probably watching every road between the coast and Three Crosses because as far as Constantine knew, there weren't very many roads leading to Three Crosses and if the Earl of March had brought hundreds of men with him, then he could easily cover all of the roads. More than likely bored of just sitting and waiting for their quarry to come to them, they'd fanned out to make sure that quarry was trapped, any way he came.

It had very nearly worked.

"Did you see who they were?" Constantine shouted.

Augustin sat forward on his horse, trying to get more speed out of the animal. "Nay," he called back. "But they were well-armed and well-protected. Whoever they are, it is an important army!"

The Earl of March would have such an army. Constantine hoped his horse could hold out all the way back to Eynon Bay, carrying two people as it was. So far, the steed was strong and keeping pace, but they were still a few miles away. That kind of pace would take its toll, eventually.

All he could do was pray.

Over another rise, down into a dale, and up again, they kept pace in front of the pursuing horses. It was possible that the army in pursuit had no idea who they really were, simply wanting to stop them and interrogate them, but with all of these men and one lone woman, the odds that the prey had come to the Earl of March were good.

The road became a little windy at one point and the horses strug-gled with their footing on the wet ground. Just as they crested another rise, the road leveled out in front of them and it was nearly a straight line all the way into Eynon Bay, which they could see clearly now. Constantine could see the distant speck of the *Gaia* out in the bay, the sunlight of late afternoon reflecting off of the water. He thought he saw a second vessel as well, but he couldn't be sure the way the water and sun were playing tricks on his vision. He urged his grunting horse faster, eager to make the sand, eager to reach his ship.

Then, the arrows started to fly.

There were many of them, too many to count, all of them singing as they hit the earth around them. Gregoria shrieked, ducking her head low and trying to cover it with a hand and not fall off, but there wasn't much she could do. She was exposed sitting where she was, covering Constantine's back, and he struggled not to feel panic because of it. An arrow aimed for him would hit her instead. He tried to lay lower on the horse, forcing her to assume a lower profile as well.

God, please... just let us make it to the ship unharmed!

More arrows. One of Constantine's men was hit in the leg. He could hear the man grunt in pain and he turned to see the man ripping the arrow from his thigh and tossing it away. This was a tough crew of men and they proved it every day. He was glad they were with him.

But it would be a bounty for the Earl of March if he captured all of them.

At this point, they could be seen from the sea, probably tiny dots being chased by more tiny dots, but he hoped that the man in com-mand of the *Gaia*, Aeolis – or even Lucifer – could see them from the spyglass and realize they were being chased. He began to pray for it, praying that his men on duty would see that they were in distress. The spyglass would be able to easily single them out and then they could move the ship in closer. They would have to leave the horses behind more than likely, but it couldn't be helped. All the Earl of March would have of Constantine le Brecque was his horse, but that was a small price to pay, considering.

And then, the sounds of distant thunder…

Only it wasn't thunder. It was nine-pounders being launched from cannons. Constantine knew the sound of that concussion well. As he watched with astonishment, both ships in the bay – now, for certain, he saw a second one – were firing their cannons. At first, Constantine thought that the *Gaia* was under fire because he couldn't clearly see the second ship but, soon enough, the cannonballs were flying over their heads, hitting the land behind them and exploding in a hail of shrapnel.

Help had, indeed, arrived.

The *Gaia* and the second ship were firing at the land, not at each other, and cannonballs were sailing overhead. The first burst of cannons was devastating for the men in pursuit; Constantine glanced behind to see men and horses being seriously damaged. It was enough to slow the group down but not stop them entirely. And as Constantine and his men neared the town, another volley of cannon fire ripped through the end of town, just as they passed through it, and tore through the lines of men who were still pursuing them.

It was enough to turn the rest of the pursuers around. They couldn't compete with volleys of cannon fire from the ships in the bay and those who hadn't been injured by the exploding nine-pounders turned tail and raced back the way they'd come. Men were picking up pieces of each other, trying to herd everyone back from where they'd come, but the cannonballs had been shattering. Wounded men and horses were on the ground, dying or crying for help, as Constantine and his men made it through the town and onto the sandy beach where four skiffs were being rowed in, full of heavily-armed men coming to help them.

"It's Shaw!" Augustin said, pointing to the dark and mighty *Savage of the Sea* as she sat in the glittering bay near the *Gaia*. "He's come!"

Constantine had been more concerned with the men pursuing them, but he quickly came to see that what was left of them had turned back. It took him a moment to realize he and his men were no longer being chased, no longer in immediate danger. Emitting a heavy sigh, one of utter relief, he dismounted his frothing horse, pulling Gregoria off with him as he turned his attention to the second dark-sailed ship in the bay.

"Bloody Beard," he muttered with mock disgust. "It is Shaw, indeed. Now, I shall have to listen to the man tell me how he saved my hide. There will be no living with him."

Augustin grinned as the men moved nearer to the water's edge, watching the skiffs moving in. He started to laugh when he saw that Shaw himself was on one of the skiffs, a broadsword in one hand and a dagger in the other, preparing to fight to the death for his fellow pirate brethren.

"Shaw!" Augustin cried, lifting his hand. "Ahoy! Thank God you came when you did!"

Shaw was armed to the teeth for a fight. He was fairly close to the shoreline now, enough so that he could see Constantine and the woman in his arms. It occurred to him that Constantine was holding the woman quite possessively, something he'd never seen Constantine do. It was a great curiosity, but something to question at a later time. At the moment, he had to make sure Constantine understood that he'd just saved his hide.

"What's that ye say?" he said, turning his head and cupping a hand to his ear. "That I'm the greatest man ye know? That there is none more daring or smarter than I?"

Constantine rolled his eyes as the skiffs came in close and the *Gaia* began to move in closer to shore so the horses could be loaded. But he made sure to fix Shaw in the eye as the man leapt off the skiff and waded through the ankle-deep water to where Constantine and Gregoria were standing.

"Aye, you dirty sea dog, you are the greatest man I know," Constantine said. "And the most daring. But I am more handsome and far more intelligent than you are."

Shaw grinned broadly as he came up on Constantine, pulling the man into a brotherly embrace before kissing him loudly on the cheek.

"I've heard ye had some trouble, lad," he said, pulling back to pat the man on the head. "I came tae help."

There was a seriousness now to the conversation as they faced each other with the realization that the danger, for the moment, was over for Constantine. The moment between them was warm and deep, a bonding moment between men who had saved one another time and time again and had lived to tell the tale.

"I was wondering when you would arrive," Constantine said. "I thought I was going to have to fight off those bastards by myself."

Shaw cocked a dark eyebrow. "So ye knew I was coming, did ye?"

"I know everything."

Shaw grinned. "Ye know that I have a special sense that tells me ye're in trouble."

Constantine laughed softly. "Aye, I know it. It's a special sense called Lucifer. He told me he sent you word."

Shaw shrugged. "'Tis a good thing he did."

Constantine nodded. "It is, indeed," he said. Then, he sobered dramatically. "I knew you would come. You always do. You always know when I am in need of you, my brother."

Shaw's dark eyes twinkled. "That storm we had last night made it so I almost dinna make it in time," he said. "It blew us into Parrog Bay where an old man told me he'd seen a *Sassenach* army near Three Crosses. Knowing ye were heading there, I came tae warn ye. I am sorry I was too late."

Constantine shook his head. "You made up for it by chasing them off my tail," he said. "If you and the *Gaia* hadn't fired cannons to chase them off, it is quite possible they could have caught us. In that respect, you have my deepest gratitude."

"There is no gratitude between us, Con. Only brotherhood."

"Agreed."

"And I would never let my brother down."

"Nor I."

Shaw's smile was back. "As ye've proven tae me, many times," he said. "Our brotherhood runs deeper than blood, laddie. I'll love ye 'til I die. And speaking of love, will ye introduce me tae the lady?"

Constantine pulled Gregoria to him, making sure she was well away from Shaw, a truly handsome devil. "Mayhap someday I will," he said. "But for now, I am keeping her all to myself."

Shaw began to follow the pair as they headed to one of the skiffs. "I saved yer hides and ye willna at least introduce me tae the woman I risked my life for?"

"Nay."

"Not even a name?"

"Not even a name."

The men around them began to chuckle, sensing the game between them. There was so much adoration and camaraderie between Constantine and Shaw that it was moments like these where that bond was felt the most deeply.

A daring brotherhood, where honor among thieves reigns supreme, and crushing their enemies was a thrilling pastime. Today, it was Shaw crushing those who would see his brother's life ended. Tomorrow, it could very well be Constantine risking all to save Shaw. But that was how it went with them.

Brothers above all, until the very end.

Epilogue

A few days later

ITWAS A DAY made of diamonds, the sunlight glittering off the waters of the sea near the outlet of the River Camel, the inlet where Constantine had been keeping the *Leucosia* for refit. But today was the day of her unveiling, and unveil she did.

Like a great, dark beast, the *Leucosia* emerged from the inlet and out into open waters. There was an entire fleet of ships to greet her as she raised her darkened sails and tread forth into the dark blue waters of the Cornwall coast, ships from both Constantine's fleet and Shaw's fleet.

The *Gaia* was there, as was the *Persephone*, the *Melinoe*, and the *Orpheus*, all four of those bigger vessels while the smaller ones like the *Ligeia* shadowed the larger ships. Shaw's vessel, *Savage of the Sea*, was also present along with three other ships in his fleet, making it a huge show of force for the Pirates of Britannia.

But they were here for a reason.

The *Leucosia* was a much-coveted vessel and simply to prevent the French or even the Spanish from sneaking up and taking aim on her, Constantine wanted a big show of force to keep the enemies at bay. He wanted the ship in the channel with no hassle, no fighting. He simply wanted to see the beauty of the sea-going ship in all her glory.

She was quite a sight.

"So that's her, is it?"

It was Shaw's question, spoken in a tone that suggested awe. On the deck of the *Gaia,* standing next to Constantine, they watched the *Leucosia* emerge from the mouth of the river. She was a massive vessel, at least three times the size of the smaller pirate vessels, and she was built for war. Constantine grinned at the appreciation he heard in Shaw's voice.

"That's why I asked you to come back to Cornwall with me," he said. "I wanted you to see her. It was a hard fight to get that lady."

Shaw snorted at the understatement. He knew what Constantine had gone through to get her. "Ballocks, she's a big bitch," he said. "I dunna blame ye for being so proud of her."

Over on Constantine's right stood Gregoria, watching the big ship emerge into the channel. Dressed in a pale blue silk embroidered with tiny roses, a gift from Constantine, she looked absolutely exquisite. The big silver cross he'd purchased for her hung around her neck, as well as strands of pearls and some other jewels she'd selected from Constantine's horde of jewelry, and she looked every inch the consort of a pirate. Except for the fact that she had no sea legs. Ever since her first trip on the *Gaia* in that terrible storm, any movement on sea made her ill. But she held herself together for this momentous occasion.

Constantine had asked it of her.

"I know nothing of ships, my lord, but she does seem quite beautiful to me," she said to Shaw.

The man leaned forward to look at her on the other side of Constantine. "I've spent three days eating meals with ye, lass, and Con has yet tae introduce us," he said. "Do ye think he ever will? If he does, ye can stop calling me 'm'lord' and address me by my name."

As Gregoria giggled, Constantine pursed his lips wryly. "I suppose I should, lest I be accused of having bad manners," he said. "I did not want to introduce the two of you until I was sure you were not going to seduce her. You're a handsome devil, you know. They call you 'Savage' for a reason."

As Gregoria snickered, Shaw lifted his eyebrows. "If I thought she would have left ye, I would have tried my hardest tae make it so, but she has eyes only for ye, Con," he teased, a twinkle in his eye. "Gregg has no interest in me."

"So you know her name, do you?"

"I've heard."

Constantine fought off a grin. "Admit it. You asked someone."

Shaw sighed. "I did. Are ye angry?"

Constantine simply shook his head. "I am not," he said. "But she belongs to me. You would do well to remember that."

Shaw grinned. "Ye know I have a lass of my own now, Con," he said. "What would I do with two?"

"Knowing you, you would find a way."

Shaw laughed softly, looking at Gregoria, who was also grinning. "Nay, Con," he said after a moment. "I have my Jane now and I couldna be happier. Speaking of Jane, I'm anxious tae return tae her, but it was worth the delay tae see the *Leucosia* put tae sea. She's a fine vessel."

Constantine glanced at Lucifer and Augustin, standing on the opposite side of Gregoria. He gave the men a vague nod, and especially to Lucifer, who nodded in return. It was as if they all shared a secret, something that was now going to be brought to the forefront. Lucifer turned to Remy, who was up on the poop deck, and lifted his hand at the man. Remy, in turn, issued a command to Kerk, who happened to be standing next to him with a bow and arrow in hand. Quickly, Kerk lit the arrow tip and fired it into the air, flaming and smoking and all. As the arrow began to arc its way back to earth, something happened over on the *Leucosia*.

Shaw's standard was suddenly raised on the mainmast, the ruddy MacDougall devil-head and sword-fisted hand flying high in the wind. It snapped and danced, announcing to all who saw it that the ship belonged to MacDougall. Confused, Shaw turned to Constantine.

"What's that about?" he asked. "Why do ye fly my banner?"

Constantine smiled faintly. "Because I am giving you the *Leucosia*," he said. Reaching over, he took Gregoria's hand and pulled her against him. "You went above and beyond the call to save both Gregg and me at Eynon Bay, Shaw. You did not have to come to Lucifer's summons, yet you did. Then you risked your life and the lives of your crew in a terrible storm to save my miserable hide from an ambush, and I shall always be grateful to you. Valor such as that deserves a reward."

Shaw was looking at the man with great surprise, turning to watch the *Leucosia* as she sailed towards the *Savage of the Sea*, ready to take her place beside Shaw's flagship. Realizing that Constantine was giving him this magnificent vessel very nearly brought a tear to his eye.

"Con…," he said, then faded off. Clearing his throat, he started again. "I dunna know what tae say, laddie. It is too much."

Constantine shook his head. "It is *not* too much," he said. "It is worthy of you."

Shaw turned to look at him again, seeing that Gregoria was beaming at him. Something about the woman just caught his eye; she was so… *happy*. Aye, he knew the story behind the ambush at Three Crosses. Constantine had told him in confidence that Gregoria had been forced into helping her brother and a fool named Lord Wembury, that they had threatened her should she not help them lure Constantine into a trap.

All Constantine's men knew of the folly was that the cup they'd been taking to Three Crosses had somehow been lost in the flight from the *Sassenach* army and nothing more. There was no mention of ever going back to Three Crosses, or of betrayal, or of anything else. To them, she was still Miles Tenby's daughter. Gregoria had confessed her sins before any real damage was done and Constantine didn't see the need to tell his men the truth. He believed the matter was between him and Gregoria, and it was settled. He was so far gone in love with the woman that he was willing to forgive her everything.

At first, Shaw wasn't entirely convinced it was the right thing to do, but three days around the pair had changed his mind. It was clear to see how deeply devoted they were with each other, so much so that even Shaw was willing to forgive Gregoria and believe that she'd made a grave mistake for which she was truly sorry. She doted on Constantine, laughed with him, and even argued with him, something that gave her Shaw's stamp of approval. A terrible scheme might have brought the two together, but that was quickly forgiven and forgotten.

Now, all Shaw saw was a couple that was terribly in love.

Constantine deserved it.

"Then I accept," he finally said. "I have never received such a proud and mighty gift. I will take great care of her, Con."

Constantine slapped him on the back, joy in the man's expression. "Excellent," he said. "And your first duty as captain of the *Leucosia* will be to marry Gregg and me. Captains can marry a couple at sea, you know. I would be honored if you would do the duty."

Shaw was grinning from ear to ear. "It will be my pleasure," he said. "My good and true pleasure. Now, let me get over to my beautiful new ship and inspect her. I love ye dearly, Con. Ye've passed her into capable hands!"

With that, he climbed over the top rail of the *Gaia*, down the rope ladder to the skiff waiting below to take him over to his vessels. As Gregoria went over to the rail to wave at him as he and his men rowed away, Constantine went to stand next to Lucifer and Augustin.

Lucifer had recovered quickly from the stab wound he'd received in Eynon. It had missed everything vital and the man had been back on his feet within a day. Now, he stood stoically as he watched Shaw row over to what was to have been his command. But he didn't mind. In truth, he understood the gifting completely.

"Well?" Constantine said. "The ship is Shaw's now."

Lucifer nodded his head. "It is."

"Regrets?"

Lucifer made a noise that sounded suspiciously like a snort. "Nay," he said. "He'll find out soon enough that every pirate in the sea is aiming for that ship. It may as well have an enormous target painted on the broadside. Better him than me."

Constantine struggled not to laugh, watching Gregoria as she continued to wave at Shaw. "We should probably warn him," he said.

Lucifer looked at him. "Why?" he asked. "Did he warn you when he gave you that beautiful sword last year, the one with the handle that came off when you tried to unsheathe it?"

Constantine well remembered that particular gift. It had been a stunning Spanish broadsword, but it had been a joke – when one tried to use it, the handle came off, revealing a tiny little blade to fight with. Constantine had been caught in a battle with it and it had been most humiliating. He'd drawn forth what he thought was a magnificent broadsword and ended up with a needle, enough of an embarrassment that the Spanish pirates he was fighting burst out in laughter when they saw it.

"I remember," he growled. "I still have not forgiven him for that."

Lucifer bit his lip at the memory. "It *was* rather humorous."

"It was humiliating."

"So, you are not going to warn him about the *Leucosia*?"

Constantine shook his head. "He will find out soon enough."

Two weeks after the marriage of Constantine and Gregoria on the deck of the *Leucosia*, Shaw had to fight off the Dureau and Nicolas Van Rompay, twice, as he made his way to a port in Ireland. It wasn't until Dureau tried to catch him off guard again and shouted to him, across an inlet with a sandbar in between them, that he wanted his ship back that Shaw began to suspect that his dear and true friend Constantine had saddled him with a cursed ship that the French were wild to reclaim. It would have been just like him to do it.

Shaw laughed about it until he could laugh no more.

With friends like that, the enemies of the Pirates of Britannia had better be on their guard.

Pirates, plunder, and brotherhood… forever.

Long live the Lords of the Sea.

THE END

Enjoy an excerpt from

Savage of the Sea

by Eliza Knight

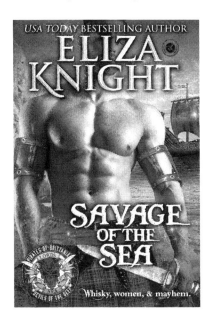

Chapter One

Edinburgh Castle, Scotland
November 1440

S HAW MACDOUGALL STOOD in the great hall of Edinburgh Castle with dread in the pit of his stomach. He was amongst dozens of other armored knights—though he was no knight. Nay, he was a blackmailed pirate under the guise of a mercenary for the day. And though he'd not known the job he was hired to do until he arrived at the castle, and still didn't really. He'd been told to wait until given an order, and ever since, the leather-studded armor weighed heavily on him, and sweat dripped in a steady line down his spine.

The wee King of Scotland, just ten summers, sat at the dais entertaining his guests, who were but children themselves. William Douglas, Earl of Douglas, was only sixteen, and his brother was only a year or two older than the king himself. Beside the lads was a beautiful young lass, with long golden locks that caught the light of the torches. The lass was perhaps no more than sixteen herself, though she already had a woman's body—a body he should most certainly *not* be looking at. And though he was only a handful of years over twenty, and might be convinced she was of age, he was positive she was far too young for him. Wide blue eyes flashed from her face and held the gaze of everyone in the room just long enough that they were left squirming. And her mouth... God, she had a mouth made to—

Ballocks! It was wrong to look at her in any way that might be construed as...desire.

There was an air of innocence about her that clashed with the cynical look she sometimes cast the earl, whom Shaw had guessed might be her husband. It wasn't hard to spot a woman unhappily married. Hell, it was a skill he'd honed while in port, as he loved to dally with disenchanted wives and leave them quite satisfied.

Unfortunately for him, he was not interested in wee virginal lasses. And so, would not be leaving *that* lass satisfied. Decidedly, he kept his gaze averted from her and eyed the men about the room.

Torches on the perimeter walls lit the great hall, but only dimly. None of the candelabras were burning, leaving many parts of the room cast in shadow—the corners in particular. And for Shaw, this was quite disturbing.

He was no stranger to battle—and not just any type of battle—he was intimately acquainted with guerilla warfare, the *pirate* way. But why the hell would he, the prince of pirates, be hired by a noble lord intimately acquainted with the king?

Shaw glanced sideways at the man who'd hired him. Sir Andrew Livingstone. Shaw's payment wasn't in coin, nay, he'd taken this mission in exchange for several members of his crew being released from the dungeons without a trial. Had he not, they'd likely have hung. Shaw had been more than happy to strike a bargain with Livingstone in exchange for his men's lives.

Now, he dreaded the thought of what that job might be.

This would be the last time he let his men convince him mooring in Blackness Bay for a night of debauchery was a good idea. It was there that two of his crew had decided to act like drunken fools, and it was also there, that half a dozen other pirates jumped in to save them. They'd all been arrested and brought before Livingstone, who'd tossed them in a cell.

And now, here he was, feeling out of place in the presence of the king and the two men, Livingstone and the Lord Chancellor, who had arranged for this oddly dark feast. They kept giving each other strange looks, as though speaking through gestures. Shaw shifted, cracking his neck, and glanced back at the dais table lined with youthful nobles.

Seated beside the young earl, the lass glanced furtively around the room, her eyes jumpy as a rabbit as though she sensed something. She sipped her cup daintily and picked at the food on her plate, peeking nervously about the room. Every once in a while, she'd give her head a little shake as if trying to convince herself that whatever it was she sensed was all in her head.

The air in the room shifted, growing tenser. There was a subtle nod from the Lord Chancellor to a man near the back of the room, who then disappeared. At the same time, a knight approached the lass with a message. She wrinkled her nose, glancing back toward the young lad to her left and shaking her head, dismissing the knight. But a second later, she was escorted, rather unwillingly, from the room.

Shaw tensed at the way the knight gripped her arm and that her idiotic boy husband didn't seem to care at all. What was the meaning of all this?

Perhaps the reason presented itself a moment later. A man dressed in black from head to toe, including a hood covering his face, entered from the rear of the great hall carrying a blackened boar's head on a platter. He walked slowly, and as those sitting at the table turned their gaze toward him, their eyes widened. In what though? Shock? Curiosity? Or was it fear?

Did Livingstone plan to kill the king?

If so, why did none of the guards pull out their swords to stop this messenger of death?

Shaw was finding it difficult to stand by and let this happen.

But the man in black did not stop in front of the king. Instead, he stopped in front of the young earl and his wee brother, placing the boar's head between them. Shaw knew what it meant before either of the victims it was served to did.

"Nay," he growled under his breath.

The two lads looked at the blackened head with disgust, and then the earl seemed to recognize the menacing gesture. Glowering at the servant, he said, "Get that bloody thing out of my sight."

Shaw was taken aback that the young man spoke with such authority, though he supposed at sixteen, he himself had already captained one of MacAlpin's ships and posed that same authority.

At this, Livingstone and Crichton stood and took their places before the earl and his brother.

"William Douglas, sixth Earl of Douglas, and Sir David Douglas, ye're hereby charged with treason against His Majesty King James II."

The young king worked hard to hide his surprise, sitting up a little taller. "What? Nay!"

The earl glanced at the king with a sneer one gives a child they think deserves punishment. "What charges could ye have against us?" Douglas shouted. "We've done nothing wrong. We are loyal to our king."

"Ye stand before your accusers and deny the charges?" Livingstone said, eyebrow arched, his tone brooking no argument.

"*What* charges?" Douglas's face had turned red with rage, and he stood, hands fisted at his sides.

Livingstone slammed his hands down on the table in front of Douglas. "Guilty. Ye're guilty."

William Douglas jerked to a stand, shoving his brother behind him, and pulled his sword from its scabbard. "Lies!" He lunged forward and would have been able to do damage to his accusers if not for the seasoned warriors who overpowered him from behind.

"Stop," King James shouted, his small voice drowned out by the screams of the Douglas lads and the shouts of the warriors.

Quickly overpowered, the noble lads were dragged kicking and screaming from the great hall, all while King James shouted for the spectacle to cease.

Shaw was about to follow the crowd outside when Livingstone gripped his arm.

"Take care of Lady Douglas."

Lady Douglas. The sixteen-year-old countess.

"Take care?" Shaw needed to hear it explicitly.

"Aye. Execute her. I dinna care how. Just see it done." The man shrugged. "We were going to let her live, but I've changed my mind. Might as well get her out of the way, too."

Livingstone wanted Shaw to kill her? As though it was acceptable for a lord to execute lads on trumped up charges of treason, but the murder of a lass, that was a pirate's duty.

Shaw ground his teeth and nodded. Killing innocent lassies wasn't part of his code. He'd never done so before and didn't want to start now. Blast it all! Six pirates for one wee lass. One beautiful, enchanting lass who'd never done him harm. Hell, he didn't even know her. Slipping unnoticed past the bloodthirsty crowd wasn't hard given they were too intent on the insanity unfolding around them. He made his way toward the arch where he'd seen the lass dragged too not a quarter hour before.

The arch led to a dimly lit rounded staircase and the only way to go was up. Pulling his *sgian-dubh* from his boot, Shaw hurried up the stairs, his soft boots barely a whisper on every stone step. At the first round, he encountered a closed door. An ear pressed against the wood proved no one inside. He went up three more stairs to another quiet room. He continued to climb, listening at every door until he reached the very top. The door was closed, and it was quiet, but the air was charged making the hair on the back of his neck prickle.

Taking no more time, Shaw shouldered the door open to find the knight who'd escorted the lass from the great hall lying on top of her on the floor. They struggled. Her legs were parted, skirts up around her hips, tears of rage on her reddened face. The bastard had a hand over her mouth and sneered up at Shaw upon his entry.

Fury boiled inside him. Shaw slammed the door shut so hard it rattled the rafters.

"Get up," Shaw demanded, rage pummeling through him at having caught the man as he tried to rape the lass.

Tears streamed from her eyes, which blazed blue as she stared at him. Her face was pale, and her limbs were trembling. Still, there was defiance in the set of her jaw. Something inside his chest clenched. He wanted to rip the whoreson limb from limb. And he knew for a fact he wasn't going to kill Lady Douglas.

"I said get up." Shaw advanced a step or two, averting his eyes for a moment as the knight removed himself from her person, letting her adjust her skirts down her legs.

Shaw waved his hand at her, indicating she should run from the room, but rather than escape, she went to the corner of the chamber and cowered.

Saints, but his heart went out to her.

Shaw was a pirate, had witnessed a number of savage acts, and the one thing he could never abide by was the rape of a woman.

The knight didn't speak, instead he charged toward Shaw with murder in his eyes.

But that didn't matter. Shaw had dealt with a number of men like him who were used to preying on women. He would be easy, and he would bear the entire brutal brunt of Shaw's ire.

Shaw didn't move, simply waiting the breath it took for the knight to be on him. He leapt to the left, out of the path of the knight's blade, and sank his own blade in quick succession into the man's gut, then heart, then neck. Three rapid jabs.

The knight fell to the ground, blood pouring from his wounds, his eyes and mouth wide in surprise. Too easy.

"Please," the lass whimpered from the corner. The defiance that had shown on her face before disappeared, and now she only looked frightened. "Please, dinna hurt me."

"I would never. Ye have my word." Shaw tried to make his words soothing, but they came out so gruff, he was certain they were exactly the opposite.

He wiped the blood from his blade onto the knight's hose and then stuck the *sgian-dubh* back into his boot. He approached the lass, hands outstretched, as he might a wild filly. "We must go, lass."

"Please, go." She wiped at the blood on her lips. "Leave me here."

"Lady Jane, is that right?" he asked, ignoring her plea for him to leave her.

She nodded.

"I need to get ye out of here. I was…" Should he tell her? "I was sent by Livingstone to…take your life. But I willna. I swear it. Come now, we must escape."

"What?" Her tears ceased in her surprise.

"Ye canna be seen. The lads, your husband…" Shaw ran a hand through his hair. "Livingstone willna let them leave alive. He doesna want *ye* to leave alive."

That defiance returned to her striking blue eyes as she stared him down. "I dinna believe ye."

"Trust me."

She shook her head and slid slowly up the wall to stand, her hands braced on the stone behind her. "Where is my husband?"

Shaw grimaced. "He's gone, lass. Come now, or ye'll be gone soon, too." He'd not been hired for this task, to take a shaking lass out of castle and hide her away. But the alternative was much worse. And he'd not be committing the murder of an innocent today.

Indeed, he risked his entire reputation by being here and doing anything at all, but he was pretty certain the two lads she'd arrived with were dead already, and along with them the rest of their party. Livingstone and Crichton weren't about to let the lass live to tell the tale or rally the rest of the Douglas clan to come after them. That line was healthy, long and powerful.

"I dinna understand," she mumbled. "Who are ye?"

"I am Shaw MacDougall."

She searched his eyes, seeking understanding and not finding it. "I dinna know ye."

"All ye need to know is I am here to get ye to safety. Come now. They'll be looking for ye soon." And him. This was a direct breach of their contract, and Livingstone would not stop until he had Shaw's head on a spike.

But Shaw didn't care. He hated the bastard and had been looking for retribution. Let that be a lesson to Livingstone for attempting to blackmail a pirate. His men would be proud to know he'd not succumbed to the blackguard's demands. As he stood there, they were already being broken out of the jail at Blackness Bay.

Stopping a few feet in front of the lass, he held out his hand and gestured for her to take it. She shook her head.

"Lady Jane, I canna begin to understand what ye're feeling right now, but I also canna stress enough the urgency of the situation. I've a horse, and my ship is not far from here. Come now, else surrender your fate to that of your husband."

"William."

"He is dead, lass. Or soon to be."

"Nay…" Her chin wobbled, and she looked ready to collapse.

"Aye. There is no time to argue. Come. I will carry ye if ye need me to."

Perhaps it would be better if he simply lifted her up and tossed her over his shoulder. Shaw made a move to reach for her when she shook her head and straightened her shoulders.

"Will ye take me to Iona, Sir MacDougall?"

"Aye. Will Livingstone know to look for ye there?"

She shook her head. "My aunt is a nun there. Livingstone may put it together at some point, but I will be safe there for now."

"Aye."

"Oh…" She started to tremble uncontrollably. "Oh my… I… I'm going to…" And then she fell into his arms, unconscious.

Shaw let out a sigh and tossed her over his shoulder as he'd thought to do just a few moments before. Hopefully, she'd not wake until they were on his ship and had already set sail. He sneaked back down the stairs, and rather than go out the front where he could hear screams of pain and shouts filled with the thirst for blood, he snuck her out the postern gate at the back of the castle. He half ran, half slid down the steep slope, thanking the heavens every second when the lass did not waken.

Though he'd arrived at the castle on a horse, he'd had one of his men ride with another and instructed him to wait at the bottom of the castle hill in case he needed to make an escape. Some might say he had a sixth sense about such things, but he preferred to say that he simply had a pirate's sense of preservation.

Livingstone was a blackguard who'd made a deal with a pirate to commit murder. A powerful lord only made dealings with a pirate when he needed muscle at his back. And when he chose to keep his own hands clean. But that didn't mean Livingstone wouldn't hesitate killing Shaw.

Well, Livingstone was a fool. And Shaw was not. There was his horse waiting for him at the bottom of the hill just as he'd asked.

"Just as ye said, Cap'n," Jack, his quartermaster—called so for being a Jack-of-all-trades—said with a wide, toothy grin. "What's that?"

Shaw raised a brow, glancing at the rounded feminine arse beside his face. "A lass. Let's go."

"Oh, taken to kidnapping now, aye?"

"Not exactly." Shaw tossed the lass up onto the horse and climbed up behind her. "Come on, Jack. Back to the ship."

They took off at a canter, loping through the dirt-packed roads of Edinburgh toward the Water of Leith that led out to the Firth of Forth and the sea beyond. But then on second thought, he veered his horse to the right. When they rowed their skiff up the Leith to get to the castle, they'd had more time. Now, time was of the essence, and riding their horses straight to the docks at the Forth where his ship awaited would be quicker. No doubt, as soon as Livingstone noticed Shaw was gone— as well as the girl—he'd send a horde of men after him. Shaw could probably convince a few of them to join his crew, but he didn't have time for that.

A quarter of an hour later, their horses covered in a sheen of sweat, Shaw shouted for his men to lower the gangplank, and he rode the horse right up onto the main deck of the *Savage of the Sea*, his pride and joy, the ship he'd captained since he was not much older than the lass he carried.

"Avast ye, maties! All hands hoy! Weigh anchor and hoist the mizzen. Ignore the wench and get us the hell out of here. To Iona we sail!" With his instructions given, Shaw carried the still unconscious young woman up the few stairs to his own quarters, pushing open the door and slamming it shut behind him.

There, he paused. If he set her on the bed, what would she think when she woke? What would he think if he saw her there? She was much too young for him, aye. But whenever he brought a wench to his quarters and laid her on the bed, it was not for any bit of *saving*, unless it was release from the tension pleasure built.

And yet, the floor did not seem like a good spot, either.

He settled for the long wooden bench at the base of his bed.

As soon as he laid her there, her eyes popped open, and she leapt to her feet. "What are ye doing? Where have ye taken me?" She looked about her wildly, reaching for nothing and everything at once. Blond locks flying wildly.

"Calm yourself, lass." Shaw raised a sardonic brow. "We sail for Iona as ye requested. And from there, we shall part ways."

She eyed him suspiciously. "And nothing more?"

He crossed his arms over his chest and studied her. As the seconds ticked past, her shoulders seemed to sag a little more, and that crazed look evaporated from her eyes. "Nothing save the satisfaction that I have taken ye from a man who would have done ye harm."

"Livingstone?"

"Aye."

Her lower lip trembled. "Aye. He will want to kill all who bear the Douglas name."

Shaw's eyes lowered to her flat belly. "Might there be another?" he asked.

She shook her head violently. "Ye saved me just before that awful man could…"

"Ye misunderstand me, my lady. I meant your husband's…" Ballocks, why did he find it hard to say the word *seed* to the lass? He was a bloody pirate and far more vulgar words, to any number of wenches, had come from his mouth.

She lifted her chin, jutting it forward obstinately. "There is nothing."

Shaw chose to take her word for it rather than discuss the intimate relationship she might have had with her boy husband and when the last time her courses had come. "Then ye need only worry about your own neck, and no one else's."

He expected her to fall into a puddle of tears, but she didn't.

The lass simply nodded and then said, "I owe ye a debt, Sir Mac-Dougall."

"Call me Savage, lass. And rest assured, I will collect."

Chapter Two

November 1441

Dear Savage of the Sea,

I deplore writing that out, but as it is the name you bid me address you, who am I to give you another? I write on this, the one year anniversary of having arrived at Iona via your impressive ship. And given I am still safely ensconced, I must thank you for seeing me brought here, as well as for keeping the secret of my whereabouts. I am reminded on this one-year mark, that I still owe you a debt, and I did not want you to think I had forgotten.

The nuns at Iona treat me well, though they are irritated I have not yet chosen to take vows. As such, I'm certain they give me the worst of all chores. But I do them with a glad heart because I am alive, and I know more so than any other woman here that life is precious. Except perhaps that of Sister Maria. I've yet to learn her story. She thinks me too young. I am almost seventeen though, and I've been married before, which I'm certain she has not. Does that not make me more of a grown up?

Well, I am rambling, and I'm certain that a man of your trade has no use for ramblings.

I bid you adieu.

Yours in debt,
Lady Marina (I have often caught myself saying my true name, so much so, that I'm certain at least three of the sisters at Iona believe my name to be Jamarina.)

March 1442

Dear Jamarina,

I quite like your new moniker. I was at sea many months, traveling near India. An exotic place to be certain, though too hot for my tastes. I've only just returned and received your missive.

It is good to know you are safe, and trust that your secret is safe with me, for we are both hunted by the same rat. Alas, I am the hawk that feeds on vermin.

Perhaps your Sister Maria has a secret as profound as yours. Perhaps she only toys with you.

I have not forgotten our debt, but I have not had cause to call upon you for it.

As you say, you are only just a lass of seventeen.

Yours in service,
What name would you give me?

June 1442

Dear Gentle Warrior,

Aye, I believe I quite like that.

I confess I was surprised that you returned my letter. I had not thought a man of your trade to possess such beautiful script.

Sister Maria is gone. In the middle of the night. Mother Superior will not tell us what happened, and neither will my aunt. I suppose she did have a dark secret. I pray I do not disappear.

Again, they have asked me if I would take vows to become a novice nun, but there is something holding me back. I shall think on it a little longer.

Yours in debt,
Jamarina

November 1442

Dearest Gentle Warrior,

I hope you are well and that I did not offend you with my last letter. If it pleases, I will not write again. But I must say thank you once more, for it has now been two years since I arrived safely at Iona.

I confess, I long to leave. I do not think a life of servitude is for me. I am a child of the Lord, to be certain, but I find myself heavy with ~~thoughts that lead me to confession~~ idle thoughts.

Yours in debt,
Jamarina

April 1443

Dearest Gentle Warrior,

I confess I am much worried over you. It has been over a year since I've heard from you.

What it must be like to sail the sea. Free from walls. Free from judgment. Free. I am still grateful for what you did for me, but I feel a heavy cloud of melancholy. A sadness and loneliness, though I am surrounded by people. Perhaps, what I long for is the open sea.

Sister Maria has come back. I should think she is hiding something, for she avoids me, though not everyone else.

Yours in debt,
Lady J

December 1443

Dearest Lass,

A pirate's life is not for thee.

I bid you good-bye until we meet again. Your last letter was read by someone other than myself.

Your Gentle Warrior

PS. I wish you well on celebrating your eighteenth year. I do not know my own birthday, so I have celebrated mine with you these past few years.

Isle of Iona
October 1445

THE NIGHTS WERE normally quiet at the abbey. Lady Jane Lindsay walked the open-air cloisters between compline and matins when everyone else was sleeping, because sleep rarely came to her.

It was an issue she'd dealt with ever since that horrible night five years before, this inability to rest. And the only thing that seemed to help was walking in the nighttime air, no matter the weather, with no one present so that she could clear her mind, stare at the stars and think of a world outside these confining walls.

Sometimes it worked, and sometimes it did not.

She was Lady Marina now, her birth name of Jane a secret between herself, her aunt and the Mother Superior. Well, and her gentle warrior. She'd not written him since that day he'd warned someone else was reading her letters. And ever since she'd stopped, the scornful gazes she'd been receiving from Mother Superior had subsided. Was it she who read the letters?

Marina had been on Iona since the day the pirate prince had left her at the shore just before dawn so none of the sisters at the abbey would be able to identify her rescuer. And though five years had passed in the company of the devoted women of God, Marina had yet to take formal vows herself. Though not for Mother Superior's lack of trying. She wasn't certain what held her back, only that she felt destined for something, and she'd yet to figure out what. Perhaps the overarching fear of discovery had been at the heart of that desire to keep herself free and separate from the women who had taken her in.

She'd once thought that she might like a life at sea. Those few days upon the *Savage of the Sea* had been the most peaceful of her life. No one had looked at her as though she were a pawn. No one had expected to use her, as had been her lot since the day she was born. Surprisingly, not even Shaw MacDougall, who she owed a debt.

For now, she knew that their lives could be in danger.

Even that rakishly handsome devil prince of pirates did not know the true danger she was in. The secret that would have made Livingstone want her dead. She'd kept that from Shaw. The less people who knew, the better.

Och, but she had thought of him often over the years. Her gentle warrior. The way he'd gazed at her with barely restrained longing, seeing the shame in his eyes for having done so. The way he'd gone against direct orders from Livingstone in order to save her. And who was she to him other than a lass?

The days she'd spent on his ship, he'd talked with her, played cards and knucklebones with her. She'd even taken two nights to read to him as the sun set. Their connection had been oddly easy and fluid. It had felt right. But then she'd had to leave him, and she wondered if maybe she'd only made up that connection after having an arrogant pig for a husband. Dare she call Shaw a friend?

She thought so. And given the fearsome pirate had been willing to write a naïve lass when she sent him letters, well, that proved it, didn't it?

Jane dropped to her knees where she was in the center of the cloister and stared up at the sky. She had to leave. And yet, she could not leave without the help of the man who'd brought her here. And there was only one way to get him to return to her. To help her.

She owed *him* a debt, and she was certain a pirate would never forget his debts. Especially those owed to him. And now, she would need him to do her another favor. But only if it were worth his while. That morning she'd managed to get a missive sent off with a local fisherman. She could only pray the messenger made it back alive, and that no one intercepted her letter this time. The man had agreed to take her message, but not for free. Especially when he heard where she wanted him to go. But the sight of her ring had been enough for him to agree. She'd given him one of her precious jewels, not only as payment, but also as proof to MacDougall that it was she who'd sent for him.

"Pray, come in time," she whispered to the night air, hoping her words reached Shaw wherever he was.

But it had been five years since she'd seen him, and well over a year since she'd gotten his last letter. She'd not replied to that one, fearful of who it was that had intercepted it, and she'd been waiting every day since then for Livingstone to come crashing through the abbey doors. But her day of reckoning was coming.

The name Livingstone had not crossed her lips since the day MacDougall had saved her from the knight's vicious attack. Not even when they'd been on the ship traveling to Iona. But it had crossed Mother Superior's tongue that morning while the sisters and Jane broke their fast. His name hung in the air, causing Jane's ears to buzz. Her worst enemy was going to be making a visit to the abbey on his pilgrimage across the country. Her hands still trembled at what Mother Superior had relayed to her.

The ladies in attendance had all been pleased to hear it, for it meant more coin would be placed in the abbey's coffers. Perhaps this coming winter, they might all have newly darned hose rather than the threadbare ones they'd used the year before. But to Jane, it had meant something else entirely—certain doom.

It meant death.

For she alone knew that Livingstone was not making a pilgrimage across the country in hopes of redeeming his soul, but instead was ferreting her out. Somehow, he must have gotten word she was seeking sanctuary at an abbey. Perhaps even this abbey.

In truth, she was surprised it had taken him this long to do so. How had he found out? Who'd told him she was here? Was it whoever read had the letter? Mother Superior? Sister Maria who'd disappeared several years before? Or was he just that clever? Perhaps in the last five years, he'd left no stone unturned but those lying atop Iona.

Mayhap for a while, he'd thought her dead, or that the pirate had kidnapped her, ravaged her and done away with her by tossing her out to sea. Part of her had hoped her gentle warrior had taken flight as a hawk and sank his claws into the blackguard.

Alas, none of her dreams that would lead her to freedom had come to fruition.

But something must have made him believe she was alive, and yet, she could not guess at who or what it could be. No one here knew of her identity, save for Mother Superior and her aunt. Even in her letters, she'd not written as Jane or given any other truly identifying information.

There was always the chance that Mother might have accidentally let some piece of information slip, for though she knew that Marina was her aunt's niece and that her name was Jane, she did not know the circumstances regarding why she must be hidden.

She did not know that Livingstone had killed Jane's husband.

That he wanted to kill her.

For Jane held a dark secret. One a man would kill for.

A secret she was willing to sell to a pirate for his protection.

A secret a pirate would be willing to barter with her for.

A secret would be the undoing of an entire kingdom.

If only she could have lived out her days in peace here. But only a naïve lass would have thought such a thing. Even when she'd come here at the age of sixteen, she'd not been naïve. She'd lived the previous three years with the most arrogant of earls—her young husband. He'd treated her like rubbish. He'd disrespected her in front of his men and made sport of seeing her look dejected because it made him feel superior. Jane had been nothing more than a pawn in their marriage bargain. Betrothed at age seven and married at age thirteen, she'd spent three miserable years with William Douglas, and the only friend she'd made was his younger brother, David.

They were both dead now.

Wee David was dead by association, for possibly knowing too much. William was dead for the latter, and for his arrogance. For he'd been the one to proclaim he knew the secret. And from that moment forth, he'd had a target on his chest.

It was only by sheer instinct that Jane had thought to ask William what the big secret was, playing on his need to brag. And then he'd told her.

Now she harbored the most dangerous secret in the country.

And Livingstone knew it.

Castle Dheomhan, Isle of Scarba

THERE WAS NOTHING to spoil a man's debauchery more than a messenger arriving with an urgent missive from a woman. An important woman if she knew where he resided. Besides the wenches lounging on his and his crewmen's laps, there was only one woman who had ever sent a missive to his pirate stronghold.

Gently knocking the two buxom wenches from his lap, who fell in a heap of drunken, naked laughter to the thick fur beneath his throne chair. The same throne chair that had been commissioned from steel and velvet with the Devils of the Deep skull and swords crest at its top and had parts that dated back to the original king of pirates, Arthur MacAlpin, from hundreds of years before.

Rock hard and half-drunk on whisky, Shaw settled his gaze on the messenger and willed his raging cock into submission. But that was almost impossible, given the inebriated state he was in and thinking of precious Jane. She'd be twenty-one now. Old enough that he didn't have to feel ashamed for thinking about her pert breasts and luscious mouth.

Was it she who'd sent this old man to him? Would she dare?

He'd not heard from her since his letter of warning, though he'd hoped to every day since.

But when he unrolled the parchment to behold the looping scrawl of his Lady Jane, he glanced at the messenger who stood cowering before him. This was not her usual girlish letter, but one full of desperation and a bargain.

Taking the steps down from his dais, he leaned down to look the fisherman in the eyes. "Dinna piss yourself."

"I willna, my…my… Your Highness."

Shaw grunted, sneering and not bothering to correct the old man. "How do I know this is not a trick?"

The fisherman stepped forward, reaching for his sporran. A bad idea in a room full of men expecting weapons to be drawn at any moment, and the old bastard was awarded with a dozen sharp blades at his throat.

The bloke raised his arms, glancing around tearfully, knees knocking. His mouth was open in a silent plea before he finally found his voice. "Please, sir, I hold proof."

Shaw waved his hand at his men. When they lowered their weapons, the fisherman continued to reach for his sporran and pulled out a golden ring of emerald and pearls. Shaw knew this ring. He'd given it to Jane as a gesture of friendship. A token of…his affection. He'd told her to send it if she ever needed him. When he'd told her he meant to collect on their debt, he'd never actually meant to take anything from the lass—other than perhaps convincing her when she was of age that she might like to grace his bed. It had taken a feat of pure willpower not to write her back when she'd said a life at sea would suit her to say he was coming to get her.

"Lady Marina," the fisherman said.

Marina… Jamarina… He let out a short laugh.

He'd not heard the name in a long time. It was the one he'd given her before she disembarked his ship. The lass had plagued his dreams for five long years. More beautiful than a woman had the right to be. He'd always felt guilty about his desire for her. For she'd been so young at the time, and pirate or nay, he had a code when it came to women. But not anymore. Now she'd be a woman grown, and the curves he'd felt when he carried her aboard his ship would have blossomed.

Shaw grunted and went back to the letter, the women on the floor pawing at his boots all but forgotten.

Dear Gentle Warrior,

I am prepared to pay my debt straightaway. 'Tis most urgent that you come now. Else, the balance will never be repaid, for there are others who wish to lay claim to the treasure I alone possess. I trust that your desire for adventure and thirst for the greatest of prizes will allow you to make haste to me. And know that I do not flatter myself that any sense of honor would bring you forth.

Most urgently yours in debt,
Lady M

"When did she give ye this?" Shaw demanded. The man stank of fish, his face the color and texture of dried leather.

"Early this morning, my laird. When I dropped off the fish at the abbey."

Shaw grunted. "And what was your payment for daring to step foot on my island?" He kept his voice calm, low, but it still had the power to cause the man to quake.

"The ring, sir."

"The ring," Shaw mused. He held the emerald jewel up to the candlelight. "So ye'll be wanting it back?"

"I'd be happy to leave with my life." The man's knees knocked together.

Shaw grinned, baring all of his teeth as he did so. "I suppose ye would." He closed his fingers around the ring. "Go then. Afore I unleash my beasts to feed on your bones. Ye were never here. Ye never saw this place. If anyone so much as lands on my beach by accident, I will hunt ye down and kill ye."

The old man nodded violently, then turned and ran toward the wide double doors that made up the entrance to Shaw's keep.

"Wait," Shaw called and two of his crew stepped in front of the old man to bar him from leaving. "Ye forgot something."

Trembling visibly, the fisherman turned, and Shaw tossed him the ring. But his reflexes, or his nerves more like, weren't expecting it, and the ring fell to the stone before his feet. There was a measure of held breath in the air, and Shaw wondered if the man would pick it up or if the moments would tick by to the appropriate count that his men knew meant free game for whatever treasure had been dropped.

Seeming to understand the urgency, or perhaps just wishing to get the hell of Shaw's island, the fisherman scooped up the ring.

But instead of rushing out, he asked, "What should I tell my lady?"

"Ye needn't tell her anything," Shaw said. "I'll be there before ye get the chance."

With that, he blew a whistle to assemble a small crew and marched past the old fisherman, thinking at the last second to grab him by the scruff and drag him down to the docks before he was robbed for having overstayed his welcome.

Soon Shaw would lay his gaze on the beautiful lass again. Only this time, she would be a woman. Had the years at the abbey done her well? Was she now a child of God as she'd often struggled with deciding upon in her letters? And if she was, would he have the ballocks to corrupt her?

At that thought, Shaw laughed aloud as he gripped the helm.

Of course, he would.

He was Shaw Savage MacDougall. He took what he wanted, when he wanted. And never had he shied from debauching a willing woman.

Better yet was the question regarding what was this prize she claimed to possess? This treasure that he would not be able to resist?

He imagined a mountain of jewels and gold. A key to the king's own treasure stores. But truth be told, those were not the treasures he'd been pining over for years since last seeing her. Nay, the treasure he wanted was *her*.

In just a few hours time, he'd know what it was she was offering.

"Where to, Cap'n?" Jack asked, eagerness in his eyes.

"Iona."

Jack frowned. "Ain't nothing there we want, Cap'n."

Shaw turned a fierce glower on his crewman. "There is indeed something I want there. And ye best not be telling me again what it is I want, else I'll have ye hanging from the jack and make good on your name."

"Aye, Cap'n. Willna overstep again."

Shaw growled. "Make certain no one else does, either."

Chapter Three

A S DAWN APPROACHED, Jane climbed the bell tower, sat on the small bench and gazed out one of the arched belfry openings that looked toward the sea. Saints, but she hoped and prayed that at some point she'd see the black sails of MacDougall's ship coming through the fog off the Firth of Lorn.

The gentle sound of the waves lapping and the slight breeze that blew through the bell tower coupled with sheer exhaustion lulled her into a state close to sleep. She huddled deeper into her cloak and let her eyelids droop to half slits, still managing to keep a partial view of the sea.

"Come for me, gentle warrior," she murmured.

Jane didn't know how much time had passed, but in the courtyard below, she watched the sisters file into the nave. She knew they would wonder where she was, but she didn't having the energy to join them, or the nerve to leave this perch in case she missed the approach of his ship.

And then she saw them—the unforgettable darkened sails of the *Savage of the Sea*. One prominent sail was ruddy in color and had a massive ship painted on it with the image of a devil's head with a sword-bearing fist crushing it.

He'd come for her.

Jane sat up taller, her eyes suddenly wide and all remnants of sleep gone from her as renewed energy flowed rampantly. She made her way to the narrow ladder and climbed down from the bell tower, passing the nun whose duty it was to ring the bell for lauds.

"What is it?" she asked, taking in the urgency in Jane's darting gaze.

"I must go," was all Jane managed to say, her breathing quick.

Down in the cloister, the sisters of Iona walked from the refectory where they'd broken their fast and prepared for lauds in the nave. None seemed to notice as she passed going in the opposite direction, as it wasn't uncommon to see Jane—or rather *Marina*—wandering around at all hours and going in any manner of direction.

When she reached the wide double doors that locked them into their sanctuary, she felt the biting grip of her aunt's fingers on her arm.

"What are ye doing, child?" Aunt Agatha whispered, her brown eyes bright with concern, face pale in the dawn light. The too-tight wimple on her head made her skin taut at the edges.

"He has come for me, Aunt. Have faith, I will be safe."

"Who has come?" Agatha's brow tried to wrinkle beyond the tight wimple.

For a moment, Jane considered not telling her aunt and just demanding to be let go. Shaw had come for her, and if she didn't meet him out on the beach, who was to say he wouldn't come knocking on the abbey doors in search of her. After all, she had bribed him with treasure. "My protector."

"God is your protector, child."

Jane struggled with how to answer, for she'd never negate her aunt's beliefs. But she was fairly certain that when Livingstone came brandishing a sword, she would not be spared. "God protects us all, aye, my aunt, but he canna protect me from who comes. Not like Savage can." Oh, no! She'd not meant to let that name slip out.

"Savage? What kind of name is that?" Her aunt gasped, covering her mouth with her hand as understanding dawned. "Nay, lass. Ye canna mean…a pirate?"

It was too late to go back on what she'd said. Besides, all her aunt had to do was look outside the abbey walls and she'd see the swift approach of the pirate ship. And it was obviously a pirate ship. "Aye, Aunt Agatha. He is the one who brought me to Iona. He saved my life. And he is the only one who can save me now."

Aunt Agatha's face lost much of its piety in that moment as her eyes burned with protective rage. "Nay! I forbid it. I canna let ye go with a man who would destroy ye. I have sworn an oath to protect ye, to keep ye here. I told your father—"

"What did ye tell my father?"

"Nothing." Agatha glanced away.

All this time, Jane had thought her father believed her dead. She'd wanted him to think she was dead. Because if he believed her alive, if he knew where she was, then he could be tortured into giving the information away.

"Aunt! How could ye? He will be in danger!"

"From a pirate."

"Nay! From the men who killed the Earl of Douglas. The same ones who want me dead."

"Your father does not believe ye're here. He believes ye safely in Rome."

"Rome?"

"Aye. I told him we sent ye there."

Well, that was something at least.

"Please, dinna go with that pirate. He will be the death of ye."

"He will not, Aunt. But Livingstone…" Jane shuddered, and just from that gesture, understanding once more dawned in her aunt's eyes. "I've said too much. 'Tis better if ye know naught. Let me go, and dinna despair. Savage saved me once before, and he will do so again. I swear to ye. I will be safe."

But her aunt was shaking her head, her lips trembling as she stared at Jane as though she'd never seen her before.

"He will ruin ye. He will drag ye down into a life a crime. Ye'll be shunned by all. Shunned by God. Excommunicated. He is a devil."

MacDougall's brethren were known as the Devils of the Deep, and he was the prince of their fleet, but would the devil have brought her to God's house? She doubted it. Despite the rough exterior, the vicious reputation, there was something more to Shaw "Savage" MacDougall than met the eye. She could feel it.

"And ye'd rather see me dead? Because if I stay here, I'll be dead and buried within the week."

Tears gathered in Agatha's eyes, and she tugged Jane into her embrace, trembling as she held her.

"Pray for me, Aunt Agatha." And with that, she wrenched up the bar on the doors and ran through the opening, knowing that this was perhaps the last time she'd see her aunt, as Mother Superior would not allow her back once she knew the truth of where Jane had gone.

The moors were damp with dew that seeped into her sturdy leather boots, and then her feet were sinking into cool sand. The ship had laid anchor some distance out, but even in the dawn light she could see a skiff being rowed toward shore, and standing in the center of it was MacDougall himself.

The man's balance had to be impeccable, his strength evident. For who could stand so stoic on small boat like that?

He seemed taller than she remembered. Broader somehow. He wore a plaid of dark reds, golds and deep green almost black, a leine of black wool, and weapons that gleamed in the dawning pink light. His wild black hair blew in the wind and bronzed skin glistened in the glowing sun. In five years, she'd somehow shrunken him in her mind, lessened his roguish good looks. A mistake, for he was more mesmerizing than ever.

Jane's heart lurched. Her breath ceased, and her legs were suddenly wobbly. Had she made a mistake? Would he offer her protection in exchange for the secrets she kept? Or would he ravish her as her mind was now conjuring up all sorts of…

Get a hold of yourself, Jane!

What if her aunt was right, and he truly was a devil? What if him helping her before was only a single chance? What if…? Saints, there were so many questions darting back and forth in her head she was growing weary and dizzy.

She wanted to sit and catch her breath, or at least figure out how to breathe again. But to do so would be to show weakness, and the only thing she knew he despised more than Livingstone was weakness.

If she didn't stand tall and steady in what she wanted and needed, it would only allow him entry to walk all over her.

And she *would* get what she needed—his protection.

So Jane stood tall, hands on her hips, chin jutted, as she waited for him to arrive on the beach. The men chanted as they rowed, and then before she could turn around and run back to the sanctuary of Iona's abbey walls, the skiff was sliding up onto the beach and MacDougall was stepping down into the water, his large leather boot sinking into the sand and leaving a footprint the size of a crater. Their eyes met for an instant, and time stood still. She remembered those well. Emerald green and piercing. The way he was looking at her, as though he would devour her whole, made her limbs tingle, and she nearly faltered in her purposeful stance.

With deliberate intent, he marched toward her. Long, muscular legs with naked knees peeking from beneath his plaid. She jerked her gaze back up to his face to see that his eyes had darkened, and he either didn't like her perusal, or he liked it very much. It was hard to tell.

Oh, heaven help her… She didn't remember him being so…tall and large.

Or handsome.

Dark, wavy hair blew in the breeze and his face held a day or two's worth of stubble. When last she'd seen him, he'd a beard covering most of his face. Now she could make out the square jaw, the wide, intimidating mouth, a distinguished nose that had been broken at least twice, and his eyes… She felt he could see straight into her soul. If he were the devil, he'd know just what she was willing to sell her soul to him for.

"My lady, Ja—Marina," he said, voice full of confidence, a wry smile on his lips, as he swept a mocking bow and took her hand, bringing it close to his mouth.

A gentleman would brush the knuckles, or hover over the skin without making contact. But Savage was no gentleman. He pressed his lips firmly to the bare skin of her knuckles and left them there a hair's breadth longer than was appropriate, enough so that she felt a shiver skid from that spot straight to her belly.

Jane swallowed hard and snatched her hand back. "Ye made good time."

"Aye," he said slowly, taking his time as he raked his intense gaze over her body. "I am most eager to collect my debt."

"And ye shall." She cleared her throat. "Now, if ye will, take me aboard your ship."

Her gentle warrior did not look so gentle now. He towered over her, his breadth blocking out the rising sun. There was a low rumble in his chest she thought might have been a laugh, and judging by the curl of his sensual mouth when he said, "Nay," she believed she was right.

Whatever game he was about, she wasn't interested in joining in. She cocked her head to the side and narrowed her eyes. "Ye would deny the treasure?"

"I would deny having ye aboard my ship." He let go of her hand then, but his gaze still held her taut enough she might as well have been pressed up against him.

"Then ye shall not collect your debt." Her nerves were so unamused, her heart leapt up into her throat, and she feared she might just start gagging.

"Lass, dinna trifle with me." He spoke low, menacingly, reaching forward to tuck her hair behind her ear.

"I would never dare trifle with a devil," she offered back, keeping herself steady.

He grinned. "Just as much spark as I remember. Now where is my treasure?"

"The treasure is up here." She tapped her head, surprised at the strength in her voice. "And I will only share it with ye, if ye take me aboard your ship."

"That is not how it works, lass."

Jane frowned. This was going to be a lot more difficult than she'd imagined. "Walk with me, MacDougall."

She didn't wait for him to answer. Instead, she turned on her heel and marched up the beach. With his legs easily two hands longer than hers, he quickly caught up.

"I dinna like to be bossed around by anyone, let alone a mere slip of a lass."

Jane let out a long sigh. "Please accept my apologies, sir. I am…" She wasn't any good at this—figuring out just how to appeal to a man to entice him into helping her. Perhaps the best course would be to simply be honest. "I am in need of your help in escaping this island. In exchange, I am willing to share with you information that has until now been known only to me and a select few others."

"Information?" The teasing turn of his lip lowered into a frown, and when next he spoke, it was not without warning. "Ye alluded to a treasure, lass. Dinna tell me ye've been lying."

She shook her head quickly. "Nay. I'm not lying. The information *leads* to a treasure. Call me the map."

"Ye deliberately misled me." She thought he might be angry, but his tone appeared more amused than anything else.

Jane chewed her lower lip, peeking up at him through her lashes, trying to gauge just how mad he might be. Aye, she'd spent some time with him, exchanged a few letters, but…perhaps she'd underestimated the bond they'd formed. He was a pirate, after all. And men of his ilk saw only gold and jewels when they looked at the world around them. "I told ye what ye needed to hear in order to get yet to come to Iona. But I didna mislead ye. 'Tis the greatest treasure in Scotland."

His eyes narrowed for a moment, and she thought he might say something more, but in the end he just said, "Tell me."

"Promise to take me away from Iona." This time, she didn't hide the hint of desperation in her voice, and she glanced over his shoulder for added emphasis.

"Why?" Real concern etched in his face giving her cause to believe that the bond they'd formed was true.

Jane gave him her full gaze then, rather than glancing down at the sand or looking through her lashes. "Livingstone. He's coming for me."

While his expression did not change, there was a subtle pulse at his jaw as though he'd clenched his teeth, a flicker of something in his eyes. "I see."

"He is coming to kill me." Unbidden tears threatened, and she managed to hold them at bay.

Again, there was that flicker in his eyes, and she swore his arm twitched as though he wanted to reach for her. Oh, how she longed to sink against him, to feel the warmth of him. One night when they were on the ship, she'd fallen asleep beside him reading. When she woke, she realized he'd not moved, instead he'd just held her. How she'd cherished that moment for the past five years.

"How can ye be certain?"

His question brought her back to the present. "Mother Superior announced to us yesterday that we'd have special guest—Livingstone. That he was on a pilgrimage across the country. But I know he is looking for me."

"Because he wants ye dead?"

"Aye."

"Because ye were there at the death feast." He stated it rather than asking.

"Partly. But also because of what I know." She ran her hands through her hair and looked down at their boots sinking into the sand. "If only I were not so…stupid."

"Lass?"

She flashed a bitter smile at him. "I shouldna have goaded William into telling me. Then I could be blissfully ignorant of it all."

"But he would still be coming for ye, and then ye'd have nothing to barter with to get ye off the island." Then his dark gaze roved over her body in a way that sent shivers rolling through her. "Well, almost nothing."

She gasped, catching his meaning, and took a step back. "Ye're a—"

"Devil?" he interrupted, stepping closer. "Aye, lass, I am, and it seems ye're willing to negotiate with me. 'Haps I dinna want whatever secrets ye hold, but instead I want…*ye*."

"I am not a pawn," she shouted, feeling anger slice through her. "I am through being a pawn."

The devil had the gall to laugh at that. All the fairytale apparitions floating before her eyes whipped from her mind faster than the lash on a pirate's back.

"We shall see, Ja-Marina. Now, tell me your secret, and I will let ye know if it is worth the price of this gentle warrior taking ye off this island."

He was mocking her. The cad. But what other choice did she have? It wasn't as if she could get off the island on her own. If she bribed the fisherman into taking her away, he might only ask for what the pirate had alluded to, and she was definitely not willing to give away her own precious gifts to the old man.

"Last month, Joan Beaufort, mother of the king, was killed in a siege at Dunbar castle. A siege laid upon them by Livingstone."

"I had heard."

"She sustained injuries in the battle, from which she died. But her husband, James Stewart, the Black Knight of Lorne, was able to escape with their children and his page."

"This is common knowledge, lass. Ye'll have to do better than that."

Jane nodded, twisting her fingers together. "The page was not his *page*."

"His squire? His cook?" Savage chuckled. "I hope ye've got something more interesting than that, love."

"He was *Alexander*."

At this, MacDougall frowned, his face darkening. "Alexander who?"

"Alexander Stewart, Duke of Rothesay, the eldest twin born on the sixteenth of October, year of our Lord 1430."

Shaw's scowl darkened. "The king's twin, the elder twin? The one who died that day?"

Jane shook her head. "He did not die."

"He did, my lady. Someone has fed ye a pack of lies, and now ye're trying to sell them to me."

"I am not lying." But she did wonder if perhaps she had been told a lie herself. "William told me before he died that the Black Knight had a page who was the spitting image of the king. That the page, was in fact, the rightful king. 'Tis why Livingstone wanted my husband and his brother dead. Because they knew and could replace the puppet Livingstone is manipulating. Now he wants me dead. But not before he tortures the truth from me."

"What truth? If ye know this, than he likely does, too."

Jane shook her head. "He will want me dead for more than that. Livingstone…" She chewed her lip again, finding her throat tight. "I know the truth about where James and Alexander, the true king, are hiding."

"How could ye know this?"

Locking her eyes on Shaw, she said, "Because, they came here seeking sanctuary. Because I told them where to go."

"And Livingstone knows they were here?"

"Aye."

"How?"

"Sister Maria."

Shaw raised a brow.

"She came back, I wrote to ye of this. But after Lorne and Alexander's visit, she left swiftly again. And now we've had word that Livingstone comes. I think she was a spy."

At this final admission, the pirate opened his mouth and then closed it again. She might not have believed she could make him speechless if she hadn't witnessed it herself.

"And where did ye tell them to hide, love?" His voice was soft, emerald eyes glittering.

"That I willna tell ye until ye let me onboard your ship. Until ye offer me protection."

He grinned, but it wasn't one filled with mirth, more like that of a pirate who'd just glimpsed his treasure and knew it would soon be his.

"There is only one way I will offer ye protection, love." His grin took on a sensual curve.

Jane squared her shoulders, thrust her chin forward. "Name your price."

"Ye…in my bed."

Jane felt as though a gale force wind had knocked her back. He would take her information and her body? "Nay." She watched his face darken and decided that perhaps another type of bargain could be hatched between them. "I shall agree to a…kiss, but nothing more."

A brow winged up at that. "I'm a pirate, lass. I dinna claim anything without fully possessing it—including a woman."

Another wayward shiver passed through her. Why did her body keep doing that? Why did that heated gaze he tossed at her have places on her body tingling that she didn't know *could* tingle? Jane swallowed hard. Was there any other choice? Perhaps she could accept his terms, with an addendum of her own. "All right, but there is only one way I'll ever enter your bed, *gentle warrior*."

His eyes glittered like sparkling jewels. "Name your price, lass."

Jane lifted her chin, meeting his gaze head on, and not wavering in the least. "Marriage."

Get Savage of the Sea now!

Enjoy an excerpt from

Lady of the Moon

by Lathryn Le Veque

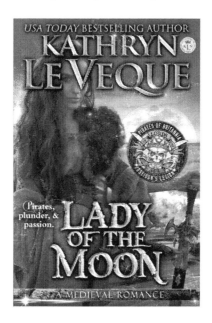

Chapter One

Year of our Lord 1444 A.D.
The Month of August

Cambourne, Cornwall

The Blackbottom Tavern

"Across the ocean of turbulent tide,

A heart that loved and was loved,

Her beauty made of moonbeams and starlight,

But her longing for home was...."

W *HACK!*

The troubadour had come too close.

A hand came up, fist balled, and slugged the hapless man right in the face. Song instantly ended, he staggered backwards but, to his credit, didn't lose his grip on his citole. The instrument remained clutched against his chest even as he lost his balance and fell on his arse, blood pouring from his injured nose.

A swell of laughter rose in the tavern's common room, men and woman cheering loudly at the troubadour's misfortune of having sung his sappy song to the wrong woman. He'd gotten too close to her, singing his song of courtly love and other things she found offensive, so she'd balled her fist and hit him. He'd probably think twice before singing to her again.

Amidst the heat and stench of the room, with smoke from a poorly designed hearth hanging about their heads like a blue fog, the woman who'd hit the troubadour was gazing at her companion across the table. In fact, her attention had never wavered from him, even when the stupid entertainer had hung over her shoulder and sang love songs that couldn't have possibly been more misplaced. Misplaced because the man seated across from her was not her lover.

He was hiring her for a job.

The man, a richly dressed lord that bespoke of his wealth and rank, leaned sideways so he could see the minstrel on the ground, now being helped to his feet by men who were laughing at him. If he'd had any doubts about the ability of the woman across the table from him, those doubts had been summarily dashed by her swift and brutal movement.

She was a brute, this one.

It was late on this evening and the tavern known as The Blackbottom Tavern, two miles from the sea on the deep and mysterious inland of Cornwall. This was a land of legends and beasts, which was why men sought shelter when the sun went down. No one wanted to be exposed in the dark to things that lurked within it. Even with a full moon, the wilds of Cornwall after dark were not a place fit for man.

But along with its danger, it was also a place that bred strong and unusual warriors, as evidenced by the woman sitting across from him. A mercenary, she was, with the looks of an angel. *Lady of the Moon* she was called because no one really knew her name. All they knew was that when night fell and the moonlight shone over the wilds of Cornwall, the Lady of the Moon moved freely and without fear. Even if Cornwall after dark wasn't fit for man, it was certainly fit for a woman.

A most remarkable woman.

"So," the man in silks said as he refocused his attention on her, "you do not like songs. I shall remember that so you do not do to me what you did to that minstrel."

The woman's gaze was steady. "Do you sing?"

The man shook his head. "Alas, I do not, and I do not intend to start with you around," he said, somewhat wryly. "Now, where were we? Ah, yes… as I was saying, you have my gratitude for agreeing to meet with me. I am willing to pay you most handsomely for a very important task regarding my son."

The bloodied troubadour was forgotten as the woman cocked a dark eyebrow. "Go on."

The man took a huge drink of the cheap ale he'd purchased. He smacked his lips. "My name is Henry de Leybourne," he told her. "I've not yet introduced myself and, for that, I do apologize. My home of Tyringham Castle is just south of St. Ives and I hold the lordship of Tyringham, St. Ives, and Trevalgan, which means I have the means to pay you a great deal for your services."

The woman's gaze moved away from him and to the several heavily-armed men who were dotted around the room, men she'd seen enter with the expensively dressed man. She didn't doubt for one moment he was who he said he was, but she was naturally leery of such men. She'd been in this business too long to instantly warm to, or trust, any man who wished to engaged her services. She needed to speak with him more to decide whether or not she even wanted to do business with him.

"I believe you," she said, although it really wasn't the truth. "You went through a great deal to summon me, Lord Tyringham. I have been receiving missives from you for the past three months, each one of them asking to meet with you. So here I am; what would you have of me?"

Tyringham cocked his head in a curious gesture. "Your name, please? All I know of you is that men call you Lady of the Moon and that your stronghold is Mithian Castle. May I have your name, lady?"

"In time. Tell me of your task first."

Tyringham suspected he had little choice; mercenaries such as the lady were often suspicious and wraith-like in the way the operated. If he said the wrong word, she would vanish like a ghost. Therefore, when he spoke, it was carefully.

It was time to get down to business.

"My son was betrothed as a young lad to a lass who lives in Penzance," he said. "Her father, Lord de Sansen, is a great friend and we brokered a marriage between our children to strengthen our alliance in

Cornwall. When our children wed, we will control the tip of Cornwall from coast to coast, from St. Ives all the way across to Penzance. You can see that it will be a very lucrative marriage."

The woman nodded faintly. "I do."

"Then you are an intelligent woman and my son is daft, for he does not see such an advantage. In fact, he wants nothing to do with her."

The woman shrugged. "What do you want me to do about it?"

"Abduct him."

Now, he had her interest. "*Abduct* him?" she repeated, puzzled. "For what purpose?"

Tyringham folded his hands on the table, looking at her quite seriously. "You will abduct him and take him to the caves of St. Agnes, where I will be waiting with his betrothed," he told her. "You know the legend of the caves, do you not? If you do not, the legend goes like this – many years ago in the wilds of Cornwall, a beautiful princess was born. She was so beautiful that an oracle foretold of the men who would go to battle to win her heart. Her father, being a wise and reasonable man, did not want men dying for his daughter, so he gave her over to a young page to tend, keeping her hidden from the world. This young boy and young girl grew to love each other over the years, but tragedy struck when the father pledged the princess to the son of his enemy. The page and the princess fled to the caves of St. Agnes where they took their own lives just as the princess' father was closing in on them. It is said that if a man and woman touch the walls of the cave where the bloodstains of the lovers are, then they will fall in love. I intend that my son and his betrothed should touch those stains so that we may cement our alliance."

The young woman was listening carefully. "That is not what I have heard of the legend," she said. "Two people, already in love, must touch the stains of their own free will and, if they do, they will remain in love with one another for all time."

Tyringham frowned. "It does not matter," he said, waving his hands about, clearly frustrated with the situation. "I intend that my son and his betrothed should touch the stains. By luck or by magic, I want him to be an agreeable groom. Something will surely happen, from my legend or from yours."

The woman eyed him, seeing that this was something that meant a great deal to him. His desperation as a father was bleeding out all over the place. "So you want me to abduct this reluctant groom and take him to the caves where you will force him to touch the stains?" she said, disbelief in her tone. "Do you then expect me to hold him at sword point until he touches the cave walls?"

Tyringham shook his head. "I will pay you to bring him to the cave," he said. "Once he is at the cave, I will handle the situation."

"It seems to me that you cannot handle the situation even now 'else you would not be trying to hire me."

She had a point. Tyringham lifted an eyebrow that suggested he was agreeing with her even if he didn't want to. "That is, mayhap, true, but I do not expect you to force him to touch the cave walls," he said. "Leave that to me. Now, is this a job you feel you can undertake?"

The woman sat back on her chair, putting her calloused hand on the hilt of the sword that was scabbarded at her side. She was very tall for a woman, with long legs encased in tight leather hose and a series of tunics over her torso that provided both coverage and protection for her strong, sinewy body. Her long, dark hair was mussed, tied at the nape of her neck with a strip of leather, while her hazel eyes gazed at Tyringham with both interest and doubt.

In truth, she appeared every inch the mercenary wench Tyringham had heard tale of, this Lady of the Moon. She looked like something out of a nightmare had it not been for that angelic face that seemed to distort the image of a blood-thirsty killer.

It's that face that sends men to their graves, Tyringham thought grimly.

"I can undertake any task," she said confidently. "But just how do you expect me to abduct him? And why can you not take him to St. Agnes yourself?"

Tyringham poured himself more ale. "Because he will run from me," he said. "My son is wily. If he suspects I am taking him to his betrothed, then he will run. He has done it before. This time, he is going to run straight into you."

"What do you mean?"

Tyringham downed more of the flat ale. "My plan is simple – I mean to tell him that his betrothed is coming to Tyringham Castle," he said. "The mere mention of her will make him run. When he does, you will be waiting for him. You will intercept him and take him straight to the caves where I will soon join you with his betrothed. What is your price?"

The young woman sighed faintly as she considered what to tell him. The harder the job, the more the price; would this son of Tyringham fight her? Easily surrender?

"Tell me of your son," she said. "Is he a knight?"

Tyringham nodded. "Rhodes de Leybourne is a very fine knight," he said. "He has served Bristol for many years as one of his most seasoned knights. I need not go in to all of the accomplishments of my son, but suffice it to say that he is a decorated knight of the highest order. His reputation in battle is unmatched."

The woman stared at him a moment, her eyes narrowing with realization. "De Russe," she finally muttered. "Your son is a Lancastrian."

"You speak as if you do not approve. Does money take sides, then? Is coinage either Yorkist or Lancastrian?"

The woman didn't say anything for a moment, perhaps trying to make that exact determination. Ultimately, it didn't matter to her who men served these days, whether they followed the House of York or the House of Lancaster. Her business crossed those lines repeatedly and she was happy to do so. Therefore, it really didn't matter to her who de Leybourne's son served.

This was business.

"Money from Yorkist or Lancastrian has equal value to me," she said. "What I want to know is if your son will resist me."

"More than likely."

"Will he fight?"

"I believe you can count on it."

"Then the price doubles."

Tyringham eyed her a moment before reluctantly digging into the robe he wore, a very expensive garment lined with fur and elaborately embroidered. There must have been hidden pockets inside of it because he pulled forth a small leather pouch and tossed it at her. Deftly, the woman caught the sack, which was jingling. There were pieces of something hard sheathed in the leather. Suspecting what was in it, she untied the top and peered inside.

It was coinage – lots of it. She even caught a glimpse of at least one gold coin among the silver. It was a substantial amount of money, probably more than what she would have asked for, so she quickly shut the pouch and tucked it away into the purse strung around her belt. For that amount of money, she would have abducted the devil himself. Now, she was far more acquiescent to do Tyringham's bidding.

"When do you intend that I should do this deed?" she asked.

Tyringham was pleased that she'd succumbed to his money. "The day after tomorrow," he told her. "I intend to return home on the morrow and tell my son that his intended is arriving from Penzance. That will drive him north, I promise you, on the road that will take him through the village of Trolvadden. Do you know it?"

The woman nodded. "I do."

"That is where you must take him. If he goes any further, the road forks and there is no knowing which direction he will take. He rides a silver rouncey with long legs that can outrun any horse in Cornwall, so be aware. Unless you catch him unaware, he will dig his spurs into his horse and you shall never catch him."

The young woman nodded, already thinking of the different ways she could knock the man off his horse. "Have no fear that I will catch him, in any case," she said. "His name is Rhodes de Leybourne, you said?"

"Aye. My only son. Do not hurt him in any way; I do not wish to take him to his bride injured."

The young woman shrugged. "If he tries to harm me, I will have little choice."

Tyringham shook his head firmly. "Do not draw a weapon on him. Hit him across the head if you must, but not a scratch upon him. Is that in any way unclear? I only wish to have him abducted, not murdered. Deliver him to me unharmed and I shall double the money I paid you."

That was an extremely attractive offer and, being that the young woman came from a family of pirates and mercenaries, she spoke that language. Money above all. She was sure it was her family motto somewhere back in the lines.

"He will not be harmed," she assured him. "Bruised, mayhap, but I will not puncture his skin with anything sharp."

Tyringham seemed satisfied by that. "Very well," he said. "Now... you will tell me something."

"What is that?"

"Your name. Tell me who you are and tell me something of your family."

The young woman pondered his question for a moment. "Why is that necessary?" she asked. "You already know where to reach me. Why must you know anything else?"

Tyringham cocked an eyebrow. "Because I want to know who I am trusting my money and my son's life to," he said. "Is that too much to ask?"

The young woman was still hesitant. "You are the one who sought me out. Obviously, you know enough about me to know that I deliver what I promise."

"If you will not tell me your name, then give me my money back. There are other mercenaries about who will not be so difficult to deal with."

The young woman didn't want to return the money. But she knew if she didn't give the man at least an answer or two, there were eight heavily-armed men with him who would happily separate her from the money their lord had paid her. Therefore, she saw no harm in divulging some information about herself... *limited* information.

"My name is Samarra le Brecque," she said. "My home is Mithian Castle, where you sent your multiple missives asking to meet with me."

Tyringham looked at her curiously. "Le Brecque," he muttered thoughtfully. "I know that name. Why do I know that name?"

Samarra knew why. Everyone along the western coast of Cornwall and far up into Wales, Ireland, and Scotland knew that name. As of late, most everyone had heard of it for reasons that were not particularly pleasant. Rather than have Tyringham figure it out later and want his money back again, she thought to be honest with him up front. Although she didn't give her name freely, she wasn't ashamed of it when she did. Nor did she lie about it.

"Poseidon's Legion," she said, her voice quiet. "It is the name of the commander of Poseidon's Legion."

Tyringham's eyes widened. "Le Brecque," he hissed. "Of course! The pirate Constantine le Brecque, the man who commands ships that raid all along the western coast!"

"That would be he."

Tyringham didn't seem pleased by the revelation. "God's Bones, I've had my share of run-ins with that man. He has raided St. Ives from time to time and my army has done battle with him. Are you his wife, then?"

Samarra chuckled, bitterly. "I am his sister," she said. Then, she leaned forward on the table, resting her forearms on it as she focused on him. "I am from a family of pirates, Lord Tyringham, which is why my sword can be bought. My brother rules the sea along with his pirate brethren but my domain is the land. I command more men than my brother and they demand to be paid well, so this coinage you have given me will make me and my men very happy. Have no fear that we will find your son and take him to St. Agnes caves. And when I do, you will, indeed, pay me double. That is the bargain you yourself struck and

I never forget a bargain. If you fail to pay, I will give your son over to my brother and let him take him out to sea as a captive. Is *that* in any way unclear? If you are going to do business with the devil, my lord, then you had better be willing to accept his terms."

Tyringham's mouth was a thin, hard line by the time she was finished. "Damnable pirates," he muttered. "I should have known that you would threaten me. Be that as it may, I will not hold a grudge. You have my money and a plan of action. Watch for my son the day after tomorrow astride his big silver beast and take him to the caves. If you do not, I will send more men than you can comprehend and burn Mithian to the ground."

Samarra looked at him for a moment before breaking down into a grin. "Are we to threaten each other all night?"

"Do you understand any other manner of conversation?"

She shook her head, putting her hand to the purse at her waist. "I understand threats and money. Those are the only languages I speak."

Tyringham scratched his cheek, thinking that this was an unusual woman, indeed. "I can give you both, fortunately," he said. "Then we understand one another?"

"We do."

Tyringham stood up, eager to be finished with this unpleasant business. For some reason, Samarra was starting to make him nervous.

"Then I shall see you at the caves in four days' time," he said. "My son's betrothed and her father are already making their way there, but I must return home to make sure my son flees to the north where you will be waiting for him."

Samarra watched the man as he stood up and straightened out his heavy clothing. "If the girl is already heading for the caves, then it seems to me that you have been planning this for a while."

"I would not have to plan anything if my son would only be agreeable."

Samarra was coming to wonder what kind of man this son was. But it was of little consequence; she liked a challenge.

"I will ensure that he is most agreeable."

Tyringham believed her.

Get Lady of the Moon now!

About Kathryn Le Veque

Medieval Just Got Real.

KATHRYN LE VEQUE is a USA TODAY Bestselling author, an Amazon All-Star author, and a #1 bestselling, award-winning, multi-published author in Medieval Historical Romance and Historical Fiction. She has been featured in the NEW YORK TIMES and on USA TODAY's HEA blog. In March 2015, Kathryn was the featured cover story for the March issue of InD'Tale Magazine, the premier Indie author magazine. She was also a quadruple nominee (a record!) for the prestigious RONE awards for 2015.

Kathryn's Medieval Romance novels have been called 'detailed', 'highly romantic', and 'character-rich'. She crafts great adventures of love, battles, passion, and romance in the High Middle Ages. More than that, she writes for both women AND men – an unusual crossover for a romance author – and Kathryn has many male readers who enjoy her stories because of the male perspective, the action, and the adventure.

On October 29, 2015, Amazon launched Kathryn's Kindle Worlds Fan Fiction site WORLD OF DE WOLFE PACK. Please visit Kindle Worlds for Kathryn Le Veque's World of de Wolfe Pack and find many action-packed adventures written by some of the top authors in their genre using Kathryn's characters from the de Wolfe Pack series. As Kindle World's FIRST Historical Romance fan fiction world, Kathryn Le Veque's World of de Wolfe Pack will contain all of the great storytelling you have come to expect.

Kathryn loves to hear from her readers. Please find Kathryn on Facebook at Kathryn Le Veque, Author, or join her on Twitter @kathrynleveque, and don't forget to visit her website and sign up for her blog at www.kathrynleveque.com.

58721624R00135

Made in the USA
San Bernardino, CA
29 November 2017